PENGUIN CLASSICS

THE LADY OF THE CAMELLIAS

ALEXANDRE DUMAS *fils* (1824–1895) was the son of the famous novelist Alexandre Dumas. In 1847 he published his first novel, *Adventures of Four Women and a Parrot*, followed a year later by *The Lady of the Camellias* and over the next decade ten other novels. After the great success of the dramatic version of *The Lady of the Camellias*, he was gradually drawn away from the novel to the stage. In 1874 he was elected to the French Academy and until his death continued to produce a long line of successful plays.

LIESL SCHILLINGER is a translator, journalist, and literary critic who writes regularly for *The New York Times Book Review* and spent many years on the editorial staff of *The New Yorker*. She lives in New York.

JULIE KAVANAGH is the author of *The Girl Who Loved Camellias: The Life and Legend of Marie Duplessis*, a biography of the courtesan who inspired *The Lady of the Camellias*. An award-winning biographer of Rudolf Nureyev (*Nureyev: The Life*) and Frederick Ashton (*Secret Muses: The Life of Frederick Ashton*), she has been London editor of both *Vanity Fair* and *The New Yorker*, and is now an editor and writer with *The Economist*'s cultural magazine *Intelligent Life*.

ALEXANDRE DUMAS
FILS

The Lady of the Camellias

Translated by
LIESL SCHILLINGER

Introduction by
JULIE KAVANAGH

PENGUIN BOOKS

PENGUIN BOOKS
Published by the Penguin Group
Penguin Group (USA) Inc., 375 Hudson Street
New York, New York 10014, USA

USA | Canada | UK | Ireland | Australia | New Zealand | India | South Africa | China
Penguin Books Ltd, Registered Offices: 80 Strand, London WC2R 0RL, England
For more information about the Penguin Group visit penguin.com

This translation first published in Penguin Books 2013

This work received support from the French Ministry of Foreign Affairs and the Cultural Services
of the French Embassy in the United States through their publishing assistance program.
Cet ouvrage publie dans le cadre du programme d'aide a la publication beneficie
du soutien du Ministere des Affaires Etrangeres et du Service Culturel de
l'Ambassade de France represente aux Etats-Unis.

LIBRARY OF CONGRESS CATALOGING-IN-PUBLICATION DATA
Dumas, Alexandre, 1824–1895.
[Dame aux camélias (Novel). English]
The Lady of the Camellias / ALEXANDRE DUMAS ; Translated by LIESL SCHILLINGER ;
Introduction by JULIE KAVANAGH.
pages cm.—(Penguin classics)
ISBN 978-0-14-310702-6
I. Title.
PQ2231.D2E513   2013
843'.8—dc23   2013005491

Printed in the United States of America
1 3 5 7 9 10 8 6 4 2

Contents

THE LADY OF THE CAMELLIAS

Introduction

The germ of *The Lady of the Camellias* was a long, impassioned poem by the twenty-three-year-old Alexandre Dumas *fils*. In 1847, after traveling in Spain and North Africa, Dumas had returned to Paris in time to see posters displayed throughout the city for a sale of great interest to him. For four days, from Wednesday, February 24, to Saturday, February 27, the entire contents of 11 boulevard de la Madeleine were to be auctioned—inlaid rosewood antiques, Sèvres vases and Saxe porcelain, bronze figurines, paintings, drawings, a library of French classics, a wardrobe of cashmere, ball gowns, and furs, as well as caskets of exquisite jewels. These were the possessions of Marie Duplessis, the famous young courtesan, who had died of tuberculosis on February 3. She, too, was twenty-three, and had been Dumas's mistress eighteen months earlier.

At the public preview on February 23, it seemed that all Paris had crammed into Duplessis's apartment, while carriages arriving from the grand faubourgs blocked the boulevard in front of the house. "Every different world was there," reported Théophile Gautier. "The best and the worst elbowed each other in the palace of this deceased queen." When Dumas joined the throng, he watched well-known courtesans being eyed by grandes dames, who were using the sale as a pretext to study these elegant women with whom they would never otherwise have allowed themselves to mingle. As he moved through familiar rooms still haunted by Duplessis's presence, he observed the prurience of people fingering her belongings and regarding every item as a trophy of prostitution. He learned that Duplessis had died in misery, the bailiffs having seized almost everything except her bed, and that night he poured his memories and impressions into an elegy he called "MD." Like all the verses collected in his book of juvenilia, *Sins of Youth*, it is a poor imitation of the French romantics and shows why Dumas *fils* had no success as a poet. And yet the eye for detail that characterizes his best writing is there, and so is his instinct for pity.

Visiting his father the following day, Dumas broke the news of Duplessis's death, reminding him that she was the girl who had once taken Dumas *père* by surprise by giving him a passionate kiss in a box of the Théâtre-Français. He talked about the poem he had written, and how going back to the apartment with all its associations had made him realize what a wonderful book could be made from her life and suffering.

"Well then," said Dumas *père*, "you should do it."

Since the publication of *The Three Musketeers* and *The Count of Monte Cristo*, Alexandre Dumas *père*, an irrepressible life force, had become a national treasure, while his son, despite the advantage of his name, was struggling to emerge from his father's immense shadow. Both had the same strapping physique, fine mustache, and features inherited from their ancestor, a Haitian slave girl—dark, crinkly hair, velvety brown eyes, and a creole tint to their skin. Dumas *fils* had turned into a typical Parisien flâneur and dandy, squandering his money on what today would be called designer clothes. He describes the look in his novella *Diane de Lys*: "Cane from Verdier, tie-pin from Janinch, watch and chain from Maclé, shirt, cravat and gloves from Boivin, suits from Staub or d'Humann." His debts in his early twenties amounted to fifty thousand francs, and he was always borrowing from his father, and relying on him to pull strings. Jovial and famously generous, Dumas *père* did his best to oblige, badgering his publishers to accept his son's "magnificent volume of poetry" by offering to write the preface. He urged his son to become his partner and collaborator, claiming this could bring him forty to fifty thousand francs a year, but Dumas *fils* was determined to forge his own writing career. "I was athirst for fame," he once confessed. *Sins of Youth*, published later the year of Duplessis's death, sold only fourteen copies, and *Adventures of Four*

Women and a Parrot, a high-spirited but unreadably long and rambling novel, made no impact either.

Father and son were constant companions, both relishing the louche pleasures of bohemian Paris and the liberties offered by society women prepared to compromise their respectability for a handsome young poet or illustrious novelist. Dumas *père*'s boyish exuberance made up for their difference in age, and his enjoyment of his son's biting wit was matched by Dumas *fils*'s admiration of his father's erudition and renown. This bond, though, was recent. For the first seven years of his childhood, Dumas *fils*'s only family had been his mother, a dressmaker, who gave birth to him at the age of thirty. A clerk without a cent, Dumas *père* could hardly support himself, let alone a mistress and a child, but he installed them both in a little apartment in Passy, and appeared from time to time. In 1831, following the success of his first play, Dumas *père* took responsibility for both his son and an illegitimate daughter from an earlier relationship. He wanted Alexandre to have the best possible education, and sent him to boarding school when he was just seven, and then to the Pension Saint-Victor, a daunting institution whose alumni included several famous men of letters. It was there that Dumas *fils* was forced to endure six years of humiliation and victimization. His schoolfellows, mostly the sons of rich, aristocratic families, taunted him for being a bastard, covered his exercise books with obscene drawings of his "mother," and brought him close to nervous collapse. Privately he scorned these boys as ridiculous versions of their fathers, destined for the same tedious, bureaucratic careers. But the experience marked him for life, and he re-created every harrowing detail in his powerful late novel *L'Affaire Clemenceau*. He wondered what the source could be of this compulsion to persecute, and whether his Caribbean blood had made him more sensitive to cruelty by carrying memories of tortures inflicted on men of a different color. These school years were the starting point for Dumas *fils*'s relentless crusades against social prejudice and injustice. "His great father, *le père prodigue*, had been all for self," said the English writer Edmund Gosse. "Alexandre would be all for others."

By May 1847, renting a room in an inn near his father's house in Saint Germain-en-Laye, Dumas *fils* had started work on the novel he was modeling on Marie Duplessis. The auction had given him his opening, and he began tinkering with facts, bringing the date forward to the middle of March and changing the address from boulevard de la Madeleine to 9 rue d'Antin (Duplessis had recently moved from No. 22). Writing in the first person, the narrator who makes his way through the crowded rooms is not the anguished Alexandre of "MD" but an urbane connoisseur appraising the superb belongings of the woman whose identity he has discovered to be that of the courtesan Marguerite Gautier. And yet he is recognizably Dumas the moralist, prepared to interrupt the story in order to deliver a lecture. The boudoir's gold and silver bottles bearing the initials and coronets of Marguerite's various lovers prompt a digression about a middle-aged prostitute who has corrupted her own daughter and arranged the abortion that leads to her death. Dumas then recalls the arrest he saw of a weeping girl clasping her baby, a scene that, like many others he had witnessed, overwhelmed him with pity, and led to what he called his "boundless compassion" for fallen women.

Indulgence toward courtesans in poetry and fiction was nothing new. It was a legacy of romanticism, and a favorite subject of his father's contemporaries Victor Hugo, Honoré de Balzac, and Alfred de Musset, all of whom Dumas *fils* knew. Drawing on this tradition, he made Marguerite Gautier a descendant of Hugo's redeemed courtesan Marion Delorme, who gives up her wealthy protectors for an impoverished young man. From an earlier literary precedent, the eighteenth-century classic *Manon Lescaut*, he borrowed his plot device, beginning with the end of the story and having the narrator learn its details from the lovesick hero. Unlike Dumas *père*, a man George Sand described as "carrying within himself a world of incidents, heroes, traitors, magicians, and adventures," Dumas *fils* was no inventor. To be successful, and to make a work his own, he needed to describe, clearly and poignantly, what he had seen. The most vibrant parts of *The Lady of the Camellias* are the observations, scenes, and conversations he simply reported—something his father understood. "I find my subjects in my dreams," Dumas *père* wrote, "my son takes his from real life. I work with my eyes shut, he with his open. I draw, he photographs."

On returning to Paris in 1844 after a spell of living in Marseille, Dumas *fils* often saw and admired a lovely girl he knew to be Marie Duplessis. In "À Propos de la Dame aux Camélias," his 1868 preface to the novel, he recalls:

> She was tall, very thin, with black hair and a pink and white complexion. Her head was small; she had long enameled eyes, like a Japanese woman's, but they were sparkling and alert. Her lips were redder than cherries, her teeth were the prettiest in the world; she looked like a little figurine made of Dresden china.

He had noticed her at the fashionable cafés and restaurants of the boulevard des Italiens; in her little blue horse-drawn carriage heading for the bois de Boulogne; at first nights at the theater or opera, where she sat with her signature bouquet of camellias, box of sweets, and opera glasses resting on the velvet ledge. There was nothing overtly seductive about her appearance; on the contrary, her favorite accessory was a cashmere shawl, which discreetly covered her shoulders and décolletage. One night at the Variétés theater, Dumas *fils* again caught sight of Duplessis sitting in her box, as he describes in notes he wrote as background for the actors in his play:

> She was alone there, or rather, she was the only person one could see . . . exchanging smiles and glances with three or four of our neighbours, leaning back, from time to time, to chat with an invisible occupant, who was no other than the aged Russian Count S—. Marie Duplessis was making signs to a fat woman with a freckled face and a flashy costume who was in one of the boxes of the higher tier opposite to her. This good lady, sitting beside a pale young woman who seemed restless and ill at ease, and whom she had presumably undertaken to "launch" in the world of gallantry, was a certain Clemence Pr-t, a milliner, whose establishment was in an apartment in the boulevard de la Made-

leine, in the house adjoining that in which Marie Duplessis occupied the mezzanine floor.

In the stalls beside Dumas *fils* was his friend Eugène Déjazet, the son of the great actress Virginie Déjazet, and a fellow young roué. Well acquainted with the *entremetteuse* Clémence Prat, Déjazet volunteered to ask Prat to arrange a meeting with Duplessis. The elderly aristocrat in the box was Count Gustav von Stackelberg, a retired diplomat and Duplessis's protector, who left the theater with her before the performance was over. The two young men then joined Prat and persuaded her to take them to boulevard de la Madeleine. The novel continues to chronicle exactly what happened next. They have dinner with Duplessis, who drinks too much champagne and becomes more raucous as the night wears on, distressing Dumas *fils* with bawdy language that sullies his idealistic image of her. She has been coughing incessantly, and when seized by a particularly violent fit, gets up from the table and runs into her dressing room. "Of those who were at supper I was the only one to be concerned," Dumas *fils* recalled in his notes to the actors. His immediate impulse was to follow her. In a candlelit room he saw Duplessis lying deathly pale on a chaise longue, struggling to catch her breath. Beside her was a silver bowl she was using as a spittoon, its water marbled with blood. Their subsequent conversation is reproduced in the novel, almost word for word. Duplessis was touched to see tears in the eyes of this intense young man as he sat beside her and kissed her hand; such tenderness and concern for her health was something her self-regarding suitors had rarely shown. She wanted to keep him in her life as a platonic friend, the relationship a courtesan values more than any other. But "Adet," as she called him (the French pronunciation of his initials), was already smitten, and craved the role of *amant de coeur*, which translates literally as "lover of the heart." As he was too young, too poor, and too possessive to be able to share her, their affair did not last long. Dumas *fils* claimed it had begun in September 1844 and ended with the letter he wrote at midnight on August 30, 1845, the dates every biographer and Dumas scholar have taken as fact. However, the evidence of a simple rental bill and the appearance of a new young lover make it highly unlikely that they were together for a year. If this attempt to extend the relationship is apocryphal, it is also perfectly understandable, if only as an admission of the profound influence Duplessis had on Dumas *fils*'s career. "It's to her that I owe my first success."

Written in less than a month, *The Lady of the Camellias* was published by the reputable firm of Cadot in 1848. According to Alfred Vandam, an English journalist living in Paris, its frankness and topicality made it the talk of the town. "It was in everyone's hands, and the press kept whetting the curiosity of those who had not read it with personal anecdotes of the heroine." The theater critic Jules Janin, who would write a memoir of Duplessis as a preface to the 1851 edition, was astonished at how much of her life was in it. "People were anxious to know the name of the heroine, her position in society, how much money she had left, the ornaments she had worn, and who her lovers had been. The public, who desire to know everything, and who in the end do know everything, gradually learned all those details, and having read the book, wished to read it again; it naturally came to pass that, the truth being known, the interest of the story was enhanced." The reason the novel was reprinted only once by Cadot was that its publication had coincided with a year of revolution in Paris. Bloody February had brought barricades into the streets, resulted in the overthrow of the monarchy, and left the country in economic crisis. Rioting had doomed popular entertainment, and Dumas *père*'s Théâtre Historique, which Dumas *fils* hoped would mount his stage adaptation of the story, had gone bankrupt by 1849. Pursued by creditors, Dumas *père*, now bankrupt himself, fled to Brussels. The son went back to being a jobbing writer, and his play of *The Lady of the Camellias* was put in a drawer.

Then came the change of regime on December 2, 1851, when Louis-Napoléon was made President of the Second Republic. Prior to that, Dumas *fils* had tried in vain to get a theater to stage his play. Finally the Vaudeville accepted it, but the censor immediately imposed a ban. This was lifted three days after the new president's appointment, and from its first night on February 2, 1852, *The Lady of the Camellias* was a theatrical sensation. Until then no dramatist had dared to put on stage a courtesan whose life had not been either distanced by history or poetized by legend. Young Dumas had not only brought the public into the world of Duplessis; he had also portrayed it exactly as he had known it, using the clothes, decor, and dialogue of modern life. "A drama of facile love has been turned into a literary event," exclaimed Jules Janin.

It was to turn into very much more than that. The pathos of the story and immediacy of its setting inspired Giuseppe Verdi to create his opera *La Traviata* in 1853 (the year the play, retitled *Camille* for an American audience, became a Broadway hit). In Verdi's hands the work is transfigured, acquiring a rapturousness, psychological subtlety, and tragic grandeur that music can convey far more powerfully than words. The opera's premiere in Venice on March 3 was a failure, but it soon became the popular hit it has remained for 160 years, the role of the heroine, Violetta, sung by every great international diva. The story of the Lady of the Camellias became a cultural phenomenon throughout the nineteenth and twentieth centuries: Marguerite Gautier has been pictured by artists and photographers from Aubrey Beardsley to Cecil Beaton, and portrayed on stage by Sarah Bernhardt, Eleonora Duse, and Isabelle Adjani, in ballets by Margot Fonteyn and Sylvie Guillem, and in films by Greta Garbo and Isabelle Huppert.

Dumas *fils* would have been astounded by the longevity of the play he had dashed off in eight days. When he wrote the preface to a new edition in 1868, he declared that the story was already "ancient history." No courtesan existed with the heart and selfless nature of Marguerite, and the profession had become a business exchange: "I'm beautiful, you're rich, give me what you have and I'll give you what I have. You don't have money? Well, good-bye." But the real reason for Dumas *fils*'s disillusion and cynicism was personal. A destructive two-year affair with a bored young married woman, a beautiful Russian countess he named the Lady of the Pearls, had annihilated his belief in romantic love. Lydia Nesselrode was the inspiration for another long, anguished, but much superior poem, "Saint

Cloud"; for the excellent novella *Diana de Lys*; for an overlong, self-pitying novel, *The Lady of the Pearls*; and for the dismayingly melodramatic reworking of *Diana de Lys* as a play. But unlike Duplessis, this lady was a toxic muse, her duplicity, lies, and callous abandonment of Dumas *fils* resulting in an embittered edge to his writing and a misogynistic attitude toward women.

There was also the fact that Dumas *fils* felt out of tune with his age. The sparkling *Belle Hélène* spirit of the Second Empire was anathema to him; a fierce moralist, he had decided to use his plays to pillory the license and laxity of the era. His 1855 play *Le Demi-Monde* (his own coinage) hardly seems the work of the same writer. A bitter satire, it is a portrait not of the bohemian world the term has come to define, but of a spurious society halfway between respectability and immorality. For Henry James, its grim realism and barbed dialogue made it a model for the drama of the time, "a singularly perfect and interesting work." Now, though, with its layers of lies, infamies, and deceit, its unconvincing plot twists, and a protagonist who is Dumas *fils* at his most priggish and cynical, *Le Demi-Monde* is as tiresomely pessimistic as it is outdated.

Dumas *fils*'s uncompromising ethics had made him sternly censorious of his father, whom he had come to blame for the dissipation of his youth: "I naturally did what I saw you do, and lived as you had taught me to live." Determined to distance himself from his father's excesses—the profligate spending, the affairs with actresses scarcely out of their teens, the births of two more "natural" children—he vented his anger about the stigma of illegitimacy in prefaces to his plays. (In one particularly extreme polemic he calls for new legislative measures on paternity, which would mean a five- to ten-year prison sentence for a young man who abandons the mother of his child.) And yet his own conduct was hardly exemplary. His daughter Colette was born four years before his marriage to Nadejda (Nadine) Naryschkine, another bored, beautiful Russian child bride, a friend and confidante of Lydia Nesselrode's. With her "tigress claws" and pathologically jealous nature, Nadine did not have the submissive nature that Dumas *fils* demanded in a wife, and their marriage was far from tranquil. This, combined with self-doubts and despair about human conduct, brought him close to suicide in the early 1860s. "I am completely worn out in body and in mind, heart and spirit," he wrote to George Sand, who would introduce him to her physician, Henri Favre, a mystic and a pioneer of psychoanalysis.

Although Favre was able to fortify Dumas *fils*'s wavering spirits, he had a disastrous influence on his work, fanning his moral fervor and encouraging him to write tediously verbose prefaces and pamphlets. Throughout the 1870s the plays became no more than homilies, their characters either voice pieces for the author or hallucinatory abstractions of vice and virtue. "His terrible knowledge suggested a kind of uniform," remarked Henry James. "It was almost like an irruption of the police." Dumas *fils* had lost touch with his public, and he knew it. In an 1879 preface to the ill-received *L'Étrangère*, he writes: "As a dramatist grows older he loses in clarity and suppleness, in the power to bring his stage alive, what he gains in his knowledge of the human heart. . . . A moment comes when he finds himself pushing the study of character and the analysis of feeling too far. He frequently becomes heavy, obscure, solemn, portentous, and, not to beat about the bush, a bore."

Two plays staged at the Comédie-Française, *Denise* (1885) and *Francillon* (1887), signaled a return to form and a reengagement with people, not symbolist types. But despite the barren years, Dumas *fils* remained his country's most successful dramatist, who won, by his 1875 election to the Académie Française, the official recognition and public respect denied his father. In today's France, however, this is no longer the case. It is Dumas *père* who is the literary giant, while his son has become the one-book author that he has always been elsewhere. His best novel, the compelling *L'Affaire Clemenceau*, whose sultry, scandalous heroine is modeled on his first infatuation, Louise Pradier, remains out of print. Only *The Lady of the Camellias* is to be found on the shelves of most bookshops and lending libraries, the other novels and plays available as badly scanned Internet editions in French.

Just as Flaubert, maddened by what Henry James called "the

boom of the particular hit," expressed a wish to buy up all the existing copies of *Madame Bovary* and burn them, Dumas *fils* came to resent the public's unquenchable appetite for his best-loved work. In a preface he was asked to write in 1886 for a lavish, illustrated quarto edition of the novel, his exasperation is evident. In earlier prefaces, and in the notes he wrote as background for actors, he had recounted everything he knew of Duplessis, but now he insisted, "I have nothing more to say." And yet the youthful memories this grand old man retained were the ones he cherished most. He admitted as much in an unpublished letter of April 1887 to Duplessis's first biographer, Romain Vienne. "If anyone had told me when I galloped in the forest of Saint-Germain with Marie that I would one day write a scholarly homage to Victor Hugo I would have been astonished. But between you and me, I would happily surrender this glory to anyone who could give me back that day, my twenties, and the Lady!"

JULIE KAVANAGH

Suggestions for Further Reading

Ariste, Paul d'. *La Vie et le Monde du Boulevard (1830–1870)* (Un Dandy: Nestor Roqueplan). Paris: Jules Tallandier, 1930.

Barnes, David S. *The Making of a Social Disease: Tuberculosis in Nineteenth-Century France.* Berkeley: University of California Press, 1995.

Boudet, Micheline. *La Fleur du Mal: la Veritable Histoire de la Dame aux Camélias.* Paris: Albin Michel, 1993.

Choulet, Jean-Marie. *Promenades à Paris et en Normandie avec la Dame aux Camélias: D'Alphonsine Plessis à La Traviata.* Paris: Editions Charles Corlet, 1998.

Claudin, Gustave. *Mes Souvenirs: Les Boulevards de 1840–1870.* Paris: Calmann Levy, 1884.

Corbin, Alain. *Women for Hire: Prostitution and Sexuality in France after 1850.* Cambridge, MA, London: Harvard University Press, 1990.

Gros, Johannes. *Une Courtisane Romantique, Marie Duplessis.* Paris: au Cabinet du Livre, 1929.

Issartel, Christiane. *Les Dames aux Camélias: De l'Histoire à la Légende.* Paris: Chene Hachette, 1981.

James, Henry. *The Scenic Art: Notes on Acting and the Drama 1872–1901.* London: Rupert Hart-Davis, 1949.

John, Nicholas. Ed. *Violetta and Her Sisters: The Lady of the Camellias: Responses to the Myth.* London: Faber and Faber, 1994.

Kavanagh, Julie. *The Girl Who Loved Camellias: The Life and Legend of Marie Duplessis.* New York: Alfred A. Knopf, 2013.

Maurois, Andre. *Three Musketeers: A Study of the Dumas Family.* Translated by Gerard Hopkins. London: Jonathan Cape, 1957.

Saunders, Edith. *The Prodigal Father*. London: Longmans, Green and Co., 1951.

Vandam, Albert. *An Englishman in Paris*. Vol 1. New York: D. Appleton & Co., 1892.

Vienne, Romain. *La Dame aux Camélias (Maris Duplessis)*. Paris: Paul Ollendorff, 1888.

A Note on the Translation

Do you remember that luscious young celebrity—Daisy something—who was such a big deal when she was twenty? She didn't act, or sing, or dance, she wasn't an heiress, but she managed to get herself known, envied, and talked about by everyone who mattered. She was, you know . . . famous for being famous. Daisy always wore expensive clothes and jewelry made by the most in-demand designers; she showed up at every opening and velvet-rope party, usually on the arm of some phenomenally rich man she was dating who had brought her there in a flashy car. You don't remember? What a pity. Apparently, her fifteen minutes of fame are over.

But really, once, nearly everyone knew all about Daisy. She was dangerously pretty, dangerously thin, lived a little too fast, and by the time she was twenty-three, she'd been in and out of rehab several times, and . . . well, things ended badly . . . and quickly. You still don't remember? Maybe this will help: She lived in Paris; Marguerite was her name in French, and though *marguerite* means "daisy," she was better known for another flower—the camellia, white or red. She carried a bouquet of them with her wherever she went, which is why people liked to call her the Lady of the Camellias. That is, Alexandre Dumas *fils* did, in the novel he wrote about her, *La Dame aux Camélias*. It is about a woman he fell passionately in love with in 1842, when he was eighteen; a famous Parisian courtesan of the 1840s named Marie Duplessis. When Marie died in 1847, her grave was strewn thickly with camellias. But when young Dumas first caught sight of her, she was a vision of youthful beauty, dressed in a white muslin summer dress and a straw hat. In the novel, he resurrected her in that outfit for a romantic country scene between Marguerite (Marie) and her besotted, obsessive lover, a naive young lawyer named Armand, who of course is cast in the image of Dumas *fils* himself.

You hold in your hands my translation of their tumultuous, doomed love affair. In my translation, I have endeavored to dust off the language of the excellent but antiquated previous English translations I have read, which make this timeless, relatable, and fiery story seem quainter, more distant, and more marmoreal than it is. It is important, while reading this novel, to understand that Marguerite and Armand are the kind of bright, self-destructive young things we still read about in magazines, watch on-screen, or brush up against today. Dumas *fils* had what we would call a "modern" sensibility, in the sense that he was unafraid to write quite baldly about behavior that would still be shocking today. While not explicit in a pornographic sense, his writing was not euphemistic, either. In a bedroom scene toward the end, when Marguerite and Armand briefly reconcile, Dumas *fils* writes with white-hot urgency that is searing to read even a century and a half after the author recorded it. Anyone who has read an outdated English translation of this novel, seen the opera it inspired (*La Traviata*, by Verdi), or watched the film it inspired (*Camille*, starring Greta Garbo) might have missed the audacity, obstinacy, sensuality, and recklessness of its characters.

In my translation, I have sought to preserve the immediacy and the frankness of the narration, as Armand relates it and as Dumas *fils* recorded it, so that its passion may come alive, while its author's idiom and settings are faithfully preserved and relayed. My goal was for twenty-first-century readers who encounter this tragic story of all-consuming love for the first time in these pages to receive the story's impact in all its dimensions, picturing it in the fully realized world of Dumas's nineteenth-century Paris, but feeling it as if it were happening in Paris, New York, or anywhere; and not centuries ago, but today . . . or even tomorrow.

LIESL SCHILLINGER

The Lady of the Camellias

CHAPTER I

It is my opinion that you cannot create a convincing character until you have made a broad study of human nature, just as you cannot speak a foreign language until you have studied it thoroughly.

Not having reached an age at which I consider myself qualified to invent a character, I content myself with simply describing one.

I therefore ask the reader to accept the truth of this story—all of whose characters, except for its heroine, are still living.

I should add that, in Paris, there are eyewitnesses to most of the facts I gather here, who would be able to confirm them should my own testimony be deemed insufficient. By a particular circumstance, I am the only one who can relate them all, as it was only I who was acquainted with the final details without which it would have been impossible to write an account that was both interesting and complete.

To return to my subject, let me tell you how these details came to my attention. On the twelfth day of the month of March, 1847, I saw in the rue Laffitte a large yellow sign announcing a sale of furniture and valuable curios. This sale was taking place after a death. The poster did not give the name of the deceased, but the sale was to take place on the rue d'Antin, No. 9, on the sixteenth, from noon to five o'clock.

Additionally, the sign specified, the apartment and its furnishings could be visited on the thirteenth and fourteenth.

I have always been fond of curios. I vowed not to miss this occasion, if only to look, not to buy.

The next day I presented myself at the rue d'Antin, No. 9.

It was early, but a good number of visitors were already in the apartment, even female visitors, who, though they were dressed in velvet and wrapped in cashmere shawls, and though they were awaited outside the doors by elegant coupés, gazed with astonishment and even admiration at the luxury that met their eyes.

Later I understood this admiration and astonishment, as, having myself begun to examine the offerings as well, I easily recognized that I was in the apartment of a kept woman. And if there is one thing society women long to see—and society women were on the premises—it is the private life of those Parisian women whose carriages splash theirs every day, who sit, like them and alongside them, in their boxes at the opera and at the Théâtre des Italiens, flaunting the insolent opulence of their beauty, their jewels, and their scandals.

The one in whose apartment I found myself was dead, so now even the most virtuous women could penetrate her bedroom. Death had purified the air surrounding this resplendent cloaca, and besides, the ladies could make excuse, if they needed to, that they had come to the sale without knowing whose home it was. They had seen some posters, and had wanted to check out the promised goods and make their selections ahead of time; nothing could be simpler. But that did not prevent them from seeking, in the midst of these marvels, traces of the life of this courtesan, about which they had, no doubt, heard so many strange accounts.

Unfortunately the mysteries had died with the goddess, and despite their best intentions these ladies were unable to find anything amid the objects on display after her death that hinted at what had been on offer while its tenant still breathed.

Nonetheless, of what remained, plenty was covetable. The furnishings were superb. Furniture of rosewood and marquetry, Sèvres vases and Chinese porcelain, Meissen statuettes, satin, velvet, and lace; nothing was lacking.

As I wandered the apartment I followed the curious noblewomen who had preceded me. They entered a room decorated with Persian wall hangings, and I, too, was about to enter, when the ladies left the room almost as quickly as they had entered it, smiling as if they were ashamed of this new wonder. This only increased my desire to enter. It was the dressing room, decked out with a multitude of toiletry articles, in which the breathtaking prodigality of the dead woman received its fullest expression.

Upon a large table that backed against the wall, its surface three feet wide and six feet long, glittered all the golden treasures of Aucoc and Odiot. It was a magnificent collection; not one of those thousand implements—so necessary to the beauty of a woman such as the one whose rooms we were visiting—was made of any metal other than gold or silver. However, it was clear that this collection could not have been obtained all at once; it had accumulated little by little, and the lover who had begun it was not the lover who had completed it.

Not being someone who can be shocked at the sight of the vanity table of a kept woman, I entertained myself by examining the intricacy of the objects, such as it was, and perceived that all these magnificently engraved utensils were marked with a variety of different monograms and crests.

I surveyed all these objects, each one of which represented a different prostitution of the poor girl, and told myself that God had been merciful to her, as he had not forced her to suffer the ordinary punishment of such a woman; he had permitted her to die in luxury and beauty, before old age set in, that first death of courtesans.

Really, what can be sadder to see than the old age of vice—above all, when it visits a woman? She retains no dignity and inspires no interest. That eternal regret, not of the wrong road taken, but of bad planning and ill-spent money, is one of the saddest things a person can hear. I knew a striking old courtesan who retained nothing of her past but a daughter who was almost as pretty as her mother had been—so her contemporaries said. That poor child, whose mother had never said, "You are my daughter," except to order her to support her in her old age as she had supported the girl in her childhood—that poor creature was named Louise, and, in obeying her mother, served her without inclination, without passion, and without pleasure, as she would have performed any trade, had anyone thought to teach her one.

The continual sight of depravity, a precocious depravity, fed by continual ill health, had extinguished in the girl the knowledge of right and wrong that God had perhaps planted in her, but that nobody had bothered to nurture.

I will always remember that young girl who walked along the boulevards almost every day at the same time. Her mother always accompanied her, as assiduously as a true mother would have accompanied her true daughter. I was very young then, and ready to accept the easy morality of my times. I remember nonetheless that the sight of this scandalous surveillance filled me with contempt and disgust.

Add to this that no virgin's face had ever conveyed such a feeling of innocence, such an expression of melancholy suffering. She resembled a statue of Resignation.

One day the face of this girl brightened. In spite of the program of debauchery that her mother had organized for her, it appeared that God had granted the sinner one happiness. And why, after all, would God, who had made her without strength, have left her with no consolation whatever for the painful burden of her life? One day she realized she was pregnant, and everything within her that remained pure and undefiled leapt for joy. The soul has strange refuges. Louise ran to her mother to announce the news that had made her so joyful. It is shameful to say this (however, we do not discuss immorality frivolously here; we relay a true fact, which we would perhaps do better to keep silent, if we did not believe that every now and then we must reveal the martyrs among those beings we condemn without understanding, whom we scorn without giving a chance to defend themselves), it is shameful, we will say, but the mother told her daughter that they barely had enough for two people as it was, and could not support three; that children in such circumstances were useless, and that a pregnancy was just so much lost time.

The next day a midwife we know only as the friend of the mother came to see Louise, who remained in bed several days afterward, and emerged thereafter paler and weaker than before.

Three months later a man took pity on her and attempted to heal her morally and physically, but the last blow had been too violent, and Louise died from complications following her miscarriage.

Her mother still lives. How? God knows.

This story returned to my thoughts as I contemplated the silver toiletry articles, and I must have passed a significant period of time in my reflections, as there was no longer anyone in the apartment except for me and a guard who kept a watchful eye from the door, to be sure I didn't make off with anything.

I walked up to this stout soul, in whom I provoked such grave anxiety.

"Sir," I said to him, "could you tell me the name of the person who resided here?"

"Miss Marguerite Gautier."

I knew that girl by name and by sight.

"What!" I said to the guard. "Marguerite Gautier is dead?"

"Yes, sir."

"When did she die?"

"Three weeks ago, I believe."

"And why are they permitting people to visit the apartment?"

"The creditors thought it would increase the selling prices. If people get a sense of the quality of the cloth and the furniture ahead of time, you understand, it boosts sales."

"So she had debts?"

"Oh! Sir. Abundant debts."

"But the sale will definitely cover them?"

"And then some."

"Who will get the surplus, then?"

"Her family."

"Then she has family?"

"So it would seem."

"Thank you, sir."

The guard, reassured of my good intentions, bowed to me, and I left.

"Poor girl!" I said to myself as I returned home. She must

have died in a pitiable state, because in her crowd, you have friends only when things are going well. In spite of myself, I grieved for the fate of Marguerite Gautier.

This may seem ridiculous to many people, but I have an inexhaustible sympathy for the plight of courtesans, and I refuse to apologize for this indulgence.

Once as I was going to the police station to pick up a passport, I saw a girl being led away by two policemen down an adjoining road. I don't know what the girl had done; all I can say is that she was shedding bitter tears while clutching a child a few months old, from whom her arrest would separate her. Since that day I have never been capable of despising a woman at first sight.

CHAPTER II

The sale was to take place on the sixteenth.

An interval of one day had been set between the open house and the sale, to give the drapers time to remove the hangings, curtains, and so on.

At that time I had recently returned from a trip. It was natural enough that nobody would have regarded the death of Marguerite as one of those juicy tidbits of news that friends make sure to tell anyone who returns to the capital of gossip. Marguerite was pretty, but the stir that such attention-getting women kick up in life fades quickly in death. They are suns that set just as they rose, without fanfare. Their deaths, when they die young, are discovered by all their lovers at the same time, because in Paris, nearly all the lovers of a well-known courtesan are intimately acquainted with one another. A few memories are shared about her, then everyone's lives continue as before, without the incident provoking a single tear.

These days, by the time you are twenty-five years old, tears come so rarely that you don't want to waste them on just anybody. It's more than enough to weep for the parents who have paid for the privilege of being mourned.

As for me, although my monogram did not appear on any of Marguerite's little necessities, this instinctive indulgence of mine—the natural pity I confessed just a little while ago—made me think of her death for a longer time than she perhaps deserved.

I recalled having very often run into Marguerite on the Champs-Élysées, where she rode without fail every day in a little blue coupé drawn by two magnificent bay horses, and remembered that I had observed in her at those times a distinction that women of her kind rarely possessed, a distinction that elevated her truly exceptional beauty.

Those unfortunate creatures are always accompanied when they go out, by whom nobody knows.

Since no man consents to publicly proclaim the nocturnal weakness he has for them, and since they are terrified of solitude, they drag along with them either women who, less fortunate than themselves, don't have a carriage, or one of those elegant old ladies who are considered elegant for no clear reason, and with whom one can speak without fear when one wants to obtain information of any sort about the women they accompany.

There was nobody like that for Marguerite. She always arrived on the Champs-Élysées alone, in her carriage, where she kept as discreet a profile as possible; in winter wrapped up in a great shawl, in summer wearing very simple dresses; and although there were plenty of people she knew along her favorite route, when by chance she smiled at them the smile was visible to them alone, a smile worthy of a duchess.

She did not ride back and forth from the Rond-Point to the entry of the Champs-Élysées, as her fellow courtesans did and do. Her two horses carried her rapidly to the Bois. There she would disembark from the carriage, walk for an hour, then climb back into her carriage and return home with her team at a swift trot.

All these circumstances, which I had sometimes witnessed, flashed before my eyes, and I mourned the death of this girl as one would mourn the complete destruction of any beautiful work of art.

In short, it was impossible to conceive of a beauty more charming than Marguerite's.

Tall and slender almost to excess, she possessed to a supreme degree the art of concealing this oversight of nature by artfully arranging the things she wore. The generous flounces of her silken gown spilled from both sides of her shawl, whose tip touched the ground; and the thick muff that concealed her hands, and which she pressed against her bosom, was cleverly positioned among the pleats of her dress such that the eye could find no fault in her contours.

Her head, a marvel, was the product of particularly felicitous coquetry. It was small, and her mother, as de Musset said, seemed to have made it small in order to make it with care.

Into an oval of indescribable grace, set a pair of black eyes with brows so perfectly arched that they look painted on; veil those eyes with long lashes that cast a shadow on the rosy hue of her cheeks when they are lowered; trace a fine nose, straight, spiritual, the nostrils slightly dilated in their ardent aspiration for the sensual life; draw a symmetrical mouth, whose lips open graciously on teeth as white as milk; color the skin with the velvet that covers peaches no hand has touched, and you will have before you the ensemble of that charming head.

Jet-black hair, naturally waved or not, descended from her forehead in two large bands, and disappeared behind her head, permitting a glimpse of her ears, upon which sparkled two diamonds, worth four to five thousand francs apiece.

The fact that her passionate life had somehow produced the virginal, childlike expression that characterized Marguerite's face was something we were forced to accept without understanding it.

Marguerite had a wonderful portrait done by Vidal, the only man whose pencil could do her justice. After her death I had this portrait in my possession for several days, and the likeness was so astonishing that it served to furnish me with specific details that had eluded my memory.

Among the details in this chapter are a few that came to me only later, but I write them down at once so as not to need to return to them, once this woman's eventful history begins.

Marguerite attended every premiere, and spent all her evenings either at the theater or at a ball. Each time a new play was performed, one could be sure to see her there, with three items she was never without, which always occupied the front of her ground-floor theater box: her opera glasses, a bag of candy, and a bouquet of camellias.

During twenty-five days of the month, the camellias were white, and during five they were red; nobody has ever known the reason for this variation in color, which I note without being able to explain it, and which her friends and the habitués of the theaters she most frequently attended often remarked upon, just as I do.

Nobody had ever seen Marguerite with any flowers but camellias. And at Mme Barjon, her florist, she had been given the nickname "the lady of the camellias," and the name had stuck.

I knew besides, as does everyone who belongs to a certain Parisian social milieu, that Marguerite had been the mistress of the most fashionable young men, that she said so openly, and that the men prided themselves on the association, which proved that both lovers and mistress were happy with each other.

However, for three years or so, after a trip to Bagnères, she had only kept company, it was said, with an old foreign duke, enormously rich, who had tried to separate her as much as possible from her old life, something to which she seemed to have submitted with reasonably good grace.

Here is what I was told on this subject.

In the spring of 1842, Marguerite was so weak, so changed, that the doctors ordered her to take a rest cure and she left for Bagnères.

Among the invalids was the daughter of this duke, who not only had the same illness but also resembled Marguerite in the face, to the point that you could have taken them for sisters. But the young duchess was in the final stages of consumption, and a few days after Marguerite's arrival she died.

One morning the duke, who had stayed at Bagnères as one does linger on the soil where one has buried a part of one's heart, caught sight of Marguerite around the curve of a tree-lined road.

It seemed to him as if he were seeing the shade of his child pass by, and, walking toward her, he took her by the hands, embraced her in tears, and, without asking who she was, begged permission to see her and to love in her the living image of his dead daughter.

Marguerite, who was alone at Bagnères except for her maid, and who in any case had no fear of compromising herself, granted the duke what he asked.

There were some people at Bagnères who knew her, and who approached the duke in an official capacity to warn him of Mlle Gautier's true nature. This news came as a blow to the old man, because in that respect any resemblance to his daughter ceased, but it was already too late. The young woman had become a necessity of his heart and his only reason, his only excuse, to go on living.

He made her no reproach—he did not have the right—but he asked her if she felt she was capable of changing her way of life, offering in exchange for this sacrifice all the compensation she could desire. She agreed.

It must be admitted that at this moment Marguerite, whose fundamental nature was lively, was sick. She had come to regard her past as one of the principal causes of her illness, and a sort of superstition made her hope that God would allow her to keep her beauty and health if she would repent and reform.

And, in truth, the waters, the long walks, honest fatigue, and rest had very nearly restored her to health when summer came to an end.

The duke accompanied Marguerite to Paris, where he continued to come see her as he had done at Bagnères.

This liaison, of which nobody knew the true origin or motivation, caused a great stir here, and the duke, who previously had been known for his great wealth, now became known for his prodigality.

The duke's intimacy with the young woman was put down to libertinage, so common among rich old men. Everything was assumed, except for what actually was happening.

However, the feelings that this father had for Marguerite had such innocent roots that any connection with her other than a connection of the heart would have seemed like incest to him, and he never spoke a word to her that his daughter might not have heard.

But let's not make out our heroine to be any finer than she was. We shall say, therefore, that as long as she remained in Bagnères, it was not hard for her to keep the promise she had made the duke, and she kept it; but once back in Paris, this girl who had been accustomed to a life of dissipation, balls, even orgies, felt as if she would die of boredom in her solitude, which was interrupted only by periodic visits from the duke, and memories of her former life burned in her mind and heart like scorching gusts.

Add to this that Marguerite had come back from this trip more beautiful than ever, that she was twenty years old, and that the illness that had been tamed, but not vanquished, lingered, provoking those fiery passions that nearly always result from an inflammation of the chest.

The duke suffered great pain, therefore, on the day when his friends, who were always on the watch for scandal involving the young woman with whom he was compromising himself, so they said, came to tell him that whenever she was sure he would not be coming to see her, she had guests over, and that those visits often lasted the whole night.

Upon being questioned, Marguerite confessed everything to the duke, and advised him without a moment's hesitation to stop troubling himself with her, because she did not have the strength to keep the agreement they'd made, and did not want to continue receiving the kindnesses of a man she was deceiving.

For eight days the duke stayed away; it was the most he could do. But on the eighth day, he came to beg Marguerite to receive him again, promising he would accept her just the way she was as long as he could see her, and swearing to her that on pain of death he would never reproach her.

This is where things stood three months after Marguerite's return—which is to say, in November or December of 1842.

CHAPTER III

On the sixteenth, at one o'clock, I presented myself at the rue d'Antin.

From the gate you could hear the cries of the auctioneers. The apartment was filled with curious onlookers.

All the notoriously elegant celebrities were there, being surreptitiously inspected by the fashionable ladies who once again were using the pretext of the sale to indulge their right to get a closer look at women with whom they would never have had occasion to mingle, and whose simple pleasures they perhaps secretly envied.

Mme la Duchesse de F . . . jostled with Mlle A . . . , one of the saddest specimens among our modern courtesans; Mme la Marquise de T . . . hesitated to buy a piece of furniture that was being bid upon by Mme D . . . , the most elegant and noted adulteress of our time; the Duc d'Y . . . , who leaves Madrid only to ruin himself in Paris, and leaves Paris only to ruin himself in Madrid, and who, with all his excesses, doesn't even exhaust the principal on his income, chatted with Mme M . . . , one of our wittiest raconteurs, who when she feels like it, writes down what she says and signs her name to it, while exchanging confidential glances with Mme de N . . . , that lovely perambulator of the Champs-Élysées, who is almost always dressed in pink or blue and whose carriage is drawn by two giant black horses, which Tony had sold her for ten thousand francs and which sum she had paid him, in her way; and finally Mlle R . . . , who earned through sheer talent twice what society ladies fetched with their dowries and three times what other women brought in with their arts, had come, despite the cold, to make some purchases, and she was not the one who drew the least attention.

We could also give the initials of a number of people who were reunited in this living room and were astonished to find themselves thrown together; but we fear we might weary the reader.

Let us merely say that everyone was suffused with a mad gaiety, and that among those present, many had known the dead woman, and seemed not to remember that fact.

There was much hearty laughter; the auctioneers shouted at earsplitting volume; the salesmen who had invaded the benches in front of the selling tables tried in vain to quiet things down so they could conduct their business calmly. Never had a reunion been noisier or more varied.

I was gliding inobtrusively into the middle of this depressing tumult when I recalled that there was an area near the bedroom in which the poor creature had died where her furniture was being sold to pay off her debts. Having come more with the intention of looking than buying, I studied the faces of the auctioneers, whose expressions bloomed radiantly every time an object reached a price they had never dreamed possible.

Honest people who had speculated on the prostitution of this woman, who had profited a hundred percent from her, who had followed the last moments of her life in gossip circulars, and who had come after her death to gather the fruits of their honorable calculations and at the same time to serve the interests of their shameful credit.

How right the ancients were who had the same god for merchants and for thieves!

Dresses, shawls, jewels sold with incredible speed. None of that held any interest for me, so I kept waiting.

Suddenly I heard the cry:

"One volume, perfect-bound, gilded on the spine, entitled: 'Manon Lescaut.' There's something written on the first page. Ten francs."

"Twelve," said a voice after a rather long silence.

"Fifteen," I said.

Why? I do not know. No doubt for this "something written."

"Fifteen," repeated the auctioneer.

"Thirty," said the first bidder, in a tone that seemed to defy anyone to challenge him.

It became a battle.

"Thirty-five!" I shouted, in the same tone.

"Forty."

"Fifty."

"Sixty."

"A hundred."

I swear that if my goal had been to cause a sensation, I would have completely succeeded, because with this bid a great silence took over, and everyone started looking at me to figure out who this fellow was who seemed so intent on acquiring this book.

Apparently the emphasis I put on my last word convinced my antagonist, and he abandoned this battle, which had served only to make me pay ten times what the volume was worth. Leaning toward me, he said to me quite graciously, if somewhat tardily, "I yield, sir."

Nobody else having spoken, the book went to me.

Lest a new wave of stubbornness overtake me, which my pride might have enjoyed, but which my purse would have taken ill, I wrote down my name, had the book put to the side, and left. I must have given plenty to think about to the people who witnessed this scene, who undoubtedly asked themselves why on earth I had paid a hundred francs for a book I could have gotten anywhere for ten or fifteen francs at the most.

An hour later I sent for my purchase.

On the first page was written in ink, in an elegant script, a dedication to the recipient of the book. This dedication carried these sole words:

MANON TO MARGUERITE,
  Humility

It was signed: Armand Duval.

What did this word mean: *humility*?

Would Manon recognize in Marguerite, in M. Armand Duval's opinion, a superiority of vice, or of heart?

The latter interpretation seemed more likely, as the former would have been nothing but an insolent liberty that Marguerite could not have appreciated, whatever her opinion of herself.

I went out again and thought no more of the book until that night, as I was going to bed.

Certainly *Manon Lescaut* is a touching story, of which not one detail is unknown to me, and yet whenever I find that book in my hand, my sympathy for it draws me, I open it, and for the hundredth time I live again with Abbé Prévost's heroine. That heroine is so real that I feel as if I have known her. In this new circumstance, the comparison made between her and Marguerite gave an unexpected character to my reading, and, out of pity, my indulgence for the poor girl who had left behind this volume grew into something almost like love. Manon had died in a desert, it is true, but in the arms of the man who had loved her with all the energy of his soul, who, when she was dead, laid her in a grave, watered her with his tears, and buried his own heart with her; whereas Marguerite, a sinner like Manon, and perhaps a convert like her, had died in the bosom of sumptuous luxury, and, if I could believe my own eyes, in the bed of her own past, but amid a desert of the heart far more arid, far more vast, far more pitiless than that in which Manon had been buried.

And in fact Marguerite, as I learned from friends who knew of the final circumstances of her life, had not had one single truly consoling visit at her bedside throughout the two months of her lingering and painful death struggle.

And then, from Manon and Marguerite, my thoughts traveled to certain women I knew who lightheartedly pursued the same path to destruction, which hardly ever varies its route.

Poor creatures! If it's wrong to love them, the least we can do is to pity them. You pity the blind man who has never seen the rays of the sun, the deaf man who has never heard the sounds of nature, the mute who has never been able to give voice to his soul, and yet, under the false pretext of modesty, you choose not to pity that blindness of the heart, that deafness of the soul, that muteness of conscience, which drive a miserable afflicted woman mad and make her incapable, however much she might wish it, of seeing goodness, of hearing the Lord, and of speaking the pure language of love and faith.

Victor Hugo created *Marion Delorme*, Alfred de Musset created *Frederic and Bernerette*, Alexandre Dumas created *Fernande*, the thinkers and poets of the ages have bestowed the gift of mercy upon the courtesan, and sometimes a great man has rehabilitated them by virtue of his love, and sometimes even with his name.

If I insist in this way upon this point, it is because among those who will read me, many perhaps are already inclined to throw down this book, fearing they will find nothing in it but an apology for vice and prostitution, and the youth of the author no doubt adds to this concern. But let those who would think this way disabuse themselves, and let them continue reading, if this is the only fear that holds them back.

I am quite simply convinced of one principle, which is this: For a woman whose education has not taught her goodness, God almost always opens the way to two paths that lead to it—the path of suffering, and the path of love. They are difficult; those who walk them end up with bleeding feet, their hands scraped raw, and brambles along the road snag the trappings of their vice until they arrive at their end with that nudity at which one does not blush in the presence of the Lord.

Anyone who encounters these hardy travelers must support them, and tell everyone that they have encountered them, because by spreading this news, they show the way.

It is not a question of baldly placing two markers at the outset of life's journey, one of them bearing the inscription "The Good Path," the other the warning "The Bad Path," and telling those who present themselves to choose. One must, like Christ, show the side roads that will lead those who have been tempted onto the second path back to the first; and above all, one must not make the first steps of the road back too painful or seem too arduous to undertake.

Christianity supplies the marvelous parable of the prodigal son to teach us indulgence and forgiveness. Jesus was full of compassion for souls wounded by mortal passions, and whose wounds he liked to salve, dressing them with balm he drew from the wounds themselves. In this way, he said to the magdalen, "Much will be forgiven because you have loved much." A sublime pardon that awoke a sublime faith.

Why would we make ourselves more inflexible than Christ? Why, in clinging obstinately to opinions of people who affect severity in order to be thought strong, would we spurn, as they do, souls that bleed with wounds that, like the diseased blood of an invalid, surge with the evil of their pasts, and require nothing more than a friendly hand to tend them and heal their hearts?

It is my own generation that I address, those for whom the theories of Monsieur Voltaire happily no longer hold, those who, like me, understand that for fifteen years humanity has been caught up in one of its most audacious moments. The knowledge of good and evil has been gained once and for all; faith is being rebuilt; respect for holy things has returned to us; and if the world has not achieved perfection in every respect, it is at least better. The efforts of all men of intelligence strive toward the same goal, and all great wills apply themselves to the same principle: Let us be good, let us be young, let us be sincere! Evil is nothing but vanity; let us take pride in the good, and, above all, let us not despair.

Let us not despise the woman who is neither mother nor daughter nor wife. Let us not limit our esteem to family life, narrow our tolerance to simple egotism. Given that heaven rejoices more at the repentance of one sinner than over a hundred good men who have never sinned, let us endeavor to make heaven rejoice. We may be rewarded with interest. Let us leave along the path the alms of our forgiveness for those whose earthly desires have marooned them, so that a divine hope may save them, and, as the wise old women say when they prescribe a remedy of their own invention, if it doesn't help, at least it can't hurt.

Certainly it must seem presumptuous of me to seek to draw

such grand conclusions from the slender matter I treat here, but I am one of those who believe that the whole resides in the part. The child is small, and contains the man; the brain is a cramped space that houses all thought; the eye is only a dot, and encompasses miles.

CHAPTER IV

Two days later, the sale was completely over. It had brought in a hundred and fifty thousand francs.

The creditors had divided two-thirds among themselves, and the family, which consisted of a sister and a little nephew, inherited the rest.

This sister's eyes had opened wide when the businessman had written to tell her that she was the inheritor of fifty thousand francs.

It had been six or seven years since this young woman had seen her sister, who had vanished one day without anyone's being able to discover thereafter, from her or from others, the least detail about the life she had led following the moment of her disappearance.

She arrived in Paris with all speed, and great was the astonishment of those who had known Marguerite when they saw that her sole inheritor was a plump and pretty country girl who until that moment had never left her village.

Her luck was made in one fell swoop, without her knowing the source of this unhoped-for fortune.

She returned to the country, someone told me later, burdened with great sadness by the death of her sister, a burden that was nonetheless lightened by the rate of four and a half percent interest she had managed to secure on the principal.

All these details reverberating around Paris—that hub of scandal—soon began to be forgotten, and I myself was almost forgetting the role I had played in these events when a new incident brought Marguerite's entire history to my attention and acquainted me with details so touching that I felt compelled to write the history I am writing now.

For three or four days the apartment had been on the rental market, emptied of all its auctioned furniture, when one morning someone rang at my home.

My servant, or rather my porter, who performed domestic duties, went to the door and brought me a visiting card, telling me that the person who had given it to him desired to speak with me.

I glanced at the card, and read there these two words: *Armand Duval.*

I struggled to remember where I had seen that name before, and I recalled the first page of the volume of *Manon Lescaut.*

What could the person who had given this book to Marguerite want with me? I gave instruction to let the man who was waiting enter immediately.

I soon saw a young blond man, tall, pale, dressed in a traveling suit he seemed to have worn for several days and not even bothered to brush upon his arrival in Paris, as it was covered in dust.

Monsieur Duval, strongly moved, made no effort to hide his emotion, and it was with tears in his eyes and a tremor in his voice that he told me, "Sir, you will forgive, I beg, my visit and my attire; but apart from the fact that among people our age such things are not too embarrassing, I wanted so much to see you today that I didn't even stop at the hotel where I sent my trunks, and hurried to your home, afraid that, though the hour is early, I might not find you here."

I begged M. Duval to sit by the fire, which he did while withdrawing from his pocket a handkerchief, in which, for a moment, he hid his face.

"You must not be able to imagine," he resumed, sighing sadly, "what this unknown visitor might want of you, at such an hour, so oddly dressed, and weeping like this. I have come quite simply, sir, to ask you a great favor."

"Speak, sir; I am at your service."

"You attended the sale of Marguerite Gautier?"

At this name, the emotion that had gripped this young man overcame him, and he was forced to raise his hands to his eyes.

"I must appear ridiculous to you," he added. "Excuse me again for that, and believe that I will never forget the patience with which you are listening to me."

"Sir," I replied, "if the service that I apparently am able to render you will serve to ease a little the sorrow you are feeling, tell me quickly how I can be of use, and you will find in me a man happy to oblige you."

M. Duval's pain was affecting, and despite myself I wanted to do what I could to help him.

He then said to me, "You bought something at Marguerite's sale?"

"Yes, sir, a book."

"*Manon Lescaut*?"

"Correct."

"Do you still have this book?"

"It is in my bedroom."

Upon this news, Armand Duval seemed relieved of a great weight, and thanked me as if I had already done him a great favor merely by keeping this volume.

I got up, went to my bedroom to get the book, and gave it to him.

"That's definitely the one," he said, looking at the dedication on the first page and leafing through it. "That's definitely the one."

Two large tears fell on the pages.

"Ah, well, sir," he said, raising his head to me, not even trying to hide from me anymore the fact that he'd been crying and was about to cry again, "do you have a great attachment to this book?"

"Why, sir?"

"Because I have come to ask you to give it to me."

"Excuse my curiosity," I said, "but you, therefore, are the one who gave it to Marguerite Gautier?"

"I am."

"The book is yours, sir; take it. I am happy to be able to return it to you."

"But," M. Duval resumed in embarrassment, "the least I can do is to refund the price you paid for it."

"Permit me to offer it to you as a gift. The price of a single book in a sale like this one is a caprice, and I no longer remember how much I paid for it."

"You paid a hundred francs."

"That's true," I said, embarrassed in turn. "How do you know that?"

"It's quite easy. I was hoping to arrive in Paris in time for Marguerite's sale, and I arrived only this morning. I wanted absolutely to have some object that came from her, and I ran to the auctioneer to ask permission to look at the list of articles that had been sold and the names of the buyers. I saw that this volume had been bought by you, and resolved to beg you to give it to me, even though the price you had paid for it made me fear you were not attached to it as a mere souvenir, but rather had some particular interest in possessing it."

By speaking this way, Armand evidently seemed to fear I might have known Marguerite in the way he had known her.

I endeavored to reassure him.

"I knew Mlle Gautier by sight only," I told him. "Her death made the same impression on me that the death of any pretty young woman would make on any young man who had once taken pleasure in the sight of her. I wanted to buy something at her sale, and stubbornly began to bid on this volume—I don't know why; for the sheer pleasure of enraging a gentleman who was set upon it, and seemed to be defying me to get it. I repeat to you therefore, sir, this book is at your disposal, and I beg you again to accept it as a gift, not to take it from me as I might take it from an auctioneer, so that it may represent for us the beginning of a longer acquaintance and a closer friendship."

"All right, sir," Armand said to me, extending his hand and shaking mine. "I accept, and I will be grateful to you all my life."

I very much wanted to ask Armand about Marguerite, as the book's dedication, the young man's journey, and his desire to possess this volume inflamed my curiosity; but I feared that if I were to quiz my visitor it would seem that I had refused his

money in order to gain the right to interfere in his private affairs.

You would have thought that he had read my mind, because
he said to me, "You have read this volume?"

"In its entirety."

"What did you think of the two lines I wrote?"

"I instantly perceived that in your eyes the poor girl to whom
you had given this volume was outside the common order, because I could not see these lines as empty compliment."

"And you were right, sir. This girl was an angel. Hold on,"
he said. "Read this letter."

And he handed me a document that seemed to have been
read many times.

I opened it; here is what it contained:

My dear Armand, I received your letter. You remain in good
health, and I thank God for that. Yes, my friend, I am ill, and
with one of those illnesses that are merciless; but the interest that
you are kind enough to take in me greatly reduces my suffering.
I will not live long enough to have the happiness of clasping the
hand that wrote the fine letter I just received, and whose words
would heal me, if anything could. I will not see you again, as I
am near death, and hundreds of leagues separate you from me.
My poor friend! Your Marguerite of other days is much changed,
and it is perhaps better that you not see her again than that you
see her as she is now. You ask me if I forgive you; oh! With all
my heart, my friend, because the pain you caused me was nothing but a proof of the love you had for me. It has been a month
since I have kept to my bed, and I care so much for your esteem
that every day I write down the diary of my life, from the moment we left each other to the moment I will no longer have the
strength to write.

If the interest that you take in me is genuine, Armand, on your
return go visit Julie Duprat. She will give you this journal. You
will find in it the explanation and the excuse for what has come
between us. Julie is very good to me; we speak of you often. She
was there when your letter arrived; we wept as we read it.

In the event you had not sent me news of yourself, she was

supposed to see to it that these papers reached you upon your arrival in France. Don't be grateful to me for them. This daily return to the only happy moments of my life has done me enormous good, and if you find in reading them an excuse for the past, I find in them a continual solace.

I would like to leave you something that always reminded me of your spirit, but everything has been taken from me, and nothing belongs to me.

Do you understand, my friend? I am going to die, and from my bedroom I can hear the guard that my creditors have appointed, walking in the living room, making sure that nobody carries anything off, and that nothing will be left me in the event that I do not die. I can hope only that they will wait until the end to begin selling.

Oh! Men are pitiless! Or perhaps I am wrong, and God is just and unyielding.

Well, dearly beloved, you will have to come to my sale, and buy something, because if I put aside the tiniest object for you and they learn of it, they would be able to charge you with possession of stolen goods.

What a sad life it is that I leave behind!

How good God would be if he would permit me to see you before I die! But in all probability, adieu, my friend; forgive me for not writing you at greater length, but those who say they are healing me wear me out with bloodlettings, and my hand refuses to write anymore.

MARGUERITE GAUTIER

In truth, the last words were barely legible.

I gave this letter back to Armand, who doubtless had reread it in his mind while I read it on paper, because he said to me as he took it, "Who would ever believe that a kept woman wrote that!" And, moved by his memories, he contemplated for some time the handwriting of this letter, and eventually brought it to his lips.

"When I think," he resumed, "that she died without my being able to see her and that I will never see her again; when I think that she made sacrifices for me that a sister would not have made, I cannot forgive myself for having let her die like this.

"Dead! Dead! And while thinking of me, while writing and speaking my name, poor, dear Marguerite!"

Armand, letting his thoughts and his tears flow freely, gave me his hand and continued, "Anyone who saw me here mourning a death like this one in this way would think I was a child; but it is because nobody knows how I made this woman suffer, how cruel I was, how good she was and how submissive. I had thought that it was for me to forgive her, but today I consider myself unworthy of the forgiveness she granted me. Oh! I would give ten years of my life to weep one hour at her feet."

It is always difficult to console someone for a pain one does not oneself know, but I felt such an active sympathy for this young man who so openly made me the confidant of his sorrows that I believed my words would not be indifferent to him, and I said, "Do you not have relatives, or friends? Take heart; go to them and they will console you. As for me, all I can do is pity you."

"It's true," he said, as he got up and began pacing around my room. "I am boring you. Excuse me, I had forgotten that my pain could mean but little to you, and that I am importuning you about something that couldn't and shouldn't interest you at all."

"You mistake my meaning. I am entirely at your service; it is just that I regret my inability to ease your heartache. If my company and the company of my friends can distract you, if, in short, there is anything at all you need from me, I want you to know the great pleasure I will take in being helpful to you."

"Excuse me, excuse me," he said. "Pain intensifies the emotions. Let me stay here a few minutes more; I need time to dry my eyes so people on the street won't stare at me like I'm an oddity, a grown man crying like a baby. You have made me very happy by giving me this book; I will never know how to repay you."

"By according me a little of your friendship," I told Armand, "and by telling me the cause of your heartache. It's consoling to talk about what one suffers."

"You are right; but today I am overcome by the need to cry, and if I spoke with you, it would be nothing but words without end. One day I will share this story with you, and you will see if I am right to feel sorry for the poor girl. And now," he added, rubbing his eyes one last time and looking at himself in the mirror, "tell me that you don't find me too inane, and permit me to come back and see you another time."

The man's expression was so good and mild; I nearly hugged him.

As for him, his eyes began again to cloud over with tears; he saw that I noticed, and averted his gaze.

"Well then," I said to him. "Courage."

"Good-bye," he said.

And making an extraordinary effort to keep from crying, he left my home, not so much leaving as fleeing.

I raised the curtain by my window and watched him board the carriage that awaited him at the door; he was scarcely inside before he dissolved into tears and hid his face in his handkerchief.

CHAPTER V

A fairly long time passed before I heard talk of Armand, but the subject of Marguerite, on the other hand, came up quite often.

I don't know if you've noticed, but once the name of someone who is supposed to be unknown to you, or at least indifferent to you, is spoken before you, details begin to cluster around this name, little by little, and you begin to hear your friends speak of things they had never before discussed with you. It is then you discover that this person was practically connected to you, that she had passed unobserved through your life many times; you find coincidences in events people relate that seem to have an actual connection with events in your own life. I had positively never known Marguerite, though I had seen her, bumped into her, and knew her face and her habits; and yet, after that sale, her name came frequently to my ears, and, given the circumstances I related in the previous chapter, this name was blended with a heartache so profound that my astonishment grew, magnifying my curiosity.

The result of this was that every time I ran into friends with whom I had never before spoken of Marguerite, I would say, "Did you ever know someone named Marguerite Gautier?"

"The Lady of the Camellias?"

"Exactly."

"*Very well!*"

These *Very wells!* were sometimes accompanied by smirks that left no doubt as to their meaning.

"Ah, and what was she like?" I'd continue.

"A grand girl."

"That's all?"

"My God! Yes, more spirit and maybe a little more heart than the rest."

"And you know nothing in particular about her?"

"She ruined the Baron de G . . . ."

"Only him?"

"She was the mistress of the old Duc de . . . ."

"Was she really his mistress?"

"So they say. In any case, he gave her a lot of money."

Always the same generalities.

However, I would have been curious to learn something about the liaison between Marguerite and Armand.

One day I ran into one of those men who continually associate with courtesans. I asked him:

"Did you know Marguerite Gautier?"

The same *very well* was his answer.

"What kind of girl was she?"

"A fine, pretty girl. I was saddened to learn of her death."

"Didn't she have a lover named Armand Duval?"

"A tall, blond man?"

"That's true. What's Armand's story?"

"He was a guy who squandered what little resources he had on her, I believe, and was forced to leave her. They say he was crazy about her."

"And she?"

"She loved him very much, too, everyone always says, but only in the way women like that can. You shouldn't expect more from them than they're capable of giving."

"What's become of Armand?"

"I don't know. We knew him very little. He spent five or six months with Marguerite, but in the countryside. When she came back, he left."

"And you haven't seen him since?"

"Never."

Me neither. I had begun to ask myself if, at the time he presented himself at my home, the recent news of Marguerite's death had exaggerated his old love and, as a consequence, his grief, and I told myself that perhaps he had already forgotten, along with her death, the promise he had made to come back and see me.

This suspicion would have been reasonable enough had it been somebody else, but there had been a sincere tenor to Armand's despair, and, passing from one extreme to the other, I wondered if his heartache had turned into illness, and that if I hadn't had news from him, it was because he was sick, or maybe even dead.

I was interested in this young man in spite of myself. Perhaps there was a degree of egotism in this interest; perhaps I had glimpsed a touching love story beneath his pain, and perhaps, in short, it was my desire to know it that was largely responsible for my concern over Armand's silence.

Since M. Duval did not return to visit me, I resolved to visit him. It was not hard to find a pretext, but unfortunately I did not know his address, and none of the people I had questioned could tell me it.

I went to the rue d'Antin. Marguerite's doorman might know where Armand lived. He was a new doorman. He didn't know any more than I did. I then obtained the name of the cemetery where Mlle Gautier had been buried. It was the cemetery of Montmartre.

April had reappeared, the weather was lovely, and the graves no longer had the dolorous, desolate air that winter gives them; at last it was warm enough for the living to remember the dead and to visit them. I went to the cemetery, telling myself, "With one glance at Marguerite's grave I will see if Armand is still suffering, and maybe I will learn what has become of him."

I entered the caretaker's house and asked if on the twenty-second of the month of February a woman named Marguerite Gautier had been buried in the cemetery of Montmartre.

The man leafed through a fat book where all those who entered this final resting place were inscribed and enumerated, and responded that yes, on the twenty-second of February, at noon, a woman by that name had been interred.

I asked the caretaker to lead me to the grave, as this city of the dead has its streets, just like the city of the living, and there would be no way to identify her grave without a guide. The

caretaker called over a gardener, to whom he gave the necessary indications, until the gardener interrupted him, saying: "I
know, I know . . . Oh! The grave is easy enough to spot," he
continued, turning toward me.

"Why?" I asked him.

"Because its flowers are much different than the others."

"Is it you who tends it?"

"Yes, sir, and I could wish all relatives took as good care of
their departed as the young man who looks after that one."

After a few turns, the gardener stopped and said to me,
"Here we are."

Before my eyes was an expanse of flowers that no one would
ever have taken for a grave, had not a white marble slab bearing a name been proof.

This marble slab stood upright. An iron trellis demarcated
the plot of land that had been bought, and that plot was covered in white camellias.

"What do you make of that?" asked the gardener.

"It's very pretty."

"And every time a camellia fades, I'm on orders to replace it."

"And who gives you those orders?"

"A young man who cried a great deal the first time he came—
a close friend of the dead woman, no doubt, because she
seemed to be a lively sort, that one. They say she was very
beautiful. Did the gentleman know her?"

"Yes."

"The way the other man did?" the gardener asked with a
wicked smile.

"No, I never spoke to her."

"And you come here to see her; that's very good of you, because the cemetery's hardly overrun with visitors to the poor
girl."

"So nobody comes?"

"No one except for the young man, who came once."

"Just once?"

"Yes, sir."

"And he hasn't been back since?"

"No, but he'll come back upon his return."

"Then he's traveling?"

"Yes."

"And do you know where he is?"

"He is, I believe, staying with Mlle Gautier's sister."

"And what is he doing there?"

"He is seeking authorization from her to exhume the dead woman and bury her someplace else."

"Why doesn't he leave her here?"

"You know, sir, people have ideas about what to do with the dead. People like me see that every day. This plot was purchased for five years only, and this young man wants a permanent resting place for her, and a larger plot; in the new quarter it will be better."

"What do you mean by 'the new quarter'?"

"The new plots that we're selling now, on the left. If the cemetery had always been kept up the way it is now, there wouldn't have been another like it in the world; but there's still a lot to do before it's just as it should be. And then again, people are so funny."

"What do you mean?"

"I mean there are people who are proud until they come here. And this girl Gautier seems to have lived it up a little, if you'll pardon the expression. Now, the poor girl, she's dead; and there are plenty more that there's nothing to say against and whom we water every day; and, well, when the relatives of the people who are buried beside her heard who she was, didn't they object to her being here—and didn't they say plots should be set apart for women like that, like they are for the poor? Have you ever heard such a thing? I told them what I thought of them, I did; wealthy people who don't even come four times a year to visit their dead, who bring their flowers themselves . . . and just imagine the flowers they bring! They act as if a visit to somebody they're supposed to cry over were a business appointment, they carve mournful sentiments on gravestones for people they've never shed a tear for, and they make trouble for the neighborhood. Believe me if you like, sir, I did not know this young woman, I don't know what she did; and all the same, I love her, that poor little mite, and I take care of her, and I choose camellias for her at the fairest price. She's my favorite of the dead. People like me, sir, are forced to love the dead, because we're so busy that we hardly have time to love anything else."

I looked at this man, and some of my readers will understand without my needing to explain it the emotion I felt upon hearing him speak this way.

He sensed it, undoubtedly, because he went on, "They say there are people who ruined themselves for that girl, and that she had lovers who adored her; well, when I think that not one of them comes to buy her one solitary flower, that's what I think is strange and sad. And again, she has nothing to complain about, because she has her grave, and if there's only one person who remembers her, well, he can stand in for the rest. But we have poor girls here of the same type and the same age that we throw into paupers' graves, and it breaks my heart when I hear their poor bodies fall to ground. And not one soul thinks of them once they're dead! It's not always so cheerful, this trade of ours, if you've got a soft heart. What do you want? It's too much for me sometimes. I've got a nice, grown-up daughter who's twenty, and when someone brings a dead girl her age here, I think of her; and, whether it's a great lady or a tramp, I can't help but be moved.

"But no doubt I'm boring you with my tales, and you did not come here to listen to me talk. I was told to lead you to the grave of Mlle Gautier—here you are. May I be of any further assistance?"

"Do you know the address of M. Armand Duval?" I asked this man.

"Yes, he lives on rue —. At least that's where I went to get the money to buy all the flowers you see here."

"Thank you, my friend."

I cast one last glance at the flower-strewn grave, and despite myself longed to part the depths to see what the earth had done to the beautiful creature who had been surrendered to it. I walked away filled with sadness.

"Would the gentleman like to see M. Duval?" asked the gardener, walking alongside me.

"Yes."

"It's just that I'm pretty sure he's not back yet; otherwise I would have seen him here already."

"You therefore are convinced he has not forgotten Marguerite?"

"Not only am I convinced, but I would also bet that his wish to move her grave is nothing more than the desire to see her again."

"What do you mean?"

"The first thing he said to me when he came to the cemetery was, 'What do I have to do to see her again?' That could only take place if the grave were moved, and I explained to him all the forms he would need to fill out to make the change, because, you know, to transfer the dead from one grave to another, you must first identify them, and only the family is authorized to make that identification, and it must be done in the presence of a police commissioner. It's to get this authorization that M. Duval has gone to Mlle Gautier's sister, and his first visit will obviously be to us."

We had arrived at the cemetery gate; I thanked the gardener again, put some money in his hand and went to the address he had given me.

Armand was not back.

I left word for him, asking him to come see me upon his return, or to let me know how I could find him.

The next day, in the morning, I received a letter from Duval, who informed me of his return and asked me to drop by, adding that, worn out with exhaustion, he was unable to leave his house.

CHAPTER VI

I found Armand in bed.

When he saw me he extended a burning hand.

"You have a fever," I told him.

"It's nothing; I'm tired out from my journey, that's all."

"You're coming from Marguerite's sister's house?"

"Yes, who told you?"

"I know all about it, and did you get what you wanted?"

"Yes again, but who told you about the trip and about the purpose I had in making it?"

"The gardener at the cemetery."

"Did you see the grave?"

I hardly dared answer, as the tone in which he asked the question proved to me that the man who asked it was still captive to the emotion I had witnessed, and that for a long time to come, whenever his thoughts or the words of another would bring him back to this painful subject, this emotion would overpower his will.

I contented myself therefore by responding with a nod of the head.

"Has he taken good care of it?" Armand asked.

Two fat tears rolled down the cheeks of the invalid, who turned his head to hide them from me. I pretended not to see them and tried to change the conversation.

"You've been gone three weeks," I said.

Armand passed his hand across his eyes and said, "Just three weeks."

"Your trip was long."

"Oh! I wasn't traveling all the time. I was sick fifteen days; otherwise I would have come back a long time ago, but I'd hardly got there when fever took me, and I was forced to keep to my bed."

"And you left again before you had recovered."

"If I'd stayed eight days more in that part of the country, I would have died there."

"But now that you're back, you've got to take care of yourself; your friends will come see you. Me, first of all, if you permit."

"In two hours I will get up."

"What folly!"

"I must."

"What do you have to do that's so urgent?"

"I must go see the police commissioner."

"Why don't you send someone else on this mission that's bound to make you sicker still?"

"It's the only thing that can cure me. I must see her. Ever since I learned of her death, and above all ever since I saw her grave, I can't sleep. I cannot comprehend that this woman I left so young and so beautiful is dead. I must assure myself of it in person. I must see what God has made of this creature I loved so much, and perhaps the horror of the sight will replace the despair of my memory. You will accompany me, won't you, if it is not too tedious for you?"

"What did you tell her sister?"

"Nothing. She seemed astonished that a stranger would want to buy a plot and have a tomb made for Marguerite, and immediately signed the authorization I asked for."

"Believe me, you must put this off until you are fully recovered."

"Oh! I'll be fine; don't worry. Anyway, I would go crazy if I didn't finish off this task that I've determined to do; my sorrow makes it imperative. I swear to you, I will be calm again only once I have seen Marguerite. Perhaps it's a thirst brought on by the fever that consumes me, an insomniac dream, a product of my delirium, but if seeing her meant I would have to become a

Trappist monk afterward like M. de Rancé, I would still want
to see her."

"I understand," I told Armand. "I am at your disposal. Have
you seen Julie Duprat?"

"Yes. Oh! I saw her the very day of my first return."

"Did she give you the documents Marguerite had left for
you?"

"Here they are."

Armand pulled out a roll of papers from beneath his pillow,
and put it back immediately.

"I know by heart what those papers contain," he told me.
"For three weeks I have reread them ten times a day. You will
read them too, but later, when I'm calmer, and when I will be
able to make you understand everything these confessions reveal about her heart and her love. At the moment I have a favor
to ask you."

"Which is?"

"You have a carriage downstairs?"

"Yes."

"Could you please take my passport and go ask at the post
office if there are any letters for me? My father and my sister
must have written to me in Paris, and I left with such precipi-
tate haste that I didn't take time to check before I left. Once
you're back we'll go together to alert the police commissioner
to tomorrow's ceremony."

Armand gave me his passport, and I went to rue Jean-Jacques
Rousseau.

There were two letters for Duval; I took them and came
back.

When I returned, Armand was dressed and ready to go out.

"Thank you," he said, taking his letters. "Yes," he added,
after having looked at the addresses. "Yes, it's from my father
and my sister. They must have been perplexed by my silence."

He opened the letters, and seemed more to divine their contents than to read them, as they were four pages each, and he
folded them back up after an instant.

"Let's go," he said. "I'll write back tomorrow."

We went to see the police commissioner, to whom Armand gave the authorization from Marguerite's sister.

In exchange the commissioner gave him a release to give to the caretaker of the cemetery; it was agreed that the transfer would take place the next day at ten in the morning, that I would drop by Armand's an hour beforehand, and that we would go together to the cemetery.

I, too, was curious to attend this spectacle, and I swear I did not sleep at all that night.

Judging from the thoughts that haunted me, it must have been a long night for Armand as well. When I entered his home the next day at nine o'clock, he was horribly pale but seemed to be calm.

He smiled at me and gave me his hand.

His candles had burnt down to the end, and before going out, Armand took up a thick letter, addressed to his father, in which he no doubt had confided his impressions of the night.

Half an hour later we arrived at Montmartre.

The commissioner was already waiting for us.

We walked slowly in the direction of Marguerite's grave. The commissioner was first in line; Armand and I followed a few steps behind.

From time to time I could feel my companion's arm shudder convulsively, as if he had been overtaken by sudden shivering. I would look at him then, and he would understand my look and smile at me, but from the time we left his home we did not exchange one word.

A little before we reached the grave, Armand stopped to wipe his face, which was beaded with perspiration.

I took advantage of this break to breathe, because I myself felt as if my heart were squeezed in a vise.

What is the source of the melancholy pleasure one takes in this sort of spectacle! When we arrived at the grave, the gardener had removed all the flowerpots, the wrought-iron trellis had been removed, and two men were digging up the earth.

Armand leaned against a tree and watched.

It seemed as if all his life were passing before his eyes.

Suddenly one of the two shovels struck stone.

With this noise Armand recoiled as from an electric shock and gripped my hand with such force that he hurt me.

A gravedigger took a broad shovel and emptied the grave little by little; then when there was nothing left but the rocks that covered the coffin, he threw them behind him one by one.

I watched Armand, fearing at every minute that the intense emotions he was so visibly undergoing might break him; but he kept watching, his eyes fixed and open as if in rapture, and only a gentle tremor in his cheeks and lips proved he was the victim of a violent nervous shock.

As for me, I can say only one thing, which is that I was sorry I had come.

When the bier was completely uncovered, the commissioner said to the gravediggers, "Open it."

The men obeyed as if it were the simplest thing in the world.

The coffin was made of oak, and they began to unscrew the upper casing that covered it. The dampness of the earth had rusted the screws, and it was not without effort that the coffin was opened. An odor of infection seeped out, in spite of the aromatic plants that had been strewn within.

"O my God! My God!" murmured Armand, and again he turned pale.

Even the gravediggers drew back.

A large white shroud covered the corpse, outlining some of its sinuous curves. This shroud was almost completely eaten away at one end; a foot of the dead woman stuck through.

I was very nearly sick, and at the hour in which I write these lines, the memory of this scene appears to me again in its daunting reality.

"Let's hurry," the commissioner said.

One of the two men extended a hand and began undoing the shroud, and seizing one end he brusquely uncovered the face of Marguerite.

It was terrible to see; it is horrible to describe.

Her eyes were nothing more than two holes, her lips had disappeared, and her white teeth were crowded one against the other. Her long, dry black hair was stuck to her temples, veiling somewhat the green cavities of her cheeks, and yet I could recognize in this visage the white, pink, and joyful face I had so often seen.

Armand, unable to avert his gaze from this face, had brought his handkerchief to his mouth and was biting it.

As for me it seemed as if a circlet of iron were bound around my head, a veil covered my eyes, buzzing filled my ears, and all I could do was open a small vial I had brought by chance and inhale deeply the salts it contained.

In the midst of this daze, I heard the commissioner say to M. Duval, "Do you make the identification?"

"Yes," the young man replied dumbly.

"Close it up and take it away," said the commissioner.

The gravediggers threw the shroud back over the face of the dead woman, closed the coffin, and each took it by one end and headed toward the designated place.

Armand did not move. His eyes were riveted on the empty pit; he was as pale as the corpse we had just seen. You would have said he'd been turned to stone.

I understood what was likely to happen once his grief had subsided, reduced by distance from the spectacle; as a result I left his side.

I approached the commissioner.

"Is the presence of the gentleman still necessary?" I asked, indicating Armand.

"No," he said, "and I would actually advise you to take him away, because he looks ill."

"Come," I said to Armand, taking his arm.

"What?" he said, looking at me as if he didn't recognize me.

"It's over," I said. "You've got to go, my friend—you're pale, you're cold, you'll kill yourself with this distress."

"You're right. Let's get out of here," he responded mechanically, without taking a step.

I grabbed him by the arm and led him off.

He let himself be guided like a child, murmuring only now and again, "Did you see her eyes?"

And he turned around, as if that vision had summoned her back.

But his step became irregular; he was no longer able to advance except by jolts. His teeth chattered; his hands were cold; a violent nervous agitation spread across his entire body.

I spoke to him; he did not answer.

All he could do was let himself be guided.

He had hardly sat down when the shivering increased, and he had a true nervous fit, in the middle of which, for fear of frightening me, he murmured while pressing my hand, "It's nothing, it's nothing; I just wish I could cry."

I heard his chest heave, and a flush spread to his eyes, but tears would not come.

I made him breathe the smelling salts that had served me, and when we arrived at his place, only the shivering still manifested itself.

With help from the servant I put him to bed, had a big fire lit in his bedroom, and ran to find my doctor, to whom I related what had just happened.

He hurried over.

Armand was purple. He was delirious, and stammered incoherent words, in which only the name Marguerite could be distinctly heard.

"Well?" I said to the doctor when he had examined the patient.

"He has brain fever, no more, no less, and that's a good thing, because I believe, God forgive me, that otherwise he would have gone mad. Luckily the physical illness will kill the psychological illness, and in one month he will be delivered from one, and perhaps from the other."

CHAPTER VII

Illnesses like the one Armand had contracted are convenient in that if they don't kill you on the spot, they are quickly conquered.

Fifteen days after the events I have just described, Armand was much better, and we had formed a firm friendship. I had hardly left his room the entire time he was sick.

Spring had scattered its flowers in profusion, its leaves, its birds and its songs, and my friend's window opened cheerfully onto his garden, whose restorative scents drifted up to him.

The doctor had given him permission to leave his bed, and we often chatted, sitting by the open window, at the hour when the sun is at its hottest, from noon until two o'clock.

I took care not to speak to him of Marguerite, still fearing that the name might awaken a dormant unhappy memory in the seemingly calm patient; but Armand, on the contrary, seemed to take pleasure in speaking of her, not the way he had done in the past, with tears in his eyes, but with a gentle smile that reassured me about his mental state.

I had noticed that since his last visit to the cemetery, where the spectacle had taken place that had brought on this violent crisis, his psychological pain seemed to have been dwarfed by the illness, and for him the death of Marguerite no longer belonged to the past. A sort of consolation had come from the certainty he had obtained, and to chase away the dark image that frequently came to him, he sank into happy memories of his relationship with Marguerite, and seemed to want to think of none but those.

His body was too worn out from his attack and from his

recovery from the fever to permit him to surrender to violent emotion, and the joys of the springtime and of the world around him led his thoughts, despite himself, to cheerful visions.

He still stubbornly refused to tell his family of the danger he was in, and until he had recovered, his father was unaware of his illness.

One night we had stayed by the window longer than usual; the weather had been magnificent, and the sun had set in a twilight of shimmering azure and gold. Although we were in Paris, the foliage that surrounded us seemed to isolate us from the world, even if from time to time the sound of a carriage faintly interrupted our conversation.

"It was at about this time of the year, on the evening of a day like this one, that I met Marguerite," Armand told me, caught up in his thoughts and not in what I was telling him.

I said nothing.

He turned toward me and said, "I must tell you this story; you will get a book out of it that no one will believe, but that perhaps will be interesting to write."

"You can tell me about it later, my friend," I said. "You're not well enough yet."

"The evening is warm, I've eaten my chicken breast," he said to me, smiling. "I don't have a fever, we've got nothing to do. I'm going to tell you everything."

"Since you feel so strongly, I'll listen."

"It's a very simple story," he added, "and I will tell it to you in the order that things happened. If you do something with it later, feel free to tell it differently."

Here is what he told me, and I have changed hardly a word of this touching narrative.

Yes, continued Armand, letting his head fall back on his armchair. Yes, it was on an evening like this one! I had spent my day in the country with one of my friends, Gaston R . . . . That night we came back to Paris, and not knowing what to do, we went to the Variétés theater.

During an intermission we went out, and in the corridor we saw a tall woman pass, and my friend bowed to her.

"Who is that you are you bowing to?" I asked him.

"Marguerite Gautier," he said.

"It seems to me she has changed; I wouldn't have recognized her," I said with an emotion that you will understand a little later.

"She's been sick; the poor girl won't last long."

I recall those words as if they had been spoken yesterday.

You must know, my friend, that for two years the sight of this girl, whenever I happened to see her, had a strange impression on me.

Without knowing why, I would become pale, and my heart would beat violently. One of my friends studies the occult sciences, and he would attribute what I experienced to "affinity of fluids"; me, I quite simply believe I was destined to fall in love with Marguerite, and that I had a presentiment of it.

She always had a powerful effect on me, which many of my friends witnessed, and which they laughed about heartily once they realized who it was that inspired it.

The first time I had seen her was on the Place de la Bourse, at the doorstep of Susse's. An open carriage had parked, and a woman dressed in white stepped out. An admiring murmur welcomed her as she entered the shop. As for me, I remained nailed in place from the moment she entered until the moment she left. Through the window I watched her choose in the boutique what she had gone there to buy. I could have gone in, but I didn't dare. I didn't know who the woman was, and I didn't want her to guess the cause of my entry into the shop and possibly take offense. However, I did not believe I would see her again.

She was elegantly dressed; she wore a muslin dress covered in ruffles, a square Indian shawl whose corners were embroidered with gold and silk flowers, an Italian straw hat, and an unusual bracelet, a thick gold chain that was just coming into fashion.

She got back into her barouche and drove off.

One of the boutique's clerks stood on the doorstep, following with his eyes the carriage of the elegant shopper. I approached him and begged him to tell me the woman's name.

"That's Mlle Marguerite Gautier," he replied.

Not daring to ask him for her address, I went away.

The memory of this vision—because it truly was a vision—did not leave my mind, unlike many other visions I'd had before, and I searched everywhere for this woman in white who was so regally beautiful.

A few days later a big production took place at the Opéra-Comique. I went, and the first person I saw in a box down by the stage was Marguerite Gautier.

The young man I was with recognized her too, because he said to me, mentioning her name, "Look at that pretty girl."

At that moment Marguerite was looking our way through her opera glasses. She spotted my friend, smiled at him, and signaled for him to come pay her a visit.

"I'm going to go over and say hello," he said. "I'll be back in a second."

I couldn't keep myself from saying, "Lucky you!"

"Why?"

"To get to go visit that woman."

"Are you in love with her?"

"No," I said, blushing, as I really didn't know what I felt, as far as that was concerned. "But I would like to meet her."

"Come with me; I'll introduce you."

"First ask her permission."

"Good God, there's no need to be shy with her; come on."

What he said pained me. I trembled to think that Marguerite might not be worthy of the feelings I had for her.

In a book by Alphonse Karr, called *Smoking*, a man follows an elegant woman one night and falls in love with her at first sight because she is so beautiful. Overcome by his desire to kiss the woman's hand, he feels in himself the strength to undertake everything, the will to conquer all, the courage to do anything. He hardly dares look at the coquettish glimpse of leg she reveals as she raises her skirt to keep the earth from besmirching her dress. As he dreams of everything he will do to win this woman, she stops on a street corner and asks him if he wants to come up to her place.

He averts his gaze, crosses the street, and returns home filled with woe.

I recalled this tale, and I, who longed to suffer for this woman, became afraid that she might accept me too quickly, and too quickly grant me a love that I wanted to gain through long pursuit or great sacrifice. That's how we're made, we men, and it's truly fortunate that the imagination bestows this sort of poetry on the senses, and that the passions of the body make this concession to the dreams of the soul.

In short, if someone had told me, "You may have this woman tonight, and tomorrow you will be killed," I would have accepted. If someone had said, "For ten louis you can be her lover," I would have refused and wept like a child who woke to see that the castle he had dreamt of in the night had disappeared.

Nonetheless I wanted to meet her; this was a way, perhaps the only way, to know what my connection to her might be.

So I told my friend I would wait to hear if she would give him permission to introduce me, and I prowled the corridors, telling myself she might see me from one moment to the next, and that I would not know what countenance to present for her scrutiny.

I tried to string together in advance the words I would say to her.

Love is so sublimely infantile!

The next instant my friend came down.

"She's waiting for us," he said.

"Is she alone?" I asked.

"With another woman."

"No men?"

"No."

"Let's go."

My friend headed toward the theater door.

"It's not that way," I said.

"We're going to get candy. She asked me to get some."

We walked into a candy shop in the Opéra passage.

I would have bought out the entire shop if I could have, and I was looking around to see what to fill the bag with when my friend said, "A pound of sugared grapes."

"Do you know if she likes them?"

"She never eats any other candy; it's a well-known fact."

"Ah!" he continued once we had left. "Do you know the woman I'm about to introduce you to? Don't imagine she's a duchess—she's quite simply a kept woman, as kept as kept can be, my dear; so don't be bashful, and tell her anything that comes into your head.

"Good, good," I stammered, and followed him, telling myself I would cure myself of my passion.

As I entered the box, Marguerite was laughing raucously.

I would have preferred her to be sad.

My friend introduced me. Marguerite made a slight inclination of her head and said, "And my candy?"

"Here it is."

As she took it she looked at me. I lowered my eyes; I blushed.

She bent to the ear of her neighbor, spoke a few words to her in a low voice, and both of them burst out laughing.

Obviously I was the cause of this hilarity; my embarrassment was compounded. At that time my mistress was a simple bourgeoise who was very tender and very sentimental, whose sentimentality and melancholy letters made me laugh. I understood the pain I must have caused her by the pain I now felt, and for five minutes I loved a woman as I never had before.

Marguerite ate her grapes and paid me no further attention.

My introducer did not want to leave me in this ridiculous position.

"Marguerite," he said, "you must not be astonished if M. Duval says nothing. You overwhelm him so much that he cannot produce a word."

"I believe rather that the gentleman accompanied you here because it would have bored you to come alone."

"If that were true," I said in turn, "I would not have begged Ernest to ask your permission to introduce me."

"It was probably nothing more than a means of postponing the fatal moment."

Even if one has spent little time with girls like Marguerite, one knows the pleasure they take in sporting with and teasing people the first time they meet them. Doubtless it is payback for the humiliations they are so often forced to undergo from people they see every day.

Also, to banter with them requires a certain familiarity with their world, a familiarity I did not possess; and then again, the idea I had formed of Marguerite increased for me the power of her teasing. No aspect of this woman was indifferent to me. And so I stood up, telling her, with an alteration in my voice that was impossible for me to completely disguise, "If that's what you think of me, madam, I have no choice but to beg your pardon for my indiscretion and to take leave of you, assuring you that it will not be repeated."

Upon this, I bowed and left.

I had hardly shut the door when I heard a third peal of laughter. I would have loved for someone to stumble into me at that moment.

I returned to my stall.

The knock came, announcing that the curtain was about to go up.

Ernest returned.

"How you carried on!" he said, as he sat down beside me. "They think you're crazy."

"What did Marguerite say after I left?"

"She laughed and assured me she'd never seen anything funnier. But you shouldn't consider yourself defeated; only don't do those girls the honor of taking them seriously. They don't know what elegance and good manners are; they're like dogs you spritz with perfume who think it smells awful and go roll in the gutter."

"After all, what do I care?" I said, trying to sound nonchalant. "I'll never see the woman again, and if I liked the look of her before I knew her, that's completely changed now that we've met."

"Bah! I'm not abandoning hope of seeing you in her box, and hearing that you're ruining yourself for her. Anyway, right you'll be—she's badly brought up, but she's a lovely mistress to have."

Luckily the curtain went up and my friend quit talking. To tell you what was playing would be impossible for me. All I remember is that from time to time I raised my eyes to the loge

I had so abruptly left, and saw a succession of new visitors appear there, one after the other.

However, I was far from not thinking anymore of Marguerite. Another feeling suffused me. I felt I had to make her forget her insult and my ridicule. I told myself that if I had to spend everything I owned I would have that girl, and reclaim my right to the place I had abandoned so quickly.

Before the show was over, Marguerite and her friend left their box.

In spite of myself, I left the stall.

"You're leaving?" asked Ernest.

"Yes."

"Why?"

At this moment he noticed the box was empty.

"Go on, go on," he said. "And good luck, or, rather, better luck."

I went out.

I heard in the stairway the rustling of dresses and the sound of voices. I stood to the side and, without being seen, watched the two women and the two young men who accompanied them pass by.

On the colonnade outside the theater, a little serving woman presented herself to them.

"Go tell the coachman to wait by the door of the Café Anglais," Marguerite said. "We will go there by foot."

A few minutes later, while lurking on the boulevard, I saw Marguerite leaning on the balcony at the window of one of the restaurant's large private rooms, plucking apart the camellias in her bouquet, one by one.

One of the two men was leaning against her shoulder and speaking softly to her.

I went to the Maison-d'Or, to one of the parlors on the first floor, installed myself there, and did not lose sight of the window in question.

At one in the morning, Marguerite climbed into her carriage with her three friends.

I took a cab and followed her.

The carriage stopped at rue d'Antin, No. 9.

Marguerite got out of the carriage and went in alone.

This was, without doubt, a coincidence, but the coincidence made me very happy.

From this day on I often bumped into Marguerite at the theater, on the Champs-Élysées. Always there was the same gaiety in her, the same confusion in me.

But then two weeks passed when I did not see her anywhere. I found myself with Gaston and asked for news of her.

"The poor girl is quite sick," he responded.

"What's wrong with her?"

"She's consumptive, and as she does not lead a life that's conducive to getting better, she has taken to her bed, and she's dying."

The heart is strange; I was almost happy about this illness.

Every day I went to get news about the invalid, without, however, leaving my name or my card. That is how I learned of her convalescence and of her departure for Bagnères.

As time passed, the impression, if not the memory, seemed to erase itself little by little from my mind. I traveled; there were connections, habits, jobs that took the place of those thoughts; and when I thought back to that first adventure, I chose to regard it as one of those follies of youth that one laughs about soon after.

But there would have been no great reason to exult over this memory, as I had lost track of Marguerite after her departure, and as I told you, when she passed near me in the corridor of the Variétés theater, I did not recognize her.

She was veiled it is true, but, two years earlier, however veiled she might have been, I would not have needed to see her to recognize her; I would have sensed her presence.

All of which did not keep my heart from beating when I knew it was she; and the two years that had passed without my seeing her, and the results that this separation had appeared to produce, melted into smoke at the mere touch of her gown.

CHAPTER VIII

However, Armand continued after a pause, although I realized I was still in love with her, I felt more self-assured than I had before, and mingled with my desire to find myself again with Marguerite was the determination to make her see I had become superior to her.

What detours and justifications the heart gives itself to arrive at what it wants!

Also I could not stay for a long time in the corridors, so I returned to take my place in the orchestra, glancing rapidly into the room to see which box she was in.

She was in a lower box on the main floor, and she was all alone. She had changed, as I told you; I no longer saw on her lips that indifferent smile. She had suffered; she still suffered.

Even though it was already April, she was still dressed for winter, covered in velvet.

I looked at her so obstinately that my gaze attracted hers.

She considered me a few moments, took her opera glasses to see me better, and believed, no doubt, that she recognized me, without being able to say positively who I was, since when she put down her opera glasses a smile—that charming salutation of women—played on her lips, as if in response to the bow she seemed to expect from me. But I hardly responded at all, in order to gain an advantage over her and to seem to have forgotten when she remembered.

Believing she was mistaken, she turned her head.

The curtain went up.

I have seen Marguerite at the theater many times; I never saw her pay the least attention to the performance.

As for me, the show was also of little interest, and I was concerned with nothing but her, while making every effort to keep her from perceiving it.

This is how I saw her exchange glances with the person who occupied the box across from hers; I cast my eyes on this box, and recognized in it a woman with whom I was reasonably well acquainted.

This woman was a former kept woman who had tried to succeed in the theater but had failed, and who, making use of her connections with the elegant women of Paris, had set herself up in business and bought a fashion boutique.

I recognized in her a means of reintroducing myself to Marguerite, and took advantage of a moment in which she looked my way to wish her good evening, with my hand and eyes.

What I had anticipated occurred; she summoned me to her box.

Prudence Duvernoy (that was the happy name of the milliner) was one of those fat women of forty with whom one need employ no great subtlety to discover what one wishes to know, especially when what one wishes to know is as simple as what I had to ask her.

I took advantage of a moment when she resumed her exchange with Marguerite to say, "Who are you looking at?"

"Marguerite Gautier."

"You know her?"

"Yes; I'm her milliner, and she's my neighbor."

"Then you live on the rue d'Antin?"

"Number seven. The window of her dressing room looks out on the window of mine."

"I hear she's a charming girl."

"You don't know her?"

"No, but I would like to."

"Would you like me to tell her to come to our box?"

"No, I would prefer you introduce me to her."

"At her home?"

"Yes."

"That is harder."

"Why?"

"Because she is the protégée of an old and very jealous duke."

"*Protégée* is a charming word."

"Yes, protégée," resumed Prudence. "The poor old man, he would be truly embarrassed to be her lover."

Prudence then related the story of how Marguerite had met the duke at Bagnères.

"That is the reason she is here alone?" I continued.

"Exactly."

"But who will drive her home?"

"He will."

"He will come here, then, to pick her up?"

"In a moment."

"And you, who will drive you home?"

"Nobody."

"I offer myself."

"But you are here with a friend, I believe."

"We both offer ourselves, then."

"Who's your friend?"

"He's a charming man, very amusing, who'll be delighted to make your acquaintance."

"All right, agreed; the four of us will leave after this play, because I know the last one."

"Gladly; I'll go tell my friend."

"Go ahead."

"Ah!" Prudence said to me the moment I prepared to leave, "and here's the duke entering Marguerite's box."

I looked. A man of seventy had just sat down behind the young woman and given her a bag of candy, into which she reached, smiling. Then she went to the front of her box and made a gesture to Prudence, which could be interpreted as, "Would you like some?"

"No," Prudence responded.

Marguerite took the bag and, turning around, began chatting with the duke.

The account of all these details sounds like childishness, but everything that had to do with that girl is so vivid in my memory that I cannot stop myself from recalling it today.

I went to alert Gaston of what I had just arranged for the two of us.

He accepted.

We left our stalls and went to Mme Duvernoy's box.

We had just opened the door to the orchestra when we were forced to stop to let Marguerite and the duke pass by; they were leaving.

I would have given ten years of my life to change places with that old fellow.

Once they had reached the boulevard, he seated her in a phaeton that he himself drove, and they disappeared, carried off at a trot by two superb horses.

We entered Prudence's box.

When the play was finished, we went out and hailed a simple fiacre, which drove us to the rue d'Antin, No. 7. At the door of her house, Prudence invited us to come up so she could show us her stock, which we were not familiar with, and of which she seemed to be very proud. You will guess with what alacrity I accepted.

It seemed that I was getting closer and closer to Marguerite. I soon brought the conversation back around to her.

"The old duke is at your neighbor's place?" I asked Prudence.

"Not at all; she's surely alone."

"But she will be terribly bored," said Gaston.

"We spend nearly all our evenings together, or, as soon as she comes home, she calls me. She never goes to bed before two in the morning. She can't sleep earlier than that."

"Why?"

"Because she's consumptive and nearly always has a fever."

"She doesn't have lovers?" I asked.

"I never see anyone stay when I leave, but I can't prove that nobody comes after I've gone. Often in the evening I see at her place a certain Comte de N . . . , who believes he can advance his cause by turning up at eleven o'clock and sending her as many jewels as she would like; but she wouldn't be able to identify him in a lineup. She's in the wrong; he's a very rich boy. I tell her from time to time, "My dear child, this is the man you need!" Usually she listens to me well enough, but this time she turns her back on me and replies that he is too stupid. Yes, he's stupid, I admit, but she would gain a social position, whereas this old duke could die one day to the next. Old men are selfish; his family reproaches him incessantly for his affection for Marguerite—right there are two reasons why he'll leave her nothing. I scold her, and she retorts that there will be time enough to accept the count when the duke is dead.

"It's not always amusing," Prudence continued, "to live as she does. I know it wouldn't suit me, and I would have sent that fellow packing. He's insipid, that old man—he calls her his daughter, he takes care of her as if she were a baby, he's always on her heels. I'm sure that at this moment one of his servants is prowling the street to see who leaves and, above all, who enters."

"Ah, that poor Marguerite," said Gaston, sitting down at the piano and starting to play a waltz. "I didn't know all that. All the same I've found her to have less sparkle than usual for some time."

"Shh!" said Prudence, cupping her ear.

Gaston stopped.

"She's calling me, I think."

We listened.

A voice was calling for Prudence.

"Go, gentlemen, off with you," Mme Duvernoy told us.

"Ah! That's how you show us your hospitality," said Gaston, laughing. "We will leave when the time seems right to us."

"Why would we leave?"

"I'm going to Marguerite's."

"We'll wait here."

"That's not possible."

"So then, we'll go with you."

"Even less possible."

"I know Marguerite," Gaston said. "I can certainly go visit her."

"But Armand does not know her."

"I will introduce him."

"It's impossible."

We heard again the voice of Marguerite, still calling for Prudence.

The latter ran to her dressing room. I followed her there with Gaston. She opened the window.

We hid ourselves so as not to be seen from outside.

"I've been calling you for ten minutes," Marguerite said from her window in an almost imperious tone.

"What do you want of me?"

"I want you to come over immediately."

"Why?"

"Because the Comte de N . . . is still here, and he's boring me to death."

"I can't now."

"What's stopping you?"

"I've got two young men at my place who don't want to leave."

"Tell them you have to go out."

"I've told them."

"Well then, let them stay at your place; when they see that you've gone out, they'll leave."

"After having turned everything upside down!"

"But what do they want?"

"They want to see you."

"What are their names?"

"You know one of them, M. Gaston R . . . ."

"Ah yes, I know him; and the other?"

"M. Armand Duval. You don't know him?"

"No, but bring them over anyway; I'd like anyone better than the count. I'm waiting for you; come quickly."

Marguerite closed her window; Prudence hers.

Marguerite, who had remembered my face for a moment, did not remember my name. I would have preferred a negative memory to this oblivion.

"I knew," Gaston said, "that she would be delighted to see us."

"*Delighted* is not the word," Prudence responded, putting on her shawl and her hat. "She is receiving you to make the count leave. Try to be more agreeable than him or, I know Marguerite; she'll get annoyed with me."

We followed Prudence downstairs.

I trembled; it seemed that this visit was to have a great impact on my life.

I was even more moved than I had been the night of my introduction in the box of the Opéra-Comique.

As I arrived at the door of the apartment that you know, my heart beat so furiously that all thought escaped me.

Some piano chords met our ears.

Prudence rang.

The piano fell silent.

A woman who seemed more like a companion than a housemaid came to let us in.

We walked into the living room, and from there to the boudoir, which back then looked just as it did when you saw it afterward.

A young man was leaning against the mantel. Marguerite, seated at her piano, let her fingers run over the keys, and began snippets that she did not finish.

The scene radiated ennui, provoked in the man by his embarrassment at his insignificance, in the woman by the presence of this gloomy personage.

Upon hearing Prudence's voice, Marguerite rose, and, coming to us after having exchanged a look of gratitude with Mme Duvernoy, said to us, "Come in, gentlemen, you are welcome."

CHAPTER IX

"Good evening, my dear Gaston," said Marguerite to my companion. "I am glad to see you. Why didn't you come visit me in my box at the Variétés?"

"I was afraid it would be indiscreet."

"Friends"—and Marguerite emphasized this word as if she wanted to make it clear to everyone there that, despite the familiar manner in which she welcomed him, Gaston was only, and never had been anything but, a friend—"friends are never indiscreet."

"Then permit me to introduce you to M. Armand Duval!"

"I'd already authorized Prudence to do that."

"Apart from that, madam," I said while nodding and managing to produce a few nearly intelligible sounds, "I have already had the honor of being introduced to you."

Marguerite's charming eye seemed to search her memory, but she didn't remember at all, or seemed not to.

"Madam," I then resumed, "I am grateful that you have forgotten our first introduction, because I was quite ridiculous and must have seemed extremely tedious to you. It was two years ago, at the Opéra-Comique; I was with Ernest de . . . ."

"Ah! I remember!" Marguerite said with a smile. "It's not you who were ridiculous; it is I who was teasing you, as I am again now, a bit, but less, all the same. Have you forgiven me, sir?"

She extended her hand to me; I kissed it.

"It's true," she continued. "Imagine, I have the bad habit of wanting to embarrass people the first time I meet them. It's very silly. My doctor says it is because I am high-strung, and always sick—believe my doctor."

"But you seem to be quite well."

"Oh! I've been very sick."

"I know."

"Who told you?"

"Everyone knows; I came here often to get news of you, and I learned of your recovery with pleasure."

"Nobody ever gave me your card."

"I never left it."

"Are you the young man who came every day to ask about me during my illness, and who never wanted to give his name?"

"It is I."

"Well, you are more than indulgent; you are generous. You would not have done that, count," she added, turning toward M. de N . . . , and after having cast over me one of those looks by which women complete their assessment of a man.

"I've only known you for two months," replied the count.

"And this gentleman only knew me for five minutes. You always respond with inanities."

Women are merciless to people they don't like.

The count reddened and bit his lip.

I felt sorry for him, because he seemed to be in love just as I was, and Marguerite's blunt frankness must have made him quite unhappy, especially in front of two strangers.

"You were playing music when we walked in," I said, to change the subject. "Won't you do me the pleasure of treating me as an old friend, and keep on playing?"

"Oh!" she said, as she threw herself on the couch and gestured for us to sit there too. "Gaston knows what kind of music I play. It's all right when I'm alone with the count, but I would not want to force you to endure such torture."

"You reserve that preference for me?" replied M. de N . . . with a smile that he tried to make knowing and ironic.

"You are wrong to reproach me for it; it's the only preference I show you."

It was obvious that this poor boy would not be allowed to speak a word. He gave the young woman a truly imploring look.

"So, Prudence," she continued, "did you do what I asked you?"

"Yes."

"That's good; you can tell me about it later. We have things to discuss—don't leave before I've spoken with you."

"Doubtless we are in the way," I said. "And now that we have—or rather that I have—obtained a second introduction to cancel the memory of the first, Gaston and I will go."

"Not at all; it is not for your benefit that I said that. On the contrary, I would like you to stay."

The count pulled out an amazingly elegant watch, and checked the time. "It's time for me to go to the club," he said.

Marguerite made no response.

The count left the fireside and approached her. "Good-bye, madam."

Marguerite rose. "Good-bye, my dear count; you're leaving already?

"Yes, I was afraid I was boring you."

"You didn't bore me more today than you did any other day. When will we see you?"

"When you permit."

"Adieu, then!"

It was cruel, you will admit.

Luckily the count had a fine upbringing and an excellent nature. He contented himself with kissing the hand that Marguerite extended nonchalantly to him, and left after bowing to us.

At the moment he crossed the threshold of the door, he looked at Prudence.

She shrugged her shoulders with an air that signified, "What do you want? I've done everything I could."

"Nanine!" Marguerite cried. "Light the way for the count."

We heard the door open and close.

"At last!" Marguerite cried, as she reappeared. "He's gone. That boy got horribly on my nerves."

"My dear child," said Prudence, "you are really too unkind to him, he who is so good and so attentive to you. Here on your mantel is a watch that he has given you, and which must have cost him at least a thousand écus; I'm sure of it."

And Mme Duvernoy, who had approached the mantelpiece,

played with the trinket she was talking about, and threw covet-
ous looks on it.

"My dear," said Marguerite, sitting down to her piano,
"when I weigh on one side what he gives to me and on the other
what he says to me, I find that he gets his visits very cheaply."

"That poor boy is in love with you."

"If I had to listen to all the men who are in love with me, I
wouldn't have time to eat."

And she ran her fingers over the piano, after which she
turned to us and said, "Would you like anything? Me, I'd like
to drink a little punch."

"And I'd be happy to eat a spot of chicken," said Prudence.
"Shall we have supper?"

"Perfect—let's go get some supper," said Gaston.

"No, we will have supper here."

She rang. Nanine appeared.

"Send out for supper."

"What should I get?"

"Whatever you like, but right now—right now."

Nanine left.

"Perfect," Marguerite said, leaping like a child. "We'll have
supper. How boring that count is!"

The more I saw this woman, the more she enchanted me. She
was ravishingly beautiful. Even her extreme slenderness seemed
like a grace.

I was lost in thought.

What was occurring within me I would have difficulty ex-
plaining. I was full of indulgence for the life she led, full of
admiration for her beauty. The proof of disinterestedness that
she showed in refusing to accept a man who was young, elegant, rich, and ready to ruin himself for her excused all her
past faults in my eyes.

There was something in this woman that you could call
candor.

You could see she was still in the virginal stage of vice. Her
assured step, her supple waist, her pink and flared nostrils, her
large eyes shadowed with pale blue circles, all indicated one of
those ardent natures that exhale a perfume of voluptuousness,

like those flasks from the Orient from which, however tightly they are closed, let escape the fragrance of the elixir they contain.

Whether it was her nature or a consequence of her poor health, flashes of desire flickered in the eyes of this woman whose intensity would have been a heaven-sent revelation to any man who loved her. But those who had loved Marguerite could no longer be counted, and those she had loved had yet to be counted.

In short one could see in this girl both the virgin that an accident had turned courtesan, and the courtesan that an accident could have made the most loving and pure of virgins. There was pride and an independent spirit in Marguerite still— two feelings that, when injured, are capable of producing the same effect as modesty. I said nothing; my soul seemed to fill my heart and my heart to fill my eyes.

"So," she said all at once, "you are the one who wanted news of me when I was ill."

"Yes."

"Do you know, that's a beautiful thing! How can I thank you?"

"Permit me to come to see you from time to time."

"As often as you like—from five o'clock to six; from eleven o'clock to midnight. Say, Gaston, play for me 'L'Invitation à la Valse.'"

"Why?"

"First, to give me pleasure, and next, because I can't seem to play it myself."

"What prevents you?"

"The third movement, the passage with the sharps."

Gaston rose, went to the piano, and began to play that marvelous melody by Weber, whose music was open on the stand.

Marguerite, one hand leaning on the piano, looked at the sheet music, following each note with her eyes, which she accompanied softly with her voice, and when Gaston arrived at the passage that she'd indicated, she hummed while drumming her fingers on the back of the piano, "Re, mi, re, do, re, fa, mi, re—that's what I can't do. Start over."

Gaston started again, and afterward Marguerite said to him, "Now let me try."

She took her seat and played in her own turn, but her rebel fingers always mixed up one of the notes we had just read.

"It's incredible," she said, in a truly childish intonation, "that I can't play this passage right! Can you believe that I sometimes stay up practicing it until two in the morning! And when I think that that imbecile count can play it by heart and play it well, that's what makes me furious with him, I believe."

And she started over, always with the same result.

"The devil take Weber, music, and all pianos!" she said, flinging the music across the room. "Doesn't he understand I can't play eight sharps in a row?"

And she crossed her arms while looking at us and tapping her foot.

The blood rushed to her cheeks, and a light cough parted her lips.

"Come now, come now," said Prudence, who had taken off her hat and was smoothing her hair in front of the mirror. "You will get yourself into a state and hurt yourself. Let's have our supper, that's a better idea; and I'm dying of hunger."

Marguerite rang the bell again, then sat down once more at the piano and began to faintly sing a bawdy song, whose accompaniment she did not muddle at all.

Gaston knew the song, and they turned it into a kind of duet.

"Don't sing those bawdy tunes," I said to Marguerite, familiarly, and with a supplicating air.

"Oh! How virtuous you are!" she said to me, smiling and extending her hand.

"It's not for my sake; it's for yours."

Marguerite made a gesture that seemed to say, "Oh! I've been through with virtue for some time now."

At this moment Nanine appeared.

"Is supper ready?" asked Marguerite.

"Yes, madam, in a moment."

"Speaking of which," said Prudence, "you haven't seen the apartment. Come, I'll give you a tour."

You know, the living room was quite a marvel.

Marguerite went along with us for a bit, then she called to Gaston and went with him to the dining room to see if supper was ready.

"Goodness," Prudence said loudly, looking at an étagère, and taking down a Saxon figurine, "I never knew you had this little fellow!"

"Which one?"

"A little shepherd holding a birdcage."

"Take it if you like it."

"Ah! But I'd hate to deprive you of it."

"I was going to give it to my chambermaid. I think it's hideous, but if you like it, take it."

Prudence noticed only the fact of the gift, and not the manner in which it was given. She put her little fellow to the side, and led me into the dressing room, where, as she showed me two miniatures that hung there, she said, "So this is the Comte de G . . . , who was very in love with Marguerite; he's the one who launched her career. Do you know him?"

"No. And this one?" I asked, pointing at another miniature.

"That's the little Vicomte de L . . . . He was forced to leave town."

"Why?"

"Because he was pretty much ruined. That's another one who loved Marguerite!"

"And she doubtless loved him very much?"

"She's such a queer girl, you never know what to make of her. On the evening of the day he left, she was at the theater as usual, and yet she cried at the time of his departure."

At this moment Nanine appeared and announced that supper was served.

When we entered the dining room, Marguerite was leaning against the wall, and Gaston, holding her hands, was speaking to her softly.

"You're crazy," Marguerite was saying. "You know very well that I don't want you in that way. You don't spend two years getting to know a woman like me before asking to be her lover. Women like us give everything at once, or never. So gentlemen, suppertime."

And, extricating her hands from Gaston's, Marguerite seated him at her right, me at her left, then said to Nanine, "Before you sit down, tell the cook not to open the door if anyone rings."

This instruction was given at one in the morning.

We laughed, we drank, and we ate much at this supper. Within moments the exuberance had reached the most outrageous levels, and the sort of witticisms that a certain segment of society finds charming but that always sully the mouth of the person who speaks them broke out again and again, to the cheers of Nanine, Prudence, and Marguerite. Gaston was enjoying himself hugely; he was a boy with a lot of heart, but his mind had apparently been a little warped by his early habits. At one moment I wanted to forget everything, close my heart and my mind to the spectacle that was before me, and take full part in the frivolity that seemed to be one of the courses of this meal; but little by little I withdrew myself from its noise, my glass remained full, and I became almost melancholy, watching this beautiful twenty-year-old creature drink, swear like a stevedore, and laugh louder the more scandalous the conversation became.

Although this gaiety and this manner of speaking and drinking seemed to me to be the natural result of debauchery, habit, or hardy constitution in the other revelers, in Marguerite, I felt it came from a need to forget, a fever, a nervous irritability. With each glass of champagne her cheeks were covered with a feverish blush, and a cough, mild at the beginning of the supper, eventually became strong enough to make her turn her head against the back of her chair and press her hands to her chest every time she coughed.

I suffered to think of the harm these daily excesses wrought on her frail organism.

Finally something happened that I had anticipated and had dreaded. Toward the end of supper Marguerite was overcome by a coughing fit that was stronger than all those she had endured while I was there. It was as if her chest were coming to pieces inside. The poor girl turned purple, closed her eyes from the pain, and brought her handkerchief to her lips; a drop of blood reddened it. She then rose and ran to her dressing room.

"What's wrong with Marguerite?" asked Gaston.

"She laughed too much, and now she's spitting blood," said Prudence. "Oh! It's nothing; it happens to her every day. She'll come back. Leave her alone; she prefers it that way."

As for me, I could not control myself, and to the great astonishment of Prudence and Nanine, who called out after me, I went to join Marguerite.

CHAPTER X

The room where she had taken refuge was lit by only a single candle, placed on a table. Fallen back on a long sofa, her dress undone, she held one hand to her heart and let the other one hang down. On the table was a silver basin half-full of water; the water was marbled with streaks of blood.

Marguerite, very pale, her mouth parted, tried to catch her breath. At moments her chest inflated with a long sigh that, upon exhalation, seemed to relieve her a little, and left her for a few seconds with a feeling of well-being.

I drew near to her without her making a movement, sat down, and took the hand she had draped on the sofa.

"Ah! It's you?" she said with a smile.

I must have looked upset, because she added, "Are you sick too?"

"No, but you, are you still in pain?"

"Very little." And with her handkerchief she wiped away the tears that the coughing had brought to her eyes. "I am used to it now."

"You are going to kill yourself, madam," I told her in a voice full of emotion. "I wish I were your friend, or a relative, so I could keep you from harming yourself in this way."

"Ah! There's really no point in your getting alarmed," she replied in a bitter tone. "Just see if the others are worried about me—they know very well that there's nothing to be done in my case."

After saying this she rose, and taking the candle, set it on the mantel and looked at herself in the mirror.

"How pale I am!" she said, refastening her dress, and running her fingers through her disordered hair. "Ah! Bah! Let's go back to the table. Are you coming?"

I remained seated, and did not move.

Understanding the emotion that this scene had provoked in me, she came up to me and, holding out her hand, said, "Now then, come."

I took her hand; I raised it to my lips, dampening it, in spite of myself, with two long-suppressed tears.

"My goodness, but you are a child!" she said, sitting beside me. "You're crying! What's the matter with you?"

"I must seem quite ridiculous to you, but what I have just seen has caused me terrible pain."

"You're a funny one! What do you want? I can't sleep; I have to distract myself a little. And then, girls like me, one less or one more of us, what's the difference? The doctors tell me the blood I spit comes from my lungs. I pretend I believe them; that's all there is for me to do."

"Listen, Marguerite," I said, in an emphatic tone I could not restrain, "I do not know what impact you are to have on my life, but I know that, at this moment, there is nobody, not even my sister, in whom I take as great an interest as I do in you. It has been this way since the first time I saw you. In Heaven's name, take better care of yourself, and don't continue to live as you are doing."

"If I take care of myself, I will die. What sustains me is the feverish life I lead. And then again, taking care of yourself is fine for society ladies who have family and friends; but women like me, once we are no longer able to feed the vanity or pleasure of our lovers, they abandon us, and long days are followed by long nights. I know it well. Come now, I spent two months confined to my bed; after three weeks, nobody came to see me anymore."

"It's true that I am nothing to you," I went on, "but if you wished, I would look after you like a brother, I would not leave you, and I would make you better. So, when you regain your strength, you may resume the life you lead, if that's what you would like; but I am sure you would prefer a tranquil existence that would make you happier and would preserve your beauty."

"That's how you think tonight, because the wine has made you melancholy, but you will find that you do not have the patience you pride yourself on."

"Permit me to tell you, Marguerite, that you were ill for two months, and during those two months, I came every day to get news of you."

"That's true, but why didn't you come up?"

"Because I did not know you then."

"Why would anyone take pains with a girl like me?"

"Everyone takes pains with a girl; that's my opinion, at least."

"In that case, you will take care of me?"

"Yes."

"You will stay beside me every day?"

"Yes."

"And even all the nights?"

"All the time, as long as I don't bore you."

"What do you call that?"

"Devotion."

"And where does this devotion come from?"

"From an irresistible affection I have for you."

"So you are in love with me?" she said instantly. "That makes things easier."

"It's possible, but if I were to tell you about it someday, it would not be today."

"You would do better to never tell me about it."

"Why?"

"Because only two things could result from such a declaration."

"Which are?"

"Either I would not accept you, in which case you would resent me, or I would accept you, in which case you would find yourself stuck with an unfortunate mistress—a neurotic woman who's either ill and sad, or else is lighthearted with a lightheartedness that is sadder than heartbreak, a woman who spits blood and spends a hundred thousand francs a year. That's just fine for a rich old man like the duke but it's tiresome for a young man like you, and the proof of that is, all the young lovers I've had have left me quickly."

I made no response; I listened. This frankness that amounted almost to confession, the reality of this painful life that I was able to glimpse beneath the golden veil that covered it, which the poor girl fled through decadence, drunkenness, and insomnia, all of it stirred me so profoundly that I could not speak a word.

"Let us go," continued Marguerite. "We are speaking childishly. Give me your arm and let us return to the dining room. They must wonder what our absence means."

"Return if you like, but I beg your permission to remain here."

"Why?"

"Because your merriment pains me too much."

"All right, I'll be sad."

"Listen, Marguerite, let me tell you something that has been said to you often, no doubt, and which the habit of hearing may keep you from taking seriously, but which is no less true for that, and which I will never say to you again.

"Which is . . . ?" she said, with the smile that young mothers put on when they listen to some nonsensical tale from a child.

"It is that ever since I saw you, I do not know how or why, you have occupied a place in my life. I have tried to chase the vision of you from my mind, but it has always come back to me, and it is only today, when I saw you again, after two years of not having seen you, that you took an even greater hold on my heart and spirit than before, and at last, now that you have invited me in, now that I know you, now that I know all that is strange about you, you have become indispensable to me, and I will go mad, not only if you do not love me, but if you do not permit me to love you."

"Unfortunate though you are, I will tell you what Mme D . . . said: You must be rich! But you do not know that I spend six or seven thousand francs a month, and that this expense has become necessary to my life; you don't know, my poor friend, that I would ruin you in next to no time, and that your family would disown you if you were to live with a creature like me. Like me as you would like a good friend, but in no other way. Come see me—we will laugh, we will talk, but do not exaggerate my worth to yourself, because I am not worth very much. You have a good heart, you need to be loved, you are too young and too sensitive to live in our world. Take a married woman for a lover. You see that I am a good-natured girl, and that I speak to you frankly."

"Ah, what's this! What in the devil are you doing?" cried Prudence, whom we had not heard enter, and who appeared on the threshold of the room with her hair half-undone and her dress unbuttoned. I recognized in this disorder the hand of Gaston.

"We are speaking sensibly," Marguerite said. "Leave us for a little; we will rejoin you in a moment."

"Fine, fine; talk, my children," said Prudence, as she left and shut the door as if to reinforce the tone in which she had pronounced those last words.

"So, it's agreed," resumed Marguerite when we were alone. "You will not love me anymore."

"I will leave."

"Has it come to this?"

I had gone too far to take it back, and anyway, this girl overwhelmed me. Her mixture of lightheartedness, sadness, candor, prostitution, even her illness, which had heightened the sensitivity of her impressions as well as the irritability of her nerves, all gave me to understand that if, on this first occasion, I did not assert myself on this forgetful, light creature, she would be lost to me.

"Goodness, so what you were saying was serious!" she said.

"Very serious."

"But why didn't you tell me that earlier?"

"When would I have told you?"

"The day after you were introduced to me at the Opéra-Comique."

"I think you would have received me impolitely if I had come to see you."

"Why?"

"Because I had been stupid the night before."

"That's true. But nonetheless, you already loved me back then."

"Yes."

"Which did not prevent you from going to bed and sleeping tranquilly after the performance. We know what kind of great loves those are."

"Actually, you are wrong. Do you know what I did the night of the Opéra-Comique?"

"No."

"I waited for you on the doorstep of the Café Anglais. I followed the carriage that took you away, you and your three friends, and when I saw you get out of the carriage alone and go home alone to your place, I was very happy."

Marguerite began to laugh.

"What are you laughing about?"

"Nothing."

"Tell me, I beg you, or I will believe that you are making fun of me again."

"You won't get angry?"

"What right would I have to get angry?"

"Well, there was a good reason why I went home alone."

"What was it?"

"Someone was waiting for me here."

She could have stabbed me and it couldn't have hurt me more. I rose, and gave her my hand. "Good-bye," I said.

"I knew you would get angry," she said. "Men are so desperate to find things out that will only hurt them."

"But I assure you," I added coldly, as if I wanted to prove that I had been cured of my passion forever, "I assure you that I am not angry. It was quite natural that someone would have been waiting for you, just as it is quite natural that I would leave at three in the morning."

"Do you also have someone waiting for you at home?"

"No, but I must go."

"Good-bye, in that case."

"You're sending me away."

"That's the last thing in the world I would do."

"Why do you hurt me?"

"How have I hurt you?"

"You tell me that someone was waiting for you."

"I couldn't help myself from laughing at the idea that you had been so happy to see me go home alone, when there'd been such a good reason for it."

"A person often derives joy from a childish fancy, and it's cruel to destroy that fancy when, by letting it linger, you could make the person who holds it happier."

"But who do you think you're dealing with? I am neither a virgin nor a duchess. I only met you today, and I am not accountable to you for my actions. In considering the possibility that one day I might become your mistress, you will need to know that I have had other lovers besides you. If you are already making jealous scenes beforehand, what might happen afterward—if an afterward were ever to exist! I've never come across a man like you."

"That is because nobody has ever loved you as I love you."

"Come now; frankly, you really love me?"

"As much as it is possible to love, I believe."

"And how long has this been going on?"

"Since the day I saw you get out of your barouche and walk into Susse's, three years ago."

"Do you know that that's a beautiful thing you just said? And what must I do to acknowledge this great love?"

"You must love me a little," I said, my heart beating so violently that I could barely speak; because, despite the half-mocking smiles with which she had accompanied this entire conversation, it seemed to me that Marguerite was beginning to share in my agitation, and that I was nearing the hour I had awaited for such a long time.

"And the duke?"

"What duke?"

"My old jealous guardian."

"He won't know a thing."

"And if he finds out?"

"He'll forgive you."

"No he won't! He'll leave me, and what's to become of me?"

"You are already risking that abandonment for another man."

"How do you know?"

"Because of the instruction you gave not to let anyone in tonight."

"That's true, but that one is a serious friend."

"Who you are not all that committed to, if you bar your door to him at such an hour."

"You are hardly the one to reproach me, since it was in order to receive you, you and your friend, that the door was barred."

Little by little I had come nearer to Marguerite. I put my hands around her waist, and felt the light weight of her supple body against my linked hands.

"If you knew how I love you!" I said softly.

"Is it really true?"

"I swear it to you."

"Well then, if you promise to satisfy all my demands without saying a word, without criticizing me, without questioning me, perhaps I will love you."

"Everything you want!"

"But I warn you, I want to be free to do whatever suits me, without giving you the slightest information about my life. I've been looking for a young lover for a long time, someone who isn't strong-willed, who's loving but not mistrustful, who is loved by me, but who doesn't claim that as his right. I've never been able to find one. Men, instead of being satisfied with the favors one grants them after a long courtship during which they scarcely hoped to obtain that favor even once, expect their mistress to give them a full account of her present, her past, and even her future. Once they get used to her, they want to dominate her, and they become still more insistent on getting everything they want. If I decide to take a new lover now, I want him to have three qualities that are extremely rare: He must be confident, obedient, and discreet."

"I will be everything you could wish."

"We shall see."

"And when will we see each other?"

"Later."

"Why?"

"Because," Marguerite said, extracting herself from my arms and taking up a large bouquet of red camellias that had been brought in that morning, one of which she threaded through my buttonhole. "Because one cannot always execute treaties the day they are signed."

That was easy to understand.

"And when will I see you again?" I asked, holding her tight in my arms.

"When this camellia changes color."

"And when will it change color?"

"Tomorrow, between eleven o'clock and midnight. Are you happy?"

"How can you ask?"

"Not a word of this, neither to your friend, nor to Prudence, nor to anybody."

"I promise."

"Now, kiss me and let's go back to the dining room."

She gave me her lips, smoothed her hair again, and we left that room—she was singing; I was half-crazy.

In the living room she stopped and said to me softly, "It must seem strange to you that I seem ready to accept you at once— do you know where that comes from? It comes," she continued, taking my hand and placing it on her heart, whose violent and repeated palpitations I could feel, "it comes from the fact that, knowing I will live a shorter time than others, I have sworn to myself to live with greater speed."

"Don't speak to me in that way, I beg you."

"Oh! Console yourself," she continued, laughing. "As little time as I have to live, I will outlive your love for me."

And she entered the dining room, singing.

"Where is Nanine?" she said, seeing Gaston and Prudence alone.

"Bad girl! I'll kill her! All right, gentlemen, it's time for you to go."

Ten minutes later, Gaston and I left. Marguerite clasped my hand as she said good-bye, and remained with Prudence.

"Well then," Gaston asked me when we were outside, "what do you think of Marguerite?"

"She's an angel, and I'm crazy about her."

"I thought so. Did you tell her?"

"Yes."

"And did she promise to believe you?"

"No."

"Not like Prudence."

"She promised you?"

"Better than that, my friend! You wouldn't think so, but she's still in fine form, that fat Duvernoy!"

CHAPTER XI

At this point in his narrative, Armand stopped.

"Could you close the window?" he said. "I'm starting to get cold. In spite of this weather, I'm going to lie down."

I closed the window. Armand, who was still very weak, took off his dressing gown and got into bed, letting his head rest on his pillow for a few moments, like a man tired from a long run or disturbed by painful memories.

"Perhaps you have spoken too much," I told him. Would you like me to go home and let you sleep? You can tell me the rest of the story another day."

"Is it boring you?"

"On the contrary."

"I will continue, then; if you were to leave me on my own, I would not sleep."

When I returned home, he resumed, without need for reflection, so present were all these details to his mind, I didn't go to sleep; I began to reflect on the adventure of the day. The encounter, the introduction, the agreement between Marguerite and me—everything had been so fast, so unhoped-for, that there were moments when I thought I had dreamed it. And yet it was not the first time that a girl like Marguerite had promised herself to a man for the day after he had asked to see her.

I had a hard time forcing myself to admit this; the first impression my future mistress had produced on me had been so powerful it was as if she were still there. I insisted to myself that she was not like other girls, and with the vanity so common to all men, I was ready to believe she shared the same invincible attraction for me that I felt for her.

However, I had much conflicting information before my eyes, and I had often heard that Marguerite's love was a commodity that was costlier or cheaper according to the season.

On the other hand, how could that reputation be reconciled with the continual refusals she made to the young count whom we had found at her home? You will say she was not attracted to him, and since she was splendidly kept by the duke, if she were to take another lover, she would prefer it be a man she liked. In that case, why wouldn't she want Gaston, charming, witty, and rich; and why did she appear to want me, whom she had found so ridiculous the first time she'd seen me?

It is true that there are incidents of a minute's duration that can be more significant than a yearlong courtship.

Among those who were at the supper, I was the only one who had been upset to see her leave the table. I had followed her; I was so moved that I couldn't hide it. I had wept while kissing her hand. This circumstance, joined to the daily visits I had made during the two months of her illness, perhaps had allowed her to see in me a different kind of man than the ones she had known before, and maybe she had told herself that she might as well do for a love expressed in this fashion what she had already done so many times that it didn't even matter to her.

All these speculations, as you see, were reasonable enough, but whatever the cause of her consent, there was one thing that was sure: She had consented.

Now, I was in love with Marguerite. I was going to possess her; there was nothing more I could ask of her. However, I repeat to you, although she was a kept woman, in my head, perhaps to romanticize her, I had transformed this passion into a hopeless love, such that the closer the moment approached when I would no longer have need to hope, the more I doubted it would ever happen.

I did not close my eyes all night.

I could not recognize myself. I was half-crazy. Sometimes I thought I wasn't handsome enough, or rich enough, or elegant enough to possess such a woman; sometimes I felt full of vanity at the thought of this possession. Then I began to fear that

Marguerite would treat me as a passing whim, and anticipating the pain of an abrupt rupture, I told myself I would do better not to visit her that night, but to leave town after writing her to explain my fears. From that point I passed on to boundless hopes, to confidence without limit. I built incredible castles in the air; I told myself that this girl would be able to thank me for her physical and moral recovery, that I would spend all my life with her, and that her love would make me happier than the most virginal of loves.

In sum I could never tell you all the thousand thoughts that caught fire in my heart and mind, and died out bit by bit in the sleep that overtook me at dawn.

When I awoke, it was two o'clock. The weather was magnificent. I don't believe that life had ever before appeared to me so beautiful and replete. The memories of the previous night replayed in my mind, without shadows, without obstacles, joyfully accompanied by my hopes for the evening. I dressed in haste. I was happy and capable of great things. My heart often leapt to my throat from joy and love. A gentle fever ran through me. I was no longer worried about the things that had preoccupied me before I fell asleep. I could see nothing but the outcome; I thought only of the hour when I would see Marguerite again.

It was impossible for me to stay at home. My bedroom seemed too small to contain my happiness; I needed all of nature to flow over me.

I went out.

I passed by the rue d'Antin; Marguerite's carriage was waiting for her by her door. I headed toward the Champs-Élysées. I loved, without even knowing them, all the people I passed.

How good love makes you!

After spending an hour walking from the horses of Marly to the Rond-Point, and from the Rond-Point to the horses of Marly, I saw Marguerite's carriage from afar. I could not positively identify it, but I knew it was hers.

At the moment she turned onto the Champs-Élysées, she stopped, and a tall young man parted from a group of people he'd been chatting with to come talk with her.

They spoke for a few moments, the young man rejoined his friends, the horses set off again, and I, who had approached the group, recognized the man who had spoken to Marguerite, this Comte de G . . . , whose portrait I had seen, and whom Prudence had indicated as the man to whom Marguerite owed her social standing.

It was to him that she had barred the door the previous night. I assumed that she had stopped her carriage to give him the reason for this rejection, and at the same time hoped she had found some new pretext to avoid receiving him the following night.

How the rest of the day passed I do not know. I walked, I smoked, I chatted, but by ten o'clock at night I had no memory of what I'd said or whom I'd seen.

All I remember is that I returned home, that I spent three hours getting dressed, and that I looked at my clock a thousand times and at my watch, both of which unhappily kept the same time.

When the clock struck ten thirty, I told myself it was time to go.

I was living at that time on the rue de Provence. I walked along the rue du Mont-Blanc, I crossed the boulevard, took the rue Louis le Grand, the rue de Port-Mahon, and the rue d'Antin. I looked into Marguerite's windows.

There was light.

I rang.

I asked the porter if Mlle Gautier was at home.

He replied that she never returned home before eleven o'clock or eleven fifteen.

I looked at my watch.

I'd thought I'd come quite slowly, but it had taken me only five minutes to get from the rue de Provence to Marguerite's.

So I strolled this street devoid of shops, which was deserted at this time of day.

Half an hour later Marguerite arrived. She got out of her coupé and looked around as if there were somebody she expected to see.

The carriage left at a walk; the stables were not in the house.

Just as Marguerite was about to ring the bell, I approached and said to her "Good evening."

"Ah! It's you?" she said, in a tone that hardly reassured me she was happy to find me there.

"Hadn't you permitted me to come pay you a visit today?"

"That's right; I had forgotten."

This comment overthrew all the reveries of my morning, all my hopes of the day. However, I was beginning to become accustomed to her ways, and I did not leave, something I obviously would have done in the past.

We walked in.

Nanine opened the door before we got to it.

"Has Prudence come home?" asked Marguerite.

"No, madam."

"Go leave word that as soon as she gets home she should come over. In the meantime, put out the lamp in the living room, and if anybody comes, tell them I am not at home and that I will not be at home."

This was definitely a woman who was preoccupied by something, and perhaps annoyed to have someone importuning her. I did not know how to act or what to say. Marguerite headed for her bedroom; I stayed where I was.

"Come," she told me.

She took off her hat, then her velvet coat, and threw them onto the bed. Then she sank into a big armchair by the fire that she kept going all the way up to the beginning of summer, and said to me, while fiddling with her watch chain, "Well then, what news do you have for me?"

"Nothing, unless it's that I was wrong to come tonight."

"Why?"

"Because you seem to be in a bad mood, and no doubt I am boring you."

"You aren't boring me; it's just that I'm sick, I felt awful all day, I haven't slept, and I have a terrible migraine."

"Would you like me to leave so you can go to bed?"

"Oh! You can stay; if I want to go to sleep, I'll sleep just fine in front of you."

At this moment the doorbell rang.

"Who's coming now?" she said with an impatient movement.

A few moments later, the bell rang again.

"There's nobody there to open it; I'll have to go get the door myself."

She got up, saying to me, "Wait here."

She crossed the apartment, and I heard the front door open. I listened.

The person to whom she had opened the door stopped in the dining room. With the first words I recognized the voice of the young Comte de N . . . .

"How are you doing tonight?" he asked.

"Badly," Marguerite replied drily.

"Am I disturbing you?"

"Perhaps."

"How you receive me! What have I done to you, my dear Marguerite?"

"My dear friend, you have done nothing to me. I am ill; I need to go to sleep—so please do me the kindness of going away. It staggers me to be unable to come home at night without having you turn up five minutes later. What do you want? For me to be your mistress? Well, I've already told you a hundred times no, that you irritate me terribly, and that you should turn your attentions elsewhere. I repeat it to you today for the last time: I want nothing to do with you, that's final; adieu. Ah, here is Nanine returning; she will light your way. Good night."

And without another word, without listening to what the young man was stammering, Marguerite came back to her bedroom and slammed the door, through which Nanine returned almost immediately.

"Understand," Marguerite told her. "You are to always tell that fool that I'm not here, or that I do not want to receive him. I've finally had it with endlessly seeing these people who come here, always after the same thing, who pay me and consider themselves quit with me. If the women who started out in our shameful trade knew what it is, they would prefer to be chambermaids. But no; the vanity of having fine gowns, carriages, diamonds pulls us in. We believe what we hear, because even prostitution has its faith, and little by little they use up your heart, your body, your beauty. You are feared like a wild beast, scorned like a pariah, and surrounded by people who take more from you than they give you, and one day you go off and die like a dog after having lost all the others and being lost yourself."

"Now, now, madam, calm yourself," said Nanine. "Your nerves are bad tonight."

"This dress bothers me," Marguerite said, unhooking her bodice. "Give me a dressing gown. All right then, and Prudence?"

"She hasn't come home yet, but we will send her to madam as soon as she does."

"There's another one," continued Marguerite, as she took off her dress and put on a white dressing gown. "Yet another one who knows very well how to find me when she needs me, but who can't do me a service out of simple kindness. She knows I'm waiting for her answer tonight, that I must know, and that I'm anxious, and I'm sure she's run off without thinking of me at all."

"Maybe she has been detained."

"Get us some punch."

"You'll suffer for it again," said Nanine.

"All the better. Also bring me some fruit, some pâté or a chicken wing, something at once; I'm hungry."

To tell you the impression that this scene had upon me is needless; you can guess, no?

"You will have supper with me," she said to me. "While you're waiting, read a book; I'm going to go into my dressing room for a bit."

She lit the candles on a candelabra, opened a door near the foot of her bed, and disappeared.

As for me, I began to reflect on the life of this girl, and pity increased my love.

I was pacing this bedroom, deep in thought, when Prudence entered.

"Oh, you're here?" she said. "Where is Marguerite?"

"In her dressing room."

"I'll wait for her. She thinks you're charming, did you know that?"

"No."

"She didn't give you a hint?"

"Not at all."

"How do you happen to be here?"

"I've come to pay a call."

"At midnight?"

"Why not?"

"You joker!"

"All the same, she received me very rudely."

"She will receive you better in future."

"You think?"

"I'm bringing her good news."

"No harm done. So she has spoken to you about me?"

"Yesterday night, or rather, early this morning, when you left with your friend. . . . And on that subject, how is he, your friend? He's called Gaston R . . . , I think?"

"Yes," I said, unable to keep from smiling as I remembered the boast Gaston had made to me, and saw that Prudence scarcely knew his name.

"He's nice, that boy; what does he do?"

"He has an income of twenty-five thousand francs."

"Ah! Really! Well, returning to you, Marguerite asked me about you; she wanted to know who you were, what you did, which mistresses you had had—in short, everything you could want to know about a man your age. I told her everything I know, adding that you are a charming boy, and there you have it."

"Thank you; now, tell me then what business she asked you to perform yesterday."

"None; that was just to make the count leave, but today she did give me a mission, and that is the answer I'm bringing her tonight."

At this moment Marguerite came out of her dressing room, coquettishly coiffed in her nightcap, decorated with poufs of yellow ribbons, which technically are known as *choux*.

She looked ravishing.

Her feet were bare in satin slippers, and she was doing her nails. "So," she said, seeing Prudence, "did you see the duke?"

"Certainly!"

"And what did he say to you?"

"He gave it to me."

"How much?"

"Six thousand."

"Do you have it with you?"

"Yes."

"Did he look annoyed?"

"No."

"Poor man!"

This "Poor man!" was said in a tone that is impossible to convey. Marguerite took the six one-thousand-franc notes.

"And high time," she said. "My dear Prudence, do you need money?"

"You know, my child, that in two days it will be the fifteenth, so if you could lend me three or four hundred francs, you would do me a great service."

"Send for it tomorrow morning; it's too late tonight to break it."

"Don't forget."

"Don't worry. Will you have supper with us?"

"No, Charles is waiting for me at home."

"You're still crazy about him, then?"

"Positively nuts, my darling! Till tomorrow. Good-bye, Armand."

Mme Duvernoy left.

Marguerite opened a door of the étagère and tossed the banknotes into it.

"You will permit me to lie down!" she said, smiling, as she went to her bed.

"Not only do I permit it; I beg it of you."

She threw back the coverlet and got into bed.

"Now," she said, "come sit beside me and we'll have a little talk."

Prudence was right: The answer she had brought Marguerite had cheered her.

"Will you forgive my bad mood from earlier this evening?" she said, taking my hand.

"I am prepared to forgive you many more."

"And do you love me?"

"So much that I could go crazy."

"In spite of my bad nature?"

"In spite of everything."

"Swear it!"

"Yes," I said softly.

Nanine came in bearing plates, a cold chicken, a bottle of Bordeaux, strawberries, and two covered dishes.

"I didn't make any punch for you," said Nanine. "The Bordeaux is better for you. Isn't that right, sir?"

"Certainly," I responded, stirred again by these last words of Marguerite's, my eyes fixed ardently upon her.

"Good," she said. "Put all that on the little table, bring it close to the bed; we will serve ourselves. You've been up three nights in a row; you must want to sleep. Go to bed; I don't need anything more."

"Should I lock the door?"

"I should say so! And above all, leave word that nobody be allowed in tomorrow before noon."

CHAPTER XII

At five in the morning, as the daylight began to appear through the curtains, Marguerite told me, "Forgive me if I send you away, but I must. The duke comes every morning; he will be told I am sleeping when he comes, and he will likely wait until I get up."

I took Marguerite's head into my hands, her hair rippled around her, and I gave her a final kiss, saying to her, "When will I see you again?"

"Listen," she replied, "take the little golden key that's on the mantel, go open that door, bring the key back here, and leave. In the afternoon you will receive a letter with my orders, which you know you must blindly obey."

"Yes, and what if I were to ask something of you already?"

"What is it, then?"

"Let me keep this key."

"I've never done for anyone what you ask of me now."

"Well then, do it for me, because I swear that I do not love you as the others loved you."

"Well then, keep it, but I warn you that it is up to me whether this key works for you at all."

"Why?"

"Because there are other locks on the door."

"Naughty!"

"I will have them removed."

"So you love me a little?"

"I don't know how it has happened, but it seems that I do. Now go away; I am so tired I could collapse."

We remained a few moments in each other's arms and I left.

The streets were deserted; the great city still slept. A sweet freshness traversed these neighborhoods that a few hours later would be invaded by the noise of men.

This sleeping city seemed to belong to me. I searched my memory for the names of other men whose happiness I had envied until now, and felt luckier than every last one of them.

To be loved by a chaste young girl, to be the first to reveal love's strange mysteries to her, certainly that is a great happiness, but it's the simplest thing in the world. To take possession of a heart that is unaccustomed to such invasions is to enter an open and undefended city. Education and the sense of duty and family are powerful sentinels, but there are no sentinels so vigilant that they cannot be outwitted by a sixteen-year-old girl to whom nature is giving its first lessons in love, in the voice of the man she loves, nature's counsel all the more ardent because of its innocence.

The more the young girl believes in goodness, the more easily she surrenders, if not to the lover, then at least to love, because her trustfulness makes her powerless. Any man of twenty-five may achieve the victory of making her fall in love with him whenever he wishes. To see the truth in this, just look how they surround young girls with surveillance and ramparts! Convents don't have walls high enough, mothers don't have locks strong enough, religion doesn't have penance stern enough to keep all those charming birds in their cages, in which nobody takes the trouble to strew flowers. How they must long for this world that is hidden from them, how tempting they must think it is, how they must long to hear the first voice that comes through the bars to tell them secrets—and kiss the hand that lifts, for the first time, a corner of the mysterious veil.

But to be truly loved by a courtesan, that is a much harder-won victory. In their case, the body has worn out the soul, the senses have burned up the heart, dissipation has hardened the feelings. All the pretty words one tells them they have known for a long time, the methods one uses are familiar to them, and even the love they inspire they have sold. They love as a matter of business, not inclination. They are better protected by their own calculations than a virgin by her mother and her convent.

They have even invented the word *caprice* for those loves without profit that they permit themselves from time to time as a kind of holiday, as an excuse or a consolation, like those usurers who ransom a thousand individuals but believe they can redeem themselves by not asking for interest or a receipt when they lend twenty francs to some poor devil who's dying of hunger.

Then, when God grants love to a courtesan, this love, which seems at first like a reprieve, nearly always becomes a punishment for her. There is no absolution without penitence. When a creature who has all her past to rue feels herself suddenly overcome by a deep, sincere, irresistible love, of which she never would have believed herself capable, when she has acknowledged this love, how she is dominated by the man she loves! How mighty he feels with his cruel right to tell her, "You do nothing more for love than you have done for money."

Then they don't know what proofs they can supply. A child, according to fable, after having amused itself by crying "Help!" in a field to annoy the workers, was devoured by a bear one day because those he had tricked so often in the past did not believe his genuine cries for help. It is the same for those unlucky women when they truly love. They have lied so many times that nobody believes them, and they are, in the midst of their remorse, devoured by their love.

This is what inspires those great devotions, those self-sacrificing retreats from the world of which some women have left us the example.

But when the man who inspires such redemptive love has a soul generous enough to accept it without recalling the past, when he surrenders to it, when in the end he loves as he is loved, this man exhausts with one blow all earthly emotions, and his heart forever after is closed to all other loves.

I did not come by these reflections on the morning I returned home. They would have been nothing more than a presentiment of what might happen to me, and despite my love for Marguerite, I did not think of such consequences at that time; today I do. Everything being irrevocably over, they are the natural result of what took place.

But let us return to the first day of this liaison. When I returned home, I was filled with wild exuberance. As I reflected that the barriers my imagination had erected between Marguerite and me had disappeared, that I possessed her, that I occupied a small place in her thoughts, that I had in my pocket the key to her apartment and the right to use this key, I was satisfied with life, proud of myself, and I loved God, who had allowed this to happen.

One day a young man walks down a street, he bumps into a woman, he looks at her, he turns around, he walks on. This woman—he does not know her—has joys, sorrows, and loves that he has no part in. He does not exist for her, and perhaps if he were to talk to her she would mock him as Marguerite had mocked me. Weeks, months, years pass, and all of a sudden, when they have each pursued their destiny in different directions, the logic of chance brings them face-to-face. This woman becomes the mistress of this man and loves him. How? Why? Their two existences merge into one; hardly does intimacy arise between them before it seems to them that it had existed forever, and everything that came before is erased from the memory of the two lovers. It's a strange thing, let us concede.

As for me, I could no longer remember how I had lived before the preceding night. All my being was exalted by the joy of the memory of the words we had exchanged that first night. Either Marguerite was exceptionally good at deception, or she had succumbed to one of those sudden passions that reveal themselves with the first kiss, and that, as often as not, die as soon as they are born.

The more I thought about it, the more I told myself that Marguerite had no reason to feign a love she did not feel, and I told myself as well that women have two ways of loving, and that one can grow out of the other: They love either with the heart or with the body. Often a woman takes a lover only to obey her sensual urges, and discovers the mystery of ineffable love without having sought it, and thereafter can no longer live except through her heart. Whereas a young girl who had looked for nothing in marriage but the union of two pure affections often may receive the sudden revelation of physical love, that energetic resolution of the chastest impulses of the soul.

I fell asleep amid these thoughts. I was awoken by a letter from Marguerite, a letter that contained these words:

> Here are my orders: Tonight at the Vaudeville. Come during the third intermission.
>
> M.G.

I put this note in a drawer so as to always have the reality of it close at hand in case I came to doubt it, as happened many a time.

She did not tell me to come see her in the afternoon; I did not dare present myself at her place. But I had such a great desire to see her before the evening that I went to the Champs-Élysées, where, as on the previous night, I had watched her drive past and disembark.

At seven o'clock I was at the Vaudeville.

Never before had I entered a theater so early.

All the boxes were filling up, one after another. Only one remained empty: the one on the ground floor, near the stage.

At the beginning of the third act I heard the door of this box open, the one on which my eyes had been almost constantly fixed. Marguerite appeared.

She went to the front immediately, looked to the orchestra, saw me, and thanked me with her gaze.

She looked marvelously beautiful that night.

Was I the cause of this coquetry? Did she love me enough to believe that the more beautiful I found her, the happier I would be? I was not sure yet, but if that had been her intention she succeeded, because as soon as she showed herself, heads swiveled, one after another, and even the actor then on stage looked for himself to see whose appearance had provoked such agitation among the spectators.

And I had the key to this woman's apartment, and in three or four hours she would be mine again.

People find fault with those who ruin themselves over ac-

tresses and kept women; what astonishes me is that they don't
commit twenty times more follies for them than they do. One
must have lived that life, as I did, to know how strongly the
little everyday vanities they give their lovers are knit together
in the heart, and, as we have no other word for it, in the love
he bears her.

Prudence next took her place in the box, and a man I knew
as the Comte de G . . . sat at the back.

At the sight of him, a chill gripped my heart.

Without doubt Marguerite saw the reaction that this man's
presence in her box produced in me, for she smiled at me again
and, turning her back to the count, appeared to give her full
attention to the play. At the third intermission she turned and
said a word or two; the count left the box, and Marguerite
signaled for me to come see her.

"Good evening," she said when I entered, and gave me her
hand.

"Good evening," I responded, addressing both Marguerite
and Prudence.

"Have a seat."

"But I am taking somebody's place. Isn't M. le Comte de
G . . . coming back?"

"Yes; I sent him to get me candy so we can speak alone for a
moment. Mme Duvernoy is in my confidence."

"Yes, my children," said the lady. "Rest assured, I will say
nothing."

"What is wrong with you tonight?" asked Marguerite, rising, walking to the dark end of the box, and kissing me on the
forehead.

"I don't feel well."

"You should go to bed," she replied, with that ironic air that
suited her dainty and spirited head so well.

"Where?"

"At your place."

"You know very well that I would not be able to sleep there."

"All the same, you must not come and pout at us because
you've seen a man in my box."

"It is not for that reason."

"Yes it is, I know it is, and you are in the wrong, so let's speak no more of it. You will come after the show to Prudence's, and you will stay there until I call for you. Do you understand?"

"Yes."

How could I disobey?

"Do you still love me?" she asked.

"How can you ask!"

"You've thought of me?"

"All day long."

"Do you know that I am decidedly afraid I'm falling in love with you? Ask Prudence."

"Ah!" the stout creature said. "This is too much."

"Now, go back to your stall; the count is about to return, and it will not be useful for him to find you here."

"Why not?"

"Because you find it unpleasant to see him."

"No; it's just that, if you had told me you wanted to come to the Vaudeville tonight, I could have gotten you this box instead of him."

"Unfortunately he got it for me without my asking him, and offered to accompany me here. You know very well I could not refuse. All I could do was write to you where I was going so you could see me, and because I myself wanted to see you earlier than I might have otherwise; but since this is how you repay me, I will profit from this lesson."

"I was in the wrong, forgive me."

"At the proper time, return nicely to your seat, and above all, don't act jealous."

She kissed me again, and I left.

In the hallway I saw the count coming back.

I returned to my seat.

After all, M. de G . . . 's presence in Marguerite's box made sense. He had been her lover, he had bought her the box, he had accompanied her to the performance. All of this was completely natural, and from the moment I had taken a girl like Marguerite for a mistress, I was going to have to accept her ways.

But all the same, I was unhappy for the rest of the evening, and as I left I was saddened to see Prudence, the count, and Marguerite get in the barouche that awaited them by the door.

A quarter of an hour later, I was at Prudence's. She had only just returned home.

CHAPTER XIII

"You got here almost as fast as we did," Prudence said to me.

"Yes," I responded mechanically. "Where is Marguerite?"

"At home."

"Alone?"

"With M. de G . . . ."

I began to pace the room.

"What's with you?"

"Do you think I can find it pleasurable to wait here for M. de G . . . to leave Marguerite's apartment?"

"You are not being reasonable. Understand that Marguerite cannot show the count the door. M. de G . . . has been with her for a long time; he has always given her a lot of money. He still does. Marguerite spends more than a hundred thousand francs a year; she has many debts. The duke sends her what she asks for, but she does not always dare to ask him for everything she needs. She must not make trouble with the count, who gives her no less than ten thousand francs a year. Marguerite likes you very much, my dear friend, but your relationship with her, speaking both in her interest and in yours, must not become serious. With your seven or eight thousand francs you cannot maintain that girl in the luxury to which she's accustomed; it would not be enough to pay for the upkeep of her carriage. Take Marguerite as she is—for a fine, spirited, and pretty girl. Be her lover for one month, maybe two; give her bouquets, candy, and theater boxes—but don't get anything else in your head and don't make ridiculous, jealous scenes. You know very well who you're dealing with; Marguerite is not a virtuous woman. She likes you, you like her very much; don't fret about

the rest. How charming you are to play the victim! You have
the most delightful mistress in Paris! She entertains you in a
magnificent apartment, she is covered in diamonds, she won't
cost you a penny if you wish it, and you aren't content. What
the devil! You ask too much of her."

"You're right, but this is stronger than I am. The idea that
that man is her lover causes me tremendous pain."

"First of all," Prudence replied, "is he still her lover? He's a
man she needs, that's all. For two days, she closed her door to
him. He came this morning; there was nothing she could do
but accept his theater box and let him accompany her. He
drove her home, he has gone up for a moment to visit her, he
will not stay there, and so you are waiting here. All of this is
quite natural, it seems to me. That aside, the duke doesn't
bother you?"

"Yes, but he's an old man, and I'm sure Marguerite is not his
mistress. Also, a man might well tolerate one affair, but not
two. That kind of complaisance begins to look like calculation,
and brings the man who consents to it, even for love, closer to
those who, in the lower element, make a business of this sort
of understanding, and profit from it."

"Ah! My dear, you are so backwards! How many men have
I seen—and nobler men than you, richer and more elegant—
who do what I advise, and without effort, without shame, without remorse? You see it every day. How could the kept women
of Paris maintain the lifestyles they lead if they didn't have
three or four lovers at a time? There's no individual fortune,
however great, that could cover the expenses of a woman like
Marguerite. A fortune of five hundred thousand francs is enormous in France; and well, my friend, five hundred thousand
francs would not be enough, and here is why: A man who has
an income that great has a house to maintain, horses, servants,
carriages, hunts, friends; often he is married, he has children,
he races, he gambles, he travels, what do I know! All of these
habits are so established that he cannot get out of them without
giving the appearance of being ruined and creating a scandal.
Everything considered, with an income of five hundred thousand francs, he can't give a woman more than forty or fifty

thousand francs a year, and that's already a lot. So, other lovers have to make up the difference of the woman's annual expenses. With Marguerite, things are a little more convenient; by a miracle that fell from Heaven, she stumbled upon a rich old man worth ten million, whose wife and daughter are dead, who has nobody left but nephews who are themselves rich, and who gives her everything she wants without asking anything in return. But she can't ask him for more than seventy thousand francs a year, and I'm sure that if she asked him for more, despite his fortune and his fondness for her, he would refuse.

"All the young people who have twenty or thirty thousand francs a year in Paris—which is to say, hardly enough to live on in the circles they travel in—know very well that if they happen to become the lover of a woman like Marguerite, she could not pay for her apartment and her servants with what they can give her. They keep quiet because they know this; they pretend to see nothing, and when they've had enough, they leave. If they are vain enough to take everything upon themselves, they ruin themselves like fools and go kill themselves in Africa after having left a hundred thousand francs of debt in Paris. Do you think that the woman should be grateful to them for it? Not at all. On the contrary, she tells them that she sacrificed her social position to them, and that while she was with them, she lost money. Ah! You find these details shameful, don't you? Well, they are true. You are a charming boy, and I love you with all my heart, but I have lived for twenty years among kept women. I know what they are and what they're worth, and I would not want to see you take the caprice a young girl has for you too seriously.

"Beyond that, let us suppose," Prudence continued, "that Marguerite loves you enough to renounce the count and the duke. In the case that the former learns of your relationship and tells her to choose between you and him, the sacrifice she would make to be with you would be enormous; you can't deny it. What comparable sacrifice would you be prepared to make for her? When you have had your fill, when you will want no more of her, what will you do to help her regain what you will have made her lose? Nothing. You will have separated her from the world in which her fortune and her future resided, she will have given you her best years, and she will be forgotten. At that point, you will either act like a typical man, throwing her past in her face and telling her that in leaving her you do no worse than her other lovers, abandoning her to certain misery; or you will be an honest man, and believing yourself honor bound to keep her by your side, will deliver yourself to inevitable unhappiness, because this liaison, which is excusable for a young man, is impardonable for a man of mature years. It becomes an obstacle to everything; it permits neither family nor ambition, those second and last loves of man. Believe me then, my friend, take things for what they're worth, women for who they are, and don't give a kept woman the right to see herself as your creditor in anything."

It was well argued and showed a logic of which I would not have believed Prudence capable. I found nothing to reply, except that she was right. I gave her my hand and thanked her for her advice.

"Now, now," she said. "Let's put aside these gloomy theories and laugh. Life is charming, my dear; it depends on how you look at it. Talk with your friend Gaston—there's a man who seems to see love as I see it. What you must be convinced of, failing which you will be a very silly boy indeed, is that there's a beautiful girl close by who is impatiently waiting for the man who's visiting her now to leave, who is thinking of you, who has reserved her night for you, and who loves you, I am certain of it. Now come by the window with me, and let's watch the count leave; he won't delay to yield us his place."

Prudence opened a window, and we leaned side by side against the balcony.

She looked at the occasional passersby; I daydreamed.

Everything she had said to me buzzed in my head, and I could not help agreeing that she was right, but the genuine love I had for Marguerite could not accommodate itself to her reasoning. From time to time I heaved sighs that made Prudence turn to me and shrug her shoulders like a doctor who has given up hope on a patient.

"How short life must be," I said to myself, "given how

quickly different feelings come and go! I have known Marguerite for only two days, she has been my mistress since only
yesterday, and she has so taken over my thoughts, my heart,
and my life that the visit of this Comte de G . . . comes as a
great unhappiness to me."

At last the count left, climbed into his carriage, and disappeared. Prudence closed her window.

At just that moment, Marguerite called out to us.

"Come quickly; we're setting the table," she said. "We're
going to have supper."

When I entered her apartment, Marguerite ran to me, threw
her arms around me, and kissed me with all her strength.

"Are we still grumpy?" she asked me.

"No, that's over with," Prudence responded. "I gave him a
lecture, and he has promised to be good."

"And high time!"

In spite of myself, I glanced at the bed; it was not unmade.
As for Marguerite, she was already in her white dressing gown.

We sat down to eat.

Charm, sweetness, character—Marguerite had everything,
and I was forced from time to time to recognize that I did not
have the right to ask anything else of her, that many people
would have felt lucky in my place, and that, like Virgil's shepherd, all I had to do was rejoice in the good offices that a god,
or rather, a goddess had bestowed upon me.

I tried to put Prudence's theories into practice, and to be as
merry as my two companions, but what was natural for them
felt forced to me, and my nervous laughter, which fooled them,
was very close to tears.

Finally the supper came to an end, and I was alone with
Marguerite. She went, as was her custom, to sit on the carpet
in front of the fire and looked with a melancholy air at the
flame on the hearth.

She was thinking—what about? I didn't know. I looked at
her with love and almost with terror, as I contemplated what I
was ready to suffer for her sake.

"Do you know what I was thinking about? About a solution
I have come upon."

"And what is this solution?"

"I can't tell you yet, but I can tell you what will come of it. What will come of it is that in one month, I will be free, I will owe nothing, and we can go spend the summer together in the country."

"And you can't tell me by what means?"

"No; you must only love me as I love you, and everything will work out."

"And you have hit upon this solution on your own?"

"Yes."

"And you will execute it on your own?"

"Only I will have the care of it," Marguerite said to me with a smile that I will never forget, "but we will both share in the benefits."

I could not keep from blushing at this word *benefits*; I recalled Manon Lescaut eating up M. de B.'s money with Des Grieux. . . .

I responded in a rather harsh tone, while rising, "You will permit me, my dear Marguerite, not to share in the benefits of any enterprise except one that I conceive and execute myself?"

"What does that mean?"

"That means that I strongly suspect M. le Comte de G . . . of being your associate in this happy solution, of which I can accept neither the burden nor the benefit."

"You are a child. I thought you loved me; I was wrong. It's all right."

And at that moment, she got up, opened her piano, and returned to playing "L'Invitation à la Valse," up until that infamous passage that always stopped her.

Did she do it out of habit, or was it to remind me of the day we met? All I know is that as I heard this melody, the memories came flooding back, and approaching her, I took her head between my hands and kissed her.

"Can you forgive me?" I asked.

"As you see," she replied. "But keep in mind that this is only our second day together, and already I have something to forgive you for. You don't keep your promises of blind obedience very well."

"What do you want from me, Marguerite? I love you too much, and I'm jealous of the least of your thoughts. What you proposed to me just now made me crazy with joy, but the mystery attached to carrying out this project grips my heart."

"Come, let's be reasonable," she said, taking my hands and looking at me with a charming smile I found impossible to resist. "You love me, don't you? And you would be happy to spend three or four months in the country alone with me. I, too, would be happy for this solitude à deux; not only would it make me happy, but I need it for my health. I can't leave Paris for such a long time without putting my affairs in order, and the affairs of a woman like me are always very complicated, and so, I've found a way to reconcile everything, my business and my love for you—yes, for you; don't laugh, I am foolish enough to love you—and now you put on your great airs and preach at me. Child, three times a child, just remember that I love you and you'll have nothing to worry about. Are we agreed, then?"

"I agree to everything you wish; you know that."

"Then, before a month is out, we will be in some village, strolling by the waterside and drinking milk. It must seem strange to you that I would speak this way—I, Marguerite Gautier. It comes, my friend, from the fact that when this Parisian life, which appears to make me so happy, doesn't burn me up, it bores me, and I've suddenly acquired aspirations for a more peaceful existence that might remind me of my childhood. Everyone has had a childhood, whatever one has become. Oh! Don't worry—I'm not going to tell you that I'm the daughter of a retired colonel and that I grew up in Saint-Denis. I'm a poor country girl, and I didn't know how to write my own name until six years ago. That reassures you, doesn't it? Why is it that you are the first man I've come to, to ask to share the joy of this impulse? No doubt it is because I recognized that you loved me for myself and not for yourself, whereas the others have only ever loved me for themselves.

"I've been to the countryside many times, but never as I would have liked to be there. I'm relying on you for this simple happiness, so don't be unkind and deny it to me. Tell yourself this: 'She can't live to be very old, and one day I will regret that I did not grant her the first favor she asked of me, which would have been so easy to grant.'"

What could I respond to such words, especially with the memory of a first night of love, and in the expectation of a second?

An hour later, I held Marguerite in my arms, and if she had demanded that I commit a crime, I would have obeyed her.

At six in the morning I left, and before leaving I said to her, "Until tonight?"

She kissed me all the harder, but did not respond.

In the afternoon I received a letter that contained these words:

"Dear child, I am not feeling well, and the doctor has ordered me to rest. I will go to sleep early tonight and will not see you. But, to make up for it, I will expect you tomorrow at noon. I love you."

My first reaction was, "She is deceiving me!"

A cold sweat broke out on my forehead, as I already loved this woman too much for this suspicion not to tear me apart.

Nonetheless, I was going to have to expect this kind of thing nearly every day with Marguerite, and it had often occurred with my other mistresses without troubling me overmuch. Where did it come from, the hold that this woman had on my life?

And then I thought, since I had her key, why not go see her as usual? That way I would quickly know the truth, and if I found a man there, I would slap his face.

While I waited, I went to the Champs-Élysées. I stayed there for four hours. She did not appear. In the evening I went to all the theaters where she usually went. She was not in any of them.

At eleven I turned up at the rue d'Antin.

There was no light in Marguerite's windows. I rang nonetheless.

The porter asked me where I was going.

"To see Mlle Gautier," I told him.

"She isn't back."

"I will go up and wait for her."

"There's nobody at home."

Obviously there were some sort of instructions at work that I could have overridden, since I had the key, but fearing an embarrassing scene, I left.

Only, I didn't go home. I couldn't leave the street, and did not let Marguerite's building out of my sight. It seemed to me there was something I had still to find out, or at least that my suspicions would be confirmed.

Toward midnight, a coupé I knew well stopped by No. 9.

The Comte de G . . . got out and entered the house, after having sent away his carriage.

For a moment I hoped that, as had happened to me, he would be told that Marguerite was not at home, and that I would see him go away; but at four o'clock in the morning I was still waiting.

I have suffered greatly these past three weeks, but it is nothing, I think, in comparison to what I suffered that night.

CHAPTER XIV

Returning home, I began to cry like a baby. Any man who has been deceived even once knows the suffering it causes.

I told myself, under the influence of those fevered resolutions that one always believes one will have the strength to keep, that I had to end this affair immediately, and I impatiently awaited the coming of morning so I could resume my former life and return to my father and sister, a double love I could feel sure of, and which would never betray me.

However, I did not want to leave without Marguerite knowing why I was leaving. Only a man who emphatically no longer loves his mistress leaves without writing her.

I wrote and rewrote twenty letters in my head.

I was involved with a girl who was like all other kept women. I had romanticized her far too much; she had treated me like a schoolboy, using a trick of insulting simplicity to deceive me, it was clear. My pride took over. I had to leave this woman without giving her the satisfaction of knowing that the rupture had hurt me, and here is what I wrote to her in my most elegant script, with tears of rage and pain in my eyes:

"My dear Marguerite,

"I hope that yesterday's indisposition has not troubled you too greatly. I dropped by at eleven last night for news of you, and was told that you had not returned. M. de G . . . was more fortunate than I, as he presented himself a few moments later, and at four in the morning was still with you.

"Forgive the tedious hours that I subjected you to, and be assured that I will never forget the happy moments that I owe to you.

"I certainly would have been eager to learn your news today, but I am planning to return to my family.

"Adieu, my dear Marguerite; I am neither rich enough to love you as I would like, nor poor enough to love you as you would prefer. Let us forget then—you, a name that must be practically indifferent to you; I, a happiness that has become impossible for me.

"I am sending you back your key, which has never been of use to me and could be of use to you, if you often fall sick as you did yesterday."

As you see, I did not have the strength to finish the letter without a flourish of insolent irony, which proved how much in love I still was.

I read and reread the letter ten times, and the idea that it would cause Marguerite pain calmed me a little. I tried to buck myself up by imagining the emotions she would feel, and when at eight o'clock my servant entered, I gave him the letter so he could take it to her at once.

"Should I wait for a response?" Joseph asked (my servant was named Joseph, like all servants).

"If anyone asks if a response is expected, say that you know nothing and that you will wait."

I clung to the hope that she would respond.

How poor and weak we are!

The entire time my servant was gone, I was in a state of extreme agitation. Sometimes, remembering how Marguerite had given herself to me, I asked myself what right I had to write her an impertinent letter, when she could have retorted that it was not M. de G . . . who was deceiving me, but I who was deceiving M. de G . . . , a rationale that allows many women to have many lovers. Sometimes, recalling the avowals the girl had made to me, I almost persuaded myself that my letter had been too mild, and that no expressions could be strongly worded enough to scourge a woman who could laugh at a love as sincere as mine. And then I told myself I would have done better not to write her at all, and to go visit her in the afternoon; and that, in that way, I could have rejoiced in the tears I would have made her shed.

At last I asked myself how she would reply, ready to believe any excuse she might give me.

Joseph came back.

"Well? I said.

"Sir," he replied, "madam was in bed and still sleeping, but as soon as she rings, they will give her the letter, and if there is a reply, they will bring it."

She was sleeping!

Twenty times I was on the point of sending him to retrieve the letter, but I always told myself, "Perhaps they've already given it to her, and it will look like I wished I hadn't sent it."

The closer the hour approached when it was likely she might respond, the more I regretted having written.

The clock struck ten, eleven o'clock, noon.

At noon I was on the verge of keeping our rendezvous, as if nothing had happened. I no longer knew how to wriggle out of the band of iron that gripped me.

I believed, with the superstitiousness of those who wait, that if I went out for a while, I would find a reply upon my return. Impatiently awaited replies always arrive when you're not home.

I went out on the pretext of going to get lunch.

Instead of lunching at Café Foy, on the corner of the boulevard, as I usually did, I chose to lunch at the Palais-Royal, and to pass by the rue d'Antin. Every time I espied a woman in the distance, I thought it was Nanine bringing me a reply. I walked across the rue d'Antin without seeing even a policeman. I arrived at the Palais-Royal; I entered Chez Véry. The waiter brought me something to eat, or rather served me whatever he chose, as I did not eat.

Despite myself, my eyes were always fixed on the clock.

I returned home convinced that I would find a letter from Marguerite.

The porter had received nothing. I held out hope for my servant. He hadn't seen anyone since my departure.

If Marguerite was going to respond at all, she would have responded long before now.

It was then when I began to regret the wording of my letter; I should have kept totally silent, that doubtless would have made her uneasy, since, not having seen me come to the rendezvous the night before, she would have asked the reasons for my absence, and only I could have supplied them. In this way she would have had no choice but to try to exculpate herself, and that was what I wanted her to do. I already realized that I would have accepted whatever reasons she might have given me, and that it would have been better for me to accept everything than never to see her again.

I convinced myself that she would come herself to see me, but the hours passed and she did not come. Marguerite was definitely not like other women, because there are few who, receiving a letter like the one I had written, would not respond in some way.

At five o'clock I ran to the Champs-Élysées.

"If I run into her," I thought to myself, "I will affect an indifferent air, and she will be convinced that I've already stopped thinking about her."

At the corner of the rue Royale, I saw her pass by in her carriage; the encounter was so abrupt that I turned pale. I do not know if she observed my emotion; as for me, I was so upset that I saw nothing but her carriage.

I did not continue my walk along the Champs-Élysées. I looked at the theater posters instead, because I still had one more chance to see her.

There was a premiere at the Palais-Royal. Marguerite was sure to be there.

I was at the theater at seven o'clock.

All the boxes filled, but Marguerite did not appear.

I then left the Palais-Royal and went to all the theaters she visited most often—to the Vaudeville, the Variétés, the Opéra-Comique.

She was nowhere.

Either my letter had hurt her too much for her to want to go to the theater, or she was afraid she might bump into me and wanted to avoid a confrontation.

This is what my vanity was whispering to me on the boulevard when I ran into my friend Gaston, who asked me where I was coming from.

"From the Palais-Royal."

"And I from the opera," he said. "Actually I thought I might see you there."

"Why?"

"Because Marguerite was there."

"Ah! She was there?"

"Yes."

"Alone?"

"No, with one of her girlfriends."

"That's all?"

"The Comte de G . . . came for an instant into her box, but she left with the duke. Every moment I thought I would see you. There was a stall beside me that remained empty all evening, and I was convinced it had been reserved for you."

"But why would I go where Marguerite goes?"

"Because you are her lover, by God!"

"And who told you that?"

"Prudence, whom I saw yesterday. I congratulate you, my friend; she is a lovely mistress whom not everyone can have. Hold on to her, my friend; she will do you credit.

Gaston's offhand remark showed me how ridiculous my weaknesses were.

If I had seen him the night before and he had spoken to me in this way, I certainly would not have written the ridiculous letter that morning.

I was on the point of going to Prudence and sending her to tell Marguerite that I wanted to speak to her, but I was afraid that, to get even, she would respond only that she would not receive me. And I went home, after passing through the rue d'Antin.

I asked my porter again if there was a letter for me.

Nothing!

"She must have wanted to see if I would make some new move, or if I would retract my letter today," I told myself as I went to bed, "but given that I didn't write to her, she will write to me tomorrow."

That night above all I rued what I had done. I was home alone, unable to sleep, devoured by anxiety and jealousy, when if I had let things take their natural course, I would have been beside Marguerite, hearing the tender words spoken to me that I had heard only on two occasions, and which burned in my ears in my solitude.

The worst thing about my situation was that my reasoning had led me wrong, when the evidence told me that Marguerite loved me. First, there was the project she had come up with of spending a summer with me alone in the country; then there was the certainty that nothing compelled her to be my mistress, given that my fortune was insufficient to her needs and even to her whims. She therefore had no incentive but the hope of finding in me a sincere affection that could offer her a respite from the mercenary loves she lived among; but on the second day I had destroyed that hope, and repaid two nights of love with insolent irony. What I was doing was therefore more than ridiculous; it was vulgar. I had not even paid this woman, yet I was attacking her lifestyle; and didn't my retreat, on the second day, give me the air of a parasitical lover who is hoping to skip out on the bill for his dinner? What had I been thinking! It had been thirty-six hours since I'd met Marguerite; twenty-four hours since I'd been her lover, and I was playing the victim. Instead of being grateful for what she had shared with me, I wanted everything for myself alone, and wanted to force her to sever with one stroke all the connections of her past that provided the income of her future. What had I to reproach her for? Nothing. She had written to me that she was unwell, when she could have told me crudely, with that hideous frankness that certain women employ, that she was expecting a lover, and instead of choosing to believe her letter, instead of going for a long walk in all the streets of Paris except for the rue d'Antin, instead of spending my evening with my friends and presenting myself the next day at the appointed hour, I had played Othello; I had spied on her, and then sought to punish her by seeing her no more. Probably, on the contrary, she was delighted by this separation; she must have found me exceedingly stupid, and her silence came not from rancor, but from disdain.

At that point I should have given Marguerite a gift that would have left no doubt of my generosity, that would have permitted me, in treating her like a kept woman, to consider myself quit of her, but I was afraid I would give offense by the least appearance of treating the love she had for me, not to mention the love I had for her, as if it were transactional. This love was so pure that it could not be shared; the happiness we'd had, brief as it was, could not be repaid through a gift, however beautiful it might be.

That is what I repeated to myself all night, and what I was ready at any moment to go tell Marguerite. When day broke I was still not asleep. I had a fever; it was impossible for me to think of anything but Marguerite.

As you understand, I had to take decisive action, and be done with either the woman or my scruples, if she would even consent to see me again.

But you know, one always puts off decisive action. Also, not being able to stay home, and not daring to present myself at Marguerite's, I tried to think of a means of getting close to her, a means that my pride would attribute to accident, should it work.

It was nine o'clock; I ran to see Prudence, who asked me to what she owed this matutinal visit.

I did not dare to tell her frankly what had brought me there. I replied that I had got up early to book a seat on the stage-coach to C . . . , where my father lived.

"You are very lucky," she told me, "to be able to get out of the city in this beautiful weather."

I looked at Prudence, asking myself if she was making fun of me.

But her face was serious.

"Will you go say good-bye to Marguerite?" she said, still serious.

"No."

"Wise decision."

"Really?"

"Of course. Since you have broken up with her, why see her again?"

"Then you know about our breakup?"

"She showed me your letter."

"And what did she tell you?"

"She said, 'My dear Prudence, your protégé is not polite. One thinks of writing such letters but one does not write them.'"

"And in what tone did she tell you that?"

"She was laughing, and she added, 'He had supper at my place twice, and he doesn't even pay a thank-you visit.'"

That is the effect that my letter and my jealousy had produced. I was cruelly humiliated in the vanity of my love.

"And what did she do last night?"

"She went to the opera."

"I know. And then?"

"She had dinner at home."

"Alone?"

"With the Comte de G . . . , I think."

So our rupture had not changed any of Marguerite's habits.

It is because of such circumstances that certain people will say to you, "You must never think about that woman; she didn't love you."

"Well then, I'm glad to see that Marguerite is not grieving over me," I continued with a forced smile.

"And she's absolutely right. You've done what you had to do; you were more reasonable than she was, because that girl loved you, she spoke of nothing but you, and would have been capable of some great folly."

"Why didn't she reply, if she loves me?"

"Because she understood that she had been wrong to love you. Women will sometimes forgive someone who deceives them, but never someone who wounds their pride, and you always wound a woman's pride when, two days after you have become her lover, you break with her, whatever reasons you may give for this rupture. I know Marguerite, and she would rather die than respond."

"Then what should I do?"

"Nothing. She will forget you, you will forget her, and neither of you will have anything with which to reproach the other."

"But what if I wrote her to ask her to forgive me?"

"Don't do it; she will forgive you."

I almost flung myself around her neck.

A quarter hour later I was home, writing to Marguerite:

"Someone who repents for a letter he wrote yesterday, who will leave town tomorrow if you do not forgive him, would like to know at what hour he may come to beg forgiveness at your feet.

"When will you be alone? As you know, confessions must be made without outside observers."

I folded this madrigal in prose, and sent it via Joseph, who gave the letter to Marguerite herself, who told him she would reply later.

I did not leave the house for one moment except to dine, and at eleven o'clock at night I still had no response.

I resolved therefore not to suffer any longer and to leave town the next day.

As a consequence of this resolution, convinced I would not be able to sleep if I went to bed, I began packing my trunks.

CHAPTER XV

For about an hour Joseph and I had been preparing for my departure, when someone rang violently at my door.

"Should I get it?" Joseph asked me.

"Get it," I told him, asking myself who could possibly come at such an hour to see me, and not daring to believe it was Marguerite.

"Sir," Joseph told me upon returning, "two ladies are here."

"It's us, Armand," cried a voice that I recognized as Prudence's.

I came out of my bedroom.

Prudence, standing, was looking at the various curios in my living room; Marguerite was sitting on the sofa looking pensive.

When I entered, I went up to her, got on my knees, took her two hands in mine, and, terribly moved, said to her, "Forgive me."

She kissed my forehead and said, "That makes three times already that I have forgiven you."

"I was going to leave tomorrow."

"How can my visit change your resolve? I have not come to keep you from quitting Paris. I have come because I did not have time to reply to you today, and did not want you to leave thinking that I was angry with you. And Prudence didn't want me to come; she said I might disturb you."

"You, disturb me? You, Marguerite? How?"

"Why, of course, you might have had a woman here," said Prudence, "and it would not have been pleasant for her to see two ladies walk in."

During this remark of Prudence's, Marguerite watched me closely.

"My dear Prudence," I replied, "you do not know what you are saying."

"How nice your apartment is," Prudence replied. "May we see the bedroom?"

"Yes."

Prudence entered my bedroom, less to inspect it than to make up for the foolish thing she'd just said, and to leave us alone, Marguerite and me.

"Why did you bring Prudence?" I asked.

"Because she was with me at the theater, and because when I left this place, I wanted to have someone to accompany me."

"Wouldn't I have been here?"

"Yes, but apart from the fact that I did not want to disturb you, I was sure that if you came to my door, you would insist on coming up to see me, and as I would not be able to grant you that, I did not want you to leave town with the right to reproach me for a rejection."

"And why would you have been unable to invite me up?"

"Because I am being watched, and the least suspicion could do me great harm."

"Is that the only reason?"

"If there were another, I would tell you; we are no longer to keep secrets from each other."

"Marguerite, I do not want to beat around the bush. Do you love me a little?"

"Very much."

"Then why did you deceive me?"

"My friend, if I were Mme the Duchess So-and-So, or if I had two hundred thousand francs of income, if I were your mistress and I had another lover besides you, you would have the right to ask me why I deceived you. But I am Mlle Marguerite Gautier, I am forty thousand francs in debt, I have not a penny to my name, and I spend a hundred thousand francs a year, which makes your question idle and my response futile."

"Fair enough," I said, letting my head fall into Marguerite's lap, "but I—I am crazy in love with you."

"Well, my friend, you'll have to love me a little less or understand me a little better. Your letter caused me great pain. If I had been free, first of all, I would not have entertained the count the day before yesterday, or, if I had let him in, I would have come to beg your pardon, and in future would not have received any lover but you. I thought for a moment I could permit myself that happiness for six months. You did not want it; you insisted on knowing the means. My God! The means were easy enough to guess. It was a greater sacrifice than you might think I would make. I could have told you, 'I need twenty thousand francs.' You were in love with me; you would have come up with it, at the risk of holding it against me later. I would have preferred to owe you nothing, but you did not understand this scruple . . . for it *is* a scruple. Women like me, if we still have a little heart, we accord words and things a meaning and consequence unknown to other women. I repeat, then, that, on the part of Marguerite Gautier, the means she found to pay off her debts without asking you for the money necessary for it was a delicate operation from which you would have profited without needing to say a thing. If you had only met with me today, you would be only too happy with what I promised you, and you would not have asked me what I had done the day before yesterday. Sometimes we are forced to purchase a satisfaction required by our soul at the expense of our body; and we suffer all the more when, afterward, that satisfaction eludes us."

I listened, and looked at Marguerite with admiration. When I thought that this magnificent creature, whose feet I longed to kiss, had made a place for me in her thoughts, that she had given me a role in her life, and that I had not been content with what she gave me, I asked myself if men's desire has any limit, when, satisfied as promptly as mine had been, it still seeks more.

"It's true," she resumed. "Women who depend on luck as I do have immoderate desires and inconceivable passions. We leap into one thing, then another. Some men ruin themselves over us without obtaining anything in return; others can get us for a bouquet. Our hearts have whims; that is our lone distrac-

tion and our sole excuse. I gave myself to you more quickly
than to any other man, I swear it to you. Why? Because when
you saw me spit blood you took my hand, because you cried,
because you are the only human creature who has ever pitied
me. I will tell you a silly thing; but once I had a little dog who
looked at me sadly whenever I coughed; that is the only creature I ever loved.

"When he died, I cried more than I did at my mother's death.
It is true that she had beaten me for twelve years of her life.
And I loved you instantly as much as I loved my dog. If men
knew what they could win with one tear, they would love more
successfully, and we would be less destructive.

"Your letter gave you away; it showed me that you lacked the
wisdom of the heart. It did more to damage the love I had for
you than anything else you might have done. It was provoked
by jealousy, that is true, but by ironic and insolent jealousy. I
was already sad when I got that letter; I had counted on seeing
you at noon, on having lunch with you, so I could blot out by
the sight of you a memory that tormented me, which before I
met you would have been as nothing.

"Because," Marguerite continued, "you were the only person who ever made me feel instantly that I could think and
speak freely. Everyone who clusters around girls like me ana-
lyzes our every word, trying to draw consequence for themselves from our most insignificant actions. Naturally, we don't
have friends. We have selfish lovers who spend their fortunes
not on us, as they say, but on their own vanity.

"With men like that, we have to be lighthearted when they
are joyful, in fine fettle when they want to have supper, in a
skeptical mood when they are. We're forbidden to have any
feelings of our own, on pain of being jeered at and having our
credit ruined.

"We no longer belong to ourselves. We are not beings, but
things. We are first in men's pride, last in their esteem. We have
female friends, but they are friends like Prudence, former kept
women who retain a taste for extravagance that their age will
no longer afford them. So they become our friends, or, really,
our dining companions. Their friendship goes as far as utility,

but never reaches the point of disinterestedness. They will never give you any but mercenary advice. It matters little to them if we have ten lovers or more, so long as they get a few dresses or a bracelet out of it, and can go out in our carriages from time to time, and come to the theater and sit in our boxes. They get our bouquets from the night before, and they borrow our cashmere shawls. They never render us any service, however small, without getting twice what it's worth. You saw it yourself, the night when Prudence brought me the six thousand francs I'd begged her to go ask the duke to give me. She borrowed five hundred francs from me that she'll never give back, or that she'll make up in hats that will never leave their boxes.

"So we cannot have—or rather, I cannot have—any happiness but one, which is, unhappy as I sometimes am, in poor health as I always am, to find a man who is of superior enough character that he will not demand a full account of my life, and will love me more for myself than for my body. I had found that man in the duke, but the duke is old, and old age can neither protect nor console. I had thought I could accept the life that he wished for me; but what do you want? I was perishing of boredom, and as long as you're going to be consumed, you might as well hurl yourself into a fire, rather than slowly suffocate from coal smoke.

"So, I met you, you—young, ardent, happy—and tried to make you into the man I had longed for in the middle of my noisy solitude. What I loved in you was not the man you were, but the man you might yet become. You refuse to accept this role, you reject it as unworthy of you, you are a vulgar lover. Do as the others do—pay me and let's speak of this no more."

Marguerite, exhausted by this long confession, threw herself on the sofa, and to stifle a weak flight of coughing, brought her handkerchief to her lips and from there to her eyes.

"Forgive me; forgive me," I murmured. "I had understood all this, but I wanted to hear you say it, my adored Marguerite. Let us forget the rest and remember only one thing: that we belong to each other, that we are young, and that we love each other.

"Marguerite, do with me what you will; I am your slave,

your dog. But in the name of Heaven, tear up the letter I wrote you, and do not let me go away tomorrow; I would die."

Marguerite withdrew the letter from the bodice of her gown and gave it to me, saying to me with a smile of ineffable sweetness, "Here, I've brought it back to you."

I tore up the letter and kissed with tears the hand that had given it back to me.

At this moment Prudence reappeared.

"Well, Prudence, do you know what he asks of me?" said Marguerite.

"He asks you to forgive him."

"Just so."

"And you pardon him?"

"I should, but he wants one thing more."

"What, then?"

"He wants to come have supper with us."

"And do you consent?"

"What do you think?"

"I think the two of you are babies, with not a brain between you. But I also think that I'm very hungry and that the earlier you consent, the earlier we'll have supper."

"Let's go," said Marguerite. "The three of us can fit in my carriage. Take this," she added, turning toward me. "Nanine will have gone to bed. You will open the door; take my key, and try not to lose it again."

I smothered Marguerite with kisses.

Joseph came in behind her.

"Sir," he told me with the air of a man delighted with himself, "the trunks are packed."

"Entirely?"

"Yes, sir."

"Unpack them, then; I'm not going away."

CHAPTER XVI

I could have, said Armand, told you of the beginning of this liaison in a few sentences, but I wanted you to understand by what events and what steps we came to the understanding that I had to agree to everything Marguerite wished, and that she could not live with anyone but me.

It was the day after the evening she came to see me that I sent her *Manon Lescaut*.

From that moment on, as I could not change my mistress's ways, I changed mine. I wanted above all not to give myself the time to analyze the role I had just accepted, because, despite myself, I would have felt it as a great sorrow. Also, my life, usually so quiet, reshaped itself immediately into a thing of noisiness and disorder. Don't think that, disinterested as it may be, the love a kept woman has for you comes for free. Nothing is more expensive than satisfying the thousand whims for flowers, theater boxes, suppers, and country picnics that one can never refuse one's mistress.

As I told you, I did not have a large fortune. My father was and is the tax collector at C . . . . The job has a great reputation for security, which permitted him to raise the commission that was required for him to take up the position. This job brings him forty thousand francs a year, and in the ten years since he's had it, he has paid back his commission, and busied himself with putting aside my sister's dowry. My father is the most honorable man you could ever meet. My mother, when she died, left behind six thousand francs in income, which he divided between my sister and me on the day he obtained the job he had sought, and once I was twenty-one, he added an annual allowance of five thousand francs to this small income, assuring me that with eight thousand francs a year I could be very happy in Paris, if I took a job either at the bar or in medicine. So I came to Paris, I studied law, I became a lawyer, and like many young men, I tucked my diploma in my pocket and let myself enjoy the carefree life of Paris for a time. My expenses were quite modest, but still I would run through my annual income in eight months, and spend the four summer months with my father, which allowed me to live as if I had an income of twelve thousand francs, and gave me the reputation of being a good son. Besides, I did not have a penny of debt.

That was the state of my affairs when I met Marguerite.

You will understand that, in spite of myself, my manner of living became more extravagant. Marguerite had a changeable nature, and she was one of those women who never regard the thousand distractions that comprise their life as a serious expense. The result was that, wanting to spend as much time with me as possible, she would write me in the morning that she would dine with me that evening not at her house but at some restaurant, either in Paris or in the countryside. I would go pick her up, we would dine together, we would go to the theater, we often had supper together, and on any given night I would spend four or five louis, which is to say two thousand or three thousand francs per month, which shortened my year to three and half months, and made it necessary for me either to go into debt, or to leave Marguerite.

I could accept everything except that last eventuality.

Forgive me for giving you so many details, but you will see that they were the cause of the events that followed. What I am telling you is a true and simple story, to which I have attached all the naïveté of the details and the simplicity of the developments.

I understood that, since nothing in the world could induce me to forget my mistress, I would have to find a way to afford the expense she put me to. Then again, this love consumed me to the point that every moment I spent away from Marguerite felt like years, and I felt the need to burn through those mo-

ments in a passion and to live them so quickly that I would not
be altogether conscious of what I was doing.

I began by borrowing five or six thousand francs off my
small capital, and then I started gambling, because once they'd
closed down the gaming houses, gambling popped up everywhere. In the past, when you entered Frascati you had the
chance of striking it rich—you played with real money, and if
you lost you had the consolation of telling yourself you could
have won—whereas now, except in circles where a certain scru-
pulousness prevails regarding payment, the moment one wins
a substantial sum one is almost sure that one will never get it.
You will easily understand why.

Gambling can be practiced only by young men who have
enormous financial needs but who lack the necessary fortune to
support the life they lead. This is why they gamble, and here is
the natural result: Either they win, in which case the losers pay
for their horses and mistresses, which is extremely awkward;
or debts are contracted, and dealings that began across a green
cloth end in quarrels that tear apart both honor and life to
some degree, and if you're an honest man, you soon find yourself ruined by very honest young people who have no flaw except for the lack of two hundred thousand francs a year.

I don't need to tell you about those men who cheat, and of
whom one day you hear that they were forced to leave town
and were belatedly brought to justice.

I threw myself, therefore, into the fast life, noisy and volca-
nic, which had formerly frightened me when I'd thought about
it, but which had become for me the inevitable backdrop of my
love for Marguerite. What would you have expected me to do?

The nights I didn't spend on the rue d'Antin I spent alone at
home. I couldn't sleep; jealousy kept me awake, burning my
mind and blood. As long as I gambled, I was distracted for the
moment from the fever that had invaded my heart, which
transformed itself into a mania whose interest consumed me,
despite myself, until the hour struck when I was to go and see
my mistress. This is how I could recognize the power of my
love—that, whether I was winning or losing, I always left the

table pitying those I left behind, who would not find the happiness I did when they left it.

For most people gambling was a necessity. For me it was a cure.

If I could be cured of Marguerite, I would be cured of gambling.

In the midst of all that, I was fairly clearheaded; I never lost more than I could pay, and I won only what I could have spared.

Also luck favored me. Without getting into debt, I was able to spend three times more money than before I started gambling. It was not easy to resist a life that allowed me to satisfy Marguerite's thousand whims without inconvenience to myself. As for her, she loved me as much as before, and still more.

As I told you, I began at first by visiting her from midnight until six in the morning; then I was admitted occasionally into her theater boxes; then she sometimes would come dine with me. One morning I didn't leave until eight o'clock, and a day came when I didn't leave until noon.

As I awaited her moral metamorphosis, a physical transformation had worked itself on Marguerite. I had undertaken her cure, and the poor girl, guessing my aim, obeyed me to prove her gratitude. Without imposing extreme changes and without effort, I had very nearly managed to wean her from her old habits. My doctor, whom I had made her consult, had told me that only rest and calm could restore her health, so I began to supplant her suppers and insomniac nights with a healthful regimen and regular sleep. Despite herself, Marguerite started getting used to this new existence, whose salutary effects she could feel. Soon she began spending some nights at home, or if the weather was good, she would wrap herself in a shawl, cover herself with a veil, and we would go on walks, like two children, strolling the dark lanes along the Champs-Élysées in the night. She would return home tired, have a light supper, then go to bed after playing a little music, or reading—something she'd never done before. The coughing, which broke my heart every time I heard it, had almost completely disappeared. At the end of six weeks, the count was no longer in the picture; he had been definitively sacrificed. Only the duke still forced me to conceal my liaison with Marguerite, and even he had been sent away during my visits, on the pretext that madam was sleeping, and had forbidden that she be woken.

As a result of the habit, the need, even, that Marguerite had developed for my company, I was able to give up gambling at just the moment when a shrewd gambler would have quit. All being counted, I found myself, with my gains, in command of ten thousand francs, a sum that appeared to me inexhaustible.

The time of year when I was accustomed to rejoin my father and my sister had arrived, but I did not leave town. I began to receive frequent letters from one or the other of them, letters imploring me to come see them. To each letter I responded as decently as I could, repeating always that I was doing well and did not need money, two things I thought would reassure my father a little about the postponement of my annual visit.

While all this was taking place, one morning Marguerite, who had been awoken by dazzling sunshine, jumped out of bed and asked me if I would take her into the country for the day.

We sent for Prudence, and the three of us went together, after Marguerite told Nanine to inform the duke that she had decided to make the most of the day, and had gone to the countryside with Mme Duvernoy.

In addition to the fact that the presence of Mme Duvernoy was necessary to satisfy the old duke, Prudence was one of those women who are expressly made for such outings. With her unfailing high spirits and her bottomless appetite, she did not permit a moment of boredom to those who accompanied her, and she expertly saw to the eggs, the cherries, the milk, the fried rabbit, and everything else that is required for a traditional picnic on the outskirts of Paris.

There was nothing left for us to do but to decide where to go.

It was Prudence again who came to the rescue.

"Do you want to go to the true countryside?" she asked.

"Yes."

"Then let's go to Bougival, to the Point du Jour, the Widow Arnould's auberge. Armand, go rent a barouche."

An hour and a half later we had arrived at the Widow Arnould's.

You may know this auberge, a hotel where you can rent by the week, or visit on a day trip. From the garden, which rises as high as the second story of a building, you can take in a spectacular view. To the left there's the aqueduct of Marly on the horizon; to the right the view extends to an infinity of hills. The river, which barely flows in this spot, unspools like a wide, pale taffeta ribbon between the plains of Gabillon and the island of Croissy, eternally lulled by the whispering of tall poplars and the murmur of weeping willows.

At the bottom, in a broad patch of sunlight, rise little white houses with red roofs, and factories that lose their hard and commercial character from a distance, admirably completing the landscape.

And beyond that, Paris, in a haze.

As Prudence had told us, it was the true countryside, and I must say, it was a true luncheon.

It is not out of gratitude for the happiness I owed to her that I say this, but Bougival, despite its horrible name, is one of the prettiest parts of the country you could imagine. I've traveled a great deal, and I've seen many grander sights, but none more charming than this little village, nestled cheerfully at the foot of the hill that protects it.

Mme Arnould offered us a boat ride, which Marguerite and Prudence accepted with joy.

The countryside has always been associated with love, and rightly so: Nothing is a better frame for the woman one loves than a blue sky and the scents, flowers, breezes, and shining solitude of the fields or the woods. However much a man loves a woman, however much he trusts her, however much confidence in the future her past permits him, a man is always jealous, to a greater or lesser degree. If you have ever been in love, seriously in love, you must have felt that need to isolate from the world that being in whom you would like to be entirely enveloped. However indifferent she may be to her surroundings, the woman one loves seems to lose her fragrance and her plenitude when she comes into contact with other men and

things. I felt this much more than any other man. I was as much
in love as an ordinary man can be, but my lover was no ordinary lover; when it came to Marguerite Gautier—in Paris, that
is—at every step I was likely to bump into a man who had been
this woman's lover, or who might be on the following day. In
the countryside, however, among people we had never seen and
who paid no attention to us, in the bosom of nature decked out
in springtime (that annual reprieve), and removed from the
sounds of the city, I could have my lover all to myself, and love
without shame and without fear.

The courtesan in her had begun to fade away, little by little,
and I had beside me a young, beautiful woman whom I loved,
by whom I was loved, and who was named Marguerite. The
past held no more shadows; the future no more clouds. The sun
shone on my mistress as it would have shone on the chastest
fiancée. The two of us strolled in those charming places that
seem made for reciting the verses of Lamartine, or for singing
the melodies of Scudo. Marguerite wore a white dress, she
leaned on my arm, she repeated to me under the starry sky the
words she had spoken to me the night before, and the world
rumbled on at a distance without marring with its shadows the
smiling tableau of our youth and our love.

That is the dream that the day's hot sun carried to me
through the leaves of the trees, as I lay on the grass on the island where we had alighted, free of all the human connections
that usually oppressed my mind. I let my thoughts run free and
gather all the hopes they could find.

Add to this that, from the place where I was, I could see on
the riverbank a charming little two-story house with a semicir-
cular fence around it; through the fence, in front of the house,
a green lawn, smooth as velvet; and behind the building a little
woods full of mysterious nooks, whose mosses would erase
every morning the steps made there the night before.

Flowering vines hid the front stoop of this house, and embraced the facade, climbing as high as the second story.

I looked at this house so long that I ended by persuading
myself it was mine, so neatly did it complete the dream I'd been
dreaming. I pictured Marguerite and me spending the day in

the woods that covered the hillside, sitting on the lawn at night, and I asked myself if any earthly creatures were ever as lucky as we were.

"What a pretty house!" said Marguerite, who had followed the direction of my gaze and perhaps of my thoughts.

"Where?" said Prudence.

"Over there." And Marguerite pointed to the house in question.

"Ah! Ravishing," replied Prudence. "You like it?"

"Very much."

"Well then! Tell the duke to rent it for you. He will, I'm sure. I'll take care of it if you like."

Marguerite looked at me, as if to ask what I thought of this idea.

My dream had flown away with those last words of Prudence's, and had thrust me so rudely into reality that I was still stunned by the transition.

"It's an excellent idea," I stammered, without knowing what I was saying.

"Well then, I'll take care of it," Marguerite said, taking my hand and interpreting my words as it suited her. "Let's go at once to see if it's for rent."

The house was vacant and could be rented for two thousand francs.

"Would you be happy here?" she asked me.

"Is it certain that I'd be allowed to come here?"

"And why would I come bury myself here, if not for you?"

"Marguerite, let me rent this house myself."

"Are you crazy? Not only is it unnecessary; it would be dangerous—you know very well that I have the right to accept such a gift from only one man. Let it be taken care of, you big baby, and don't say a thing."

"And whenever I have a couple of free days, I'll come spend them with you," said Prudence.

We left the house and got back on the road to Paris while discussing this new decision. I held Marguerite in my arms so happily that when I got out of the carriage I began to consider my mistress's scheme with a less critical air.

CHAPTER XVII

The next day Marguerite sent me away early, saying the duke was going to come first thing in the morning, and promising that she would write as soon as he left to give me our evening arrangements.

That afternoon I received this message:

"I am going to Bougival with the duke; be at Prudence's tonight at eight o'clock."

At the appointed hour Marguerite was back home, and came to join me at Mme Duvernoy's.

"Everything is arranged," she said as she walked in.

"The house has been rented?" Prudence asked.

"Yes; he consented at once."

I did not know the duke, but I was ashamed to deceive him as I was doing.

"But that's not all!" Marguerite continued.

"What more, then?"

"I was worried about where Armand would stay."

"In the same house?" asked Prudence, laughing.

"No, at the Point du Jour, where we had lunch, the duke and I. While he took in the view, I asked Mme Arnould—that is her name, isn't it? I asked her if she had a room that would be suitable. She has just one, with a living room, foyer, and bedroom. It's everything one could ask for, I think. Sixty francs per month. Furnished so as to drive a hypochondriac to distraction. I reserved it. Did I do the right thing?"

I flung my arms around Marguerite's neck.

"It will be charming," she continued. "You have a key to the little door, and I've promised the duke a key to the gate, which

he will not take, because he will come only during the day . . .
when he comes. I believe, between you and me, that he is enchanted by this whim, which will keep me at a distance from
Paris for a while, and calm his family a bit. However, he asked
me how I, who love Paris so much, could have resolved to bury
myself in the countryside; I told him I haven't been feeling well,
and that I needed rest. He seemed only to half-believe me. That
poor old man is always in the dark. We will have to take many
precautions, my dear Armand. He will have me watched over
there, and he won't just be renting me a house; he also must pay
my debts, and unfortunately I have a few. Is all this acceptable
to you?"

"Yes," I said, as I tried to quiet all the scruples that this way
of life awoke in me from time to time.

"We took a tour of the house from top to bottom; we'll be in
bliss there. The duke has seen to everything. Ah! My darling,"
the crazy girl added as she kissed me, "you are a fortunate
man—a millionaire makes your bed for you."

"And when will you move out there?" asked Prudence.

"As soon as possible."

"Will you take your carriage and your horses with you?"

"I will take my whole household with me. You will look after my apartment during my absence."

Eight days later Marguerite had moved into the country
house, and I was installed in the Point du Jour.

Then began an existence I would be hard-pressed to describe
to you.

At the outset of her stay in Bougival, Marguerite could not
completely break her old ways, and the house was always in
festival mode. All her friends came to see her; for a month there
was not a day when Marguerite did not have eight or ten people to dinner. Prudence, for her part, brought the people she
knew, and they received all the hospitality of the house, as if
the house belonged to her.

The duke's money paid for it all, as you may imagine, yet all
the same, on occasion, Prudence would ask me for a thousand
francs, purportedly in Marguerite's name. As you know, I had
made some profit from gambling; so I charged myself to give

Prudence what Marguerite had her ask of me, and, for fear that she might need more than I possessed, I borrowed in Paris an amount equal to the sum I had borrowed in the past, and which I had scrupulously repaid.

I found myself newly richer by ten thousand francs, not counting my allowance.

However, the pleasure Marguerite took in receiving her girl-friends dimmed a bit when she considered the expenses this pleasure entailed, and above all considered the necessity to which she was sometimes put of asking me for money. The duke, who had rented this house so Marguerite could rest, stopped coming, always fearing he would be met there by an exuberant and populous crowd by which he did not want to be seen. This arose from the instance when, coming over one day for an intimate dinner with Marguerite, he found himself in the middle of a lunch for fifteen people that had not yet ended at the hour when he had intended to sit down to dinner. When he entered the dining room all unsuspecting, a wave of laughter welcomed his entry, and he beat a hasty retreat, in the face of the impertinent gaiety of the women who were there.

Marguerite had gotten up from the table, gone to find the duke in the next room, and tried, insofar as it was possible, to make him forget this incident, but the old man, his pride wounded, had resented it. He told the poor girl somewhat harshly that he was tired of paying for the excesses of a woman who did not treat him respectfully in her home, and he left quite angry.

From that day on, nothing had been heard from him. Marguerite could have sent away her friends and changed her ways, but the duke did not get in touch. Through this development I won more complete ownership of my mistress, and my dream at last felt as if it had come true. Marguerite could no longer live without me. Without worrying about what might come of it, she made our relationship public, and I no longer had to leave her house. The servants called me sir, and regarded me as their official master.

Prudence had lectured Marguerite on the subject of this new lifestyle, but the latter had responded that she loved me, that she could not live without me, and that, whatever might happen, she would not renounce the happiness of having me continually by her side, adding that anyone who wasn't happy with that was free to go away and not come back.

I overheard this conversation one day when Prudence had told Marguerite that she had something very important to say to her, and I listened at the door of the room where they had shut themselves up.

A little time after, Prudence came back.

I was at the back of the garden when she came in; she did not see me. I wondered, from the way in which Marguerite came up to her, whether a conversation similar to the one I had already overheard might again take place, and I wanted to hear this one as well.

The two women shut themselves up in a dressing room, and I listened in.

"Well?" said Marguerite.

"Well? I saw the duke."

"What did he say to you?"

"That he would happily forgive you the first incident, but that he had learned that you are living publicly with M. Armand Duval, and that he will not forgive you this. He told me, 'If Marguerite leaves this young man, I will give her everything she wants, as I did in the past. If not, she will have to give up asking me for anything at all.'"

"How did you respond?"

"I told him that I would inform you of his decision, and promised him to make you see reason. Reflect, my dear child, on the status that you will lose and which Armand will never be able to give you. He loves you with all his soul, but he does not have a fortune large enough to meet all your needs, and one day he will be forced to leave you, at which point it will be too late and the duke will no longer want to do anything for you. Would you like me to speak to Armand?"

Marguerite seemed to reflect, for she did not answer. My heart beat violently as I awaited her response.

"No," she said. "I will not leave Armand, and I will not hide myself away to live with him. Maybe it is folly, but I love him!

What do you want? Also, he has grown used to being able to love me without any obstacle; he would suffer too greatly if he were forced to leave me, if only for an hour a day. Anyway, I don't have long enough to live to make myself unhappy, and to humor the will of an old man the very sight of whom makes me grow older. Let him keep his money; I'll make do without it."

"But how?"

"I don't know."

Without a doubt, Prudence was about to make some retort, but I entered abruptly and ran to throw myself at Marguerite's feet, covering her hands with tears that overflowed from my joy at being loved so much.

"You are my life, Marguerite; you don't need that man anymore, now that I'm here. How could I ever leave you, and how could I ever repay the happiness you give me? No more limits, my Marguerite; we are in love! What does the rest matter to us?"

"Oh! Yes, I love you, my Armand!" she murmured, lacing her arms around my neck. "And I love you as I never believed I would be able to love. We are happy, we will live serenely together, and I will say good-bye forever to the life that now makes me blush. You won't ever reproach me for my past, will you?"

Tears muffled my voice. I could not respond except by clasping Marguerite to my heart.

"Let's go," she said, and turning back to Prudence, she said in a voice filled with emotion, "You are to report this scene to the duke, and add that we don't need him."

From that day on the duke was no longer in the picture. Marguerite was no longer the girl I had known. She shunned anything that might have recalled the milieu in which I had met her. Never has a woman, never has a sister shown the love and attentiveness to a husband or brother that she showed me. Her sickly constitution was impressionable and accessible to all feelings. She broke with her old girlfriends as she had with her old habits, and with her old ways of talking and spending. Anyone who saw us leave the house for an excursion on the charming little boat I'd bought would never have believed that this woman in a white dress, wearing a straw picture hat and a simple silk pelisse draped over her arm to protect herself from the water's cool dampness could be that same Marguerite Gautier whose extravagance and scandals had prompted gossip only four months before.

Alas! We were in such a hurry to be happy, it was as if we guessed that we would not be happy for long.

For two months we didn't even go to Paris. Nobody came to see us except for Prudence, and that Julie Duprat I told you about, to whom Marguerite would later give the touching narrative I relay here.

I passed entire days at the feet of my mistress. We opened the windows that looked out on the garden, and watched the summer descend joyfully upon the flowers and burst them into bloom, and under the shade of the trees, side by side, we breathed in that genuine life that neither Marguerite nor I had known until that time.

This woman fell into childlike raptures at the tiniest things. There were days when she ran into the garden like a girl of ten to chase after a butterfly or a dragonfly. This courtesan for whom men had spent more money on bouquets than is required to comfortably maintain an entire family would sit on the lawn for an hour at a time, simply to inspect the simple marguerite daisy, whose name she bore.

It was during that time that she so often read *Manon Lescaut*. I came upon her many times making notes in the book; she always told me that when a woman is in love, she cannot help acting as Manon did.

Two or three times the duke wrote to her. She recognized his handwriting and gave me the letters without reading them.

Sometimes the language of these letters brought tears to my eyes.

He had believed that closing his purse to Marguerite would bring her back to him, but when he understood the uselessness of this device, he could not believe it. He wrote again, asking for permission to come back to her, as he had done before, whatever conditions she might impose upon his return.

I of course read these urgent, repetitive letters, and ripped them up, without telling Marguerite what they contained, and without advising her to see the old man again, despite the feelings of pity for the poor man they inspired in me. But I was afraid that she might read into any sanction of a return of the duke's former visits a base desire on my part to make him resume paying the household expenses; I feared above all that she might believe me capable of rejecting responsibility for her on any of the paths where her love for me might lead her.

As a result, the duke, receiving no response, stopped writing, and Marguerite and I continued to live together with no thought of the future.

CHAPTER XVIII

To give you the details of our new life would be difficult. It was made up of a series of childlike indulgences that were delightful to us, but would be insignificant to anyone I might tell them to. You know what it is to be in love with a woman; you know how short the days are, and with what amorous indolence one passes from one day to the next. You are not unaware of the obliviousness to all other things that accompanies the birth of a strong, confident, shared passion. Any creature who is not the woman you love seems to you an entirely pointless being. One regrets having given away any portion of one's heart to other women, and one cannot imagine the possibility of ever holding any hand but the one you now hold in yours. The brain will not tolerate work or memory—anything, in short, that could distract you from the overwhelming obsession that constantly presents itself to the mind. Every day one finds in one's mistress a new charm, a previously unsuspected sensuality.

Existence becomes nothing more than the repeated fulfillment of a continuing desire; the soul is nothing but the vestal virgin charged with maintaining the sacred fire of love.

Often, once night fell, we would go to sit in the little woods that surrounded the house. There we would listen to the cheerful harmonies of the night, while we both thought of the hour to come, when we would fall into each other's arms and lie there until the next day. Other times we remained in bed the entire day, without even letting the sun enter our bedroom. The curtains were hermetically sealed, and for a moment, the outside world ceased to exist for us. Only Nanine had the right to open our door, but only to bring us our meals, and even those we took without getting out of bed, and we interrupted them continually with laughter and giddiness. This would be followed by a sleep of a few moments, for, lost in our love, we were like two stubborn divers who surface only long enough to draw air.

Sometimes, though, I was surprised to come upon Marguerite in moments of sadness, even in tears. I would ask her the cause of her sudden sorrow, and she would answer, "Our love is not an ordinary love, my dear Armand. You love me as if I had never belonged to anybody else, and I tremble to think that, later, repenting of your love and blaming me for my past, you might throw me back into the midst of the existence you snatched me from. Please remember that, now that I've tasted a new life, it would kill me to take up the old one again. Tell me that you will never leave me."

"I swear it to you!"

At these words she looked searchingly into my eyes, as if to try to read there if my vow was sincere, then flung herself into my arms and, hiding her head against my chest, said, "It's just that you don't know how much I love you!"

One night we were leaning against the balcony outside the window, looking at the moon, which seemed to extricate itself with difficulty from its bed of clouds, and listening to the wind noisily shaking the trees. We held hands, and for a solid quarter of an hour we had not spoken, when Marguerite said, "Winter is here; would you like us to go away?"

"To go where?"

"To Italy."

"So you're bored?"

"I'm afraid of winter, but above all I'm afraid of our return to Paris."

"Why?"

"For many reasons."

She continued rapidly, without giving me the reasons for her fears, "Do you want to go? I will sell everything I own; we will go live abroad. Nothing will be left of what I used to be; nobody will know who I am. Do you want to?"

"Let's go, if that makes you happy, Marguerite; let's take a trip," I said. "But why sell all the things that you'll be glad to find upon returning? I don't have a big enough fortune to accept so great a sacrifice, but I have enough for us to travel in style for five or six months, if that would entertain you at all."

"Actually, no," she said, leaving the window and going to sit on the sofa at the dark end of the room. "What's the good of going over there to spend money? I'm costing you enough here."

"It's not generous of you to reproach me for that, Marguerite."

"I'm sorry, my friend," she said, giving me her hand. "This stormy weather is hard on my nerves; I'm not saying what I mean to say."

And, after kissing me, she fell into a long reverie.

Similar scenes took place many times, and even if I did not know what it was that caused them, this did not keep me from sensing in Marguerite a feeling of anxiety about the future. She could not doubt my love; it grew every day. Yet all the same, I often saw her unhappy, and she was never able to give me any explanation for her sadness, apart from some physical excuse.

Afraid that she might be growing tired of a life that had become too monotonous for her, I would propose that we return to Paris, but she always rejected the suggestion, and assured me that she could not be as happy anywhere as she was in the countryside.

Prudence came rarely now, but to make up for it she wrote letters, which I never asked to see, although Marguerite became deeply preoccupied every time she got one. I did not know what to think.

One day Marguerite kept to her room. I walked in. She was writing.

"Who are you writing to?" I asked.

"To Prudence; would you like me to read you what I'm writing?"

Horrified by anything that might smack of suspicion, I told Marguerite that I did not need to know what she was writing; nonetheless I was sure the letter would have acquainted me with the true cause of her sadness.

The next day the weather was glorious. Marguerite proposed that we go out on the boat and visit the island of Croissy. She seemed extremely cheerful; it was five o'clock when we got home.

"Mme Duvernoy came by," Nanine said as she saw us come in.

"And she left?" Marguerite asked.

"Yes, in madam's carriage; she said that it had been arranged."

"Very good," Marguerite said spiritedly. "May it serve us well."

Two days later a letter arrived from Prudence, and for two weeks, Marguerite seemed to be over her mysterious depressions, which she didn't stop begging my pardon for, once they no longer existed.

However, the carriage did not come back.

"Why hasn't Prudence sent back your coupé?" I asked one day.

"One of the two horses is sick, and the carriage is being fixed. We might as well have all of that dealt with while we're still here, where we don't need a carriage, rather than wait until we're back in Paris."

Prudence came to see us a few days later, and confirmed what Marguerite had told me.

The two women went for a walk alone in the garden, and when I came to join them, they changed the subject.

That night, when she went out, Prudence complained of the cold and asked Marguerite to lend her a cashmere shawl.

A month passed, during which Marguerite was more joyful and loving than she had ever been.

However, the carriage never returned; the cashmere was not sent back. All this intrigued me, in spite of myself, and as I knew in which drawer Marguerite put her letters from Prudence, I took advantage of a moment when she was at the far end of the garden, went to the drawer, and tried to open it, but in vain; it was double-locked.

Then I searched through drawers where her jewels and diamonds ordinarily could be found. These opened without resistance, but the cases had disappeared, along with their contents, of course.

A sinking feeling gripped my heart.

I determined to get the truth out of Marguerite about the meaning of these disappearances, but was sure she would not own up to it.

"My good Marguerite," I said to her later, "I've come to ask your leave to go to Paris. Nobody at my residence knows where I am, and they must have received letters from my father. No doubt he is worried; I must send him a reply."

"Go, my friend," she said, "but come back quickly."

I left.

I ran at once to see Prudence.

"All right," I said to her without any preliminaries, "tell me frankly, where are Marguerite's horses?"

"Sold."

"Her cashmere shawl?"

"Sold."

"The diamonds?"

"Pawned."

"And who did the selling and pawning?"

"I did."

"Why didn't you alert me to this?"

"Because Marguerite forbade me to."

"And why didn't you ask me for money?"

"Because she didn't want me to."

"And what was this money for?"

"To pay for things."

"So she owes a lot?"

"She still owes thirty thousand francs or thereabouts. Ah! My dear, I told you, and you didn't want to believe me; well, now, consider yourself convinced. The decorator who formerly was paid by the duke was shown the door when he presented himself there, and the duke wrote him the next day that he would do nothing further for Mlle Gautier. That man wanted money; we gave him a portion of what he was due, which is where those few thousand francs I asked you for went. Then, some charitable souls informed him that his debtor, abandoned by the duke, was living with a boy with no fortune. The other creditors got wind of the same thing; they all started asking for money and demanding their goods back. Marguerite wanted to sell everything, but there wasn't time, and anyway, I would have been against it. We simply had to pay, and in order not to ask you for money, she sold her horses and her cashmeres and pawned her jewelry. Would you like the receipts from the buyers and the receipts from the pawnshop?"

And Prudence, opening a drawer, showed me these papers.

"Ah! You see," she continued with the persistence of a woman determined to speak her piece, "I was right! Ah! You thought it was enough to be in love and to go live a pastoral, ethereal existence in the country? No, my friend; no. The material world coexists alongside the ideal life, and the purest intentions are bound to the earth by ridiculous threads, but they are threads of iron, and they are not easily broken. If Marguerite has not cheated on you twenty times, it's only because she has extraordinary character. It's not for lack of my counsel, either, because it pained me to watch the poor girl lose everything. But she didn't want to! She told me she loved you and would not deceive you for anything in the world. All that is very pretty, very poetic, but it won't pay the creditors, and today she can no longer get out of this mess, except, I repeat, with thirty thousand francs."

"That's fine; I will furnish that sum."

"You will borrow it?"

"Good God, yes."

"A fine mess you'll get yourself in that way. You'll fight with your father, deplete your resources; and it's not so easy to come up with thirty thousand francs overnight. Believe me, my dear Armand; I know women better than you do. Do not commit this folly, which you will repent one day. Be reasonable. I am not telling you to leave Marguerite, but live with her as you did at the beginning of summer. Let her find the means to extricate herself from her predicament. The duke will come back to her, step by step. The Comte de N . . . , if she will take him, he told me again yesterday, will pay off all her debts and give her four or five thousand francs per month. He has two hundred thousand francs a year. That would create a secure position for her, whereas you? You will inevitably have to leave her anyway. Don't wait to do it until you are ruined, and keep in mind that the Comte de N . . . is an imbecile, and that nothing will prevent you from being Marguerite's lover. She will cry a little at first, but she'll end by getting used to it, and she'll thank you one day for what you have done. Just pretend that Marguerite is married and you're cheating on her husband, that's all.

"I told you all of this before; only, at that time, it was still just advice. Today it's practically a necessity."

Prudence was cruelly correct.

"Here's how it is," she continued, while putting away the papers she had just shown me. "Kept women always anticipate being loved, but they never anticipate being in love. Otherwise they would put money aside, and at thirty they could afford the luxury of taking a lover for free. If I had only known then what I know now! Well, say nothing to Marguerite, but take her back to Paris. You have spent four or five months alone with her, that's a marvelous thing, now all that is required of you is to shut your eyes. After two weeks she will take the Comte de N . . . as a lover, she will make economies this winter, and next summer, you will start over. That's what you need to do, my dear!"

Prudence appeared enchanted by her sage advice, which I indignantly rejected.

Not only did my love and my dignity prevent me from acting in such a way, but I was also convinced that, given the point to which things had come, Marguerite would have rather died than share herself with another.

"That's enough kidding around," I said to Prudence. "How much, definitively, does Marguerite have to have?"

"I told you, thirty thousand francs."

"And by what time must she have this sum?"

"Within two months."

"She will have it."

Prudence shrugged her shoulders.

"I will get it for you," I continued, "but you must swear to

me that you will not tell Marguerite that it was I who gave it to
you."

"Don't worry."

"And if she sends you to sell or pawn something else, let me
know."

"There's no danger of that, she has nothing left."

I went first to my residence to see if there were any letters
from my father.

There were four.

CHAPTER XIX

In his first three letters, my father expressed anxiety about my silence and asked me the cause of it; in the last, he led me to see that he had been apprised of the change in my life, and announced his imminent arrival.

I have always had a great respect and a sincere fondness for my father. I therefore responded that a little trip had been the cause of my silence, and begged him to tell me the day of his arrival in advance, so I could go see him.

I gave my servant my address in the country, instructing him to bring me the first letter he received postmarked with the city of C . . . , and then returned at once to Bougival.

Marguerite was waiting for me at the garden gate.

Her gaze looked anxious. She threw her arms around my neck, and couldn't keep from saying, "Did you see Prudence?"

"No."

"You were in Paris for some time."

"I found letters from my father which I had to respond to."

A few moments later Nanine entered all out of breath. Marguerite got up and went to speak to her in a low voice.

When Nanine had left, Marguerite said, as she sat near me and took my hand, "Why did you deceive me? You went to see Prudence?"

"Who told you?"

"Nanine."

"And how did she know?"

"She followed you."

"You told her to follow me?"

"Yes. I thought that you must have a motive to go to Paris

like that, you who have not left me for four months. I was afraid that some stroke of bad luck had come to you, or that perhaps you were going to go see another woman."

"Child!"

"I'm reassured, now that I know what you have done, but I don't know yet what you have been told."

I showed Marguerite the letters from my father.

"That's not what I am asking you for; what I would like to know is why you went to see Prudence."

"Just to see her."

"You are lying, my friend."

"All right, well, I went to ask her if the horse was doing better, and if she still needed your cashmere and your jewels."

Marguerite colored but did not respond.

"And," I continued, "I found out what use you had put the horses to, and the cashmere and the diamonds."

"And you hold it against me?"

"I hold it against you that it didn't occur to you to come ask me for what you needed."

"In a relationship such as ours, if the woman is to retain any dignity, she must make every possible sacrifice rather than ask for money from her lover and cast a venal character on her love. You love me, I'm sure of it, but you don't know how slender the thread is that secures the love people have for girls like me to their hearts. Who knows? Maybe on some day of irritation or tedium you might decide you perceive in our relationship some sort of clever calculation! Prudence is a chatterbox. What need had I of those horses! It was a savings for me to sell them; I can get along just fine without them, and I no longer have to spend anything on them. As long as you love me, that's all that I ask, and you will love me just as much without horses, without cashmere, and without diamonds."

All of this was said in a tone so natural that tears came to my eyes as I listened to her.

"But, my good Marguerite," I said, clasping my mistress's hands with love, "you must have known that one day I would learn of this sacrifice, and that the day I learned of it, I would not tolerate it."

"But why?"

"Because, dear child, I cannot accept that the affection you choose to have for me should deprive you of even one jewel. Nor do I, either, want to think that, in some moment of irritation or tedium, you might reflect that if you lived with a different man, such difficulties would not arise; nor do I want for you to regret, if only for a minute, that you live with me. In a few days your horses, your diamonds, and your cashmere will be returned to you. They are as necessary to you as oxygen is to life, and it may be ridiculous, but I love you more when you're sumptuous than when you're simple."

"So you don't love me anymore."

"You're crazy!"

"If you loved me, you would let me love you in my own way; instead you continue to see in me nothing but a girl to whom luxury is indispensable, and whom you believe yourself always forced to pay for. You are ashamed to accept the proofs of my love. In spite of yourself, you intend to leave me one day, and out of delicacy you make sure your behavior is unexceptionable. Fair enough, my friend, but I had hoped for better."

Marguerite made a movement to rise, but I held her back, saying, "I want you to be happy, and for you to have nothing to reproach me with, that is all."

"But we will part!"

"Why, Marguerite? Who can part us?" I cried.

"You, who do not want to permit me to consider your position, yet who have the vanity to keep me in mine; you, who in preserving the luxury in which I used to live, seek to preserve the moral distance that divides us; you, finally, who do not believe my affection for you is disinterested enough to share with me the income you have, on which we could live happily together, but who prefer to ruin yourself, slave that you are to an absurd preconception. Does that mean that you believe I would prefer a carriage and jewelry to your love? Do you believe happiness consists for me of the trifles that one takes pleasure in when one loves nothing, and that become worthless when one truly loves? You will pay my debts, use up your fortune, and keep me! How long will all of that last? Two or three months, and then it will be too late to attempt the life that I'm proposing to you, because in that way you would accept everything about me, which is all a man of honor may do. As it is, now you have eight or ten thousand francs a year on which we could live. I will sell what is left of what I have, and by this sale alone I will make two thousand francs a year. We will rent a pretty little apartment in which we will live, just the two of us. In the summer we'll go to the country, not to a house like this one but to a little place that's just fine for two people. You are independent, I am free, we are young. In the name of Heaven, Armand, do not throw me back into the life I was forced to lead in the past."

I could not respond; tears of acknowledgment and love flooded my eyes, and I threw myself into Marguerite's arms.

"I had wanted," she continued, "to arrange everything without telling you about it, to pay off all my debts and get my new apartment ready. In the month of October we would have returned to Paris, and I would have told you everything then; but since Prudence has told you everything, now you must give your consent beforehand, instead of after. Do you love me enough to do that?"

It was impossible to resist such great devotion. I showered Marguerite's hands with kisses and said to her, "I will do as you wish."

What she had decided was agreed.

She then was overcome with wild joy. She danced, she sang, she gushed about the simplicity of her new apartment, about the neighborhood and how we would live there, and made me part of her plans.

I saw her happy and proud of this resolve, which seemed to have brought us definitively closer together.

I wanted to be with nobody but her.

In an instant I decided what to do with my life. I would put my financial affairs in order, and I would give Marguerite the use of the income that came to me from my mother, and that seemed to me hardly sufficient recompense for the sacrifice I was accepting from her.

I still had the five thousand francs in allowance that my fa-

ther gave me, and as long as that kept coming, I would always
have enough to live on from this annual sum.

I did not tell Marguerite what I had resolved, convinced she
would refuse this gift.

The income came from a sixty-thousand-franc mortgage on
a house I'd never even seen. All I knew was that every three
months my father's notary, an old friend of the family, sent me
750 francs.

The day when Marguerite and I came to Paris to go apartment hunting, I went to see this notary and asked him how I
could transfer this income to another person.

The good man assumed I was ruined, and asked me the reason for this decision. And, rationalizing that sooner or later I
would have to tell him to whom I was making over this money,
I chose to tell him the truth at once.

He made none of the objections that his position as notary
and friend entitled him to make, and assured me that he would
take it upon himself to arrange everything for the best.

I naturally asked him to exercise great discretion on the matter when it came to my father, and then went to join Marguerite, who was waiting for me at Julie Duprat's, where she had
decided to go, instead of to Prudence's, where she was bound
to get a lecture.

We went apartment hunting. Everything we saw was either
too expensive for Marguerite's taste or too simple for mine.
However, we ended up agreeing on a place in one of the most
tranquil neighborhoods of Paris, a little detached residence set
back from the main house on the grounds of a property.

Behind this little residence extended a charming garden that
belonged to it, surrounded by walls that were high enough to
separate us from our neighbors, yet low enough not to obstruct
the view.

It was better than we had hoped for.

While I went home to revisit my apartment, Marguerite went
to see a businessman who, she said, had already done for one
of her girlfriends what she was going to ask him to undertake
for her.

She came to find me on the rue de Provence in an exhilarated mood. The man had promised to pay off all her debts, to liberate her from them, and to give her twenty thousand francs on expectation of the sale of her furniture.

You saw by the amount of money the sale yielded that this honest man would have made more than thirty thousand francs off his client.

We left for Bougival all elated, and we continued to discuss our plans for the future, which, thanks to our carefree mood and, above all, to our love, we saw in the rosiest hue.

Eight days later we were having lunch when Nanine came to alert me that my servant was there to see me.

I bid him enter.

"Sir," he told me, "your father has come to Paris, and begs you immediately to return home, where he awaits you."

This news was the simplest thing in the world, and yet, in learning of it, Marguerite and I looked at each other.

We sensed misfortune in this development.

Also, without her needing to admit this emotion, which I shared, I said to her, giving her my hand, "Have no fear."

"Come back as soon as you can," Marguerite murmured as she kissed me. "I will wait for you at the window."

I sent Joseph to tell my father that I was on my way.

Two hours later I was on the rue de Provence.

CHAPTER XX

My father, in a dressing gown, was seated in my living room, writing.

I understood at once from the way he looked at me when I entered that there was to be a serious discussion.

Nonetheless, I greeted him as if I had guessed nothing from his expression, and embraced him.

"When did you arrive, Father?"

"Last night."

"You came to stay at my place, as usual?"

"Yes."

"I regret very much that I was not here to welcome you."

I expected to see these words provoke the lecture that my father's frosty expression promised, but he made no answer, sealed the letter he had just written. and gave it to Joseph to take to the post office.

When we were alone, my father rose and said to me, while leaning against the mantel, "We have, my dear Armand, serious matters to discuss."

"I'm listening, Father."

"Do you promise to be frank?"

"That is my habit."

"Is it true that you are living with a woman named Marguerite Gautier?"

"Yes."

"Do you know what this woman was?"

"A kept woman."

"And it is because of her that you have forgotten to come see us this year, your sister and me?"

"Yes, Father, I admit it."

"So you love this woman very much?"

"As you see, Father, since she has caused me to neglect a sacred duty, for which I today humbly beg your pardon."

My father undoubtedly had not expected such categorical responses, for he seemed to reflect for a moment, after which he said, "Surely you have understood that you will not be able to go on living like this?"

"I have feared that, Father, but I have not accepted it."

"But you must have understood," my father continued, in a slightly drier tone, "that I myself will not accept it."

"I told myself that, as I would do nothing to violate the respect I owe to your name and to the traditional integrity of our family, I could continue to live as I do now, which reassured me to some extent about my fears."

Passion warred with my emotions. I was ready for any fight, even against my father, to keep Marguerite.

"Well, the moment to live differently has come."

"What? Why, Father?"

"Because you are on the brink of doing things that will injure what you believe to be the respect you have for your family."

"I can see no sense in these words."

"I will explain it to you. It is well and good that you should have a mistress—as long as you pay her as a gentleman pays for the love of a kept woman, one can ask no more—but that you should forget the holiest things for her, that you would permit the gossip of your scandalous life to spread deep into my province and stain the honorable name I have given you; that cannot be. That will not be."

"Permit me to tell you, Father, that those who have instructed you on my affairs were ill informed. I am the lover of Mlle Gautier, I live with her, it's the simplest thing in the world. I do not give to Mlle Gautier the name I received from you, I spend on her only that which my means allow, I have not gotten into debt, and I am not, in short, in any of those positions that might authorize a father to say to his son what you have just said to me."

"A father is always authorized to remove his son from an evil

path he sees his son pursuing. You have not done anything ir-
reparable yet, but you will."

"Father!"

"Sir, I know more about life than you do. No woman can
have entirely pure feelings except women who are entirely
chaste. Every Manon can turn a man into Des Grieux, however
times and morals may change. It would be pointless for the
world to keep turning if we did not learn from our mistakes
along the way. You will leave your mistress."

"It hurts me to disobey you, Father, but it's impossible."

"I must insist."

"Unfortunately, Father, there are no more Sainte-Marguerite
isles where one can banish courtesans, and if there were, I
would follow Mlle Gautier if you sent her there. What do you
want from me? Perhaps I'm in the wrong, but I can be happy
only if I remain the lover of this woman."

"Come now, Armand. Open your eyes; recognize your father
who has always loved you, and who only wishes your happiness. Is it honorable for you to live conjugally with a girl whom
all the world has had?"

"What does it matter, Father, if nobody else can have her
anymore! What does it matter, if this girl loves me, if she's been
reformed by the love she has for me and by the love I have for
her! What does it matter, in the end, since she has reformed!"

"Eh! Do you believe then, sir, that the mission of an honorable man is to rehabilitate courtesans? Do you believe that God
would impose such a grotesque purpose on life, and that the
heart should have no enthusiasm but that one? What will be
the conclusion of this marvelous cure, and what will you think
of what you have said today when you are forty? You will laugh
at your love, if you're still able to laugh, if it hasn't left too deep
a mark on your past. What would you be at this moment, if
your father had had notions like yours, and had given over his
life to heaving sighs of love instead of fixing unshakably on the
course of honor and loyalty? Think, Armand, and speak no
more of such foolishness. Come now, you will leave this
woman; your father begs you."

I made no response.

"Armand," continued my father, "in the name of your sainted mother, believe me, renounce this life that you will forget more quickly than you think, and to which you have attached impossible notions. You are twenty-four years old; think of the future. You cannot always love this woman, and she will not love you forever, either. Both of you exaggerate your love. You will bar yourself from any career. One more step and you will not be able to leave the road you've embarked on, and all your life you will suffer remorse for your youth. Leave; come spend a month or two at your sister's side. Rest and the pious love of your family will heal you quickly of this fever, for it is nothing but that.

"During this time, your mistress will console herself, she will take another lover, and when you see for yourself for whom you would have quarreled with your father and lost his affection, you will tell me that I did well to come find you, and you will bless me.

"Come, you will leave—yes, Armand?"

I felt my father was right about all other women, but I was convinced he was not right about Marguerite. However, the tone in which he had spoken those last words to me was so gentle, so imploring, that I dared not respond.

"Well then?" he said, his voice full of emotion.

"Father, I can't promise you anything," I said at last. "What you ask of me is beyond my power to give. Believe me," I continued, as I saw him make an impatient movement, "you exaggerate the consequences of this liaison. Marguerite is not the kind of girl you think she is. This love, far from setting me on an evil path, is on the contrary capable of nurturing the most honorable sentiments in me. True love always makes a man better, whatever the nature of the woman who inspires it. If you knew Marguerite, you would understand that I am not exposing myself to any danger. She is as honorable as the most honorable of women. Greedy as other women may be, she is not motivated by self-interest."

"Which does not hinder her from accepting your entire fortune; the sixty thousand francs that come to you from your mother, which you are giving to her, are, mark my words, your sole fortune."

My father had probably saved this peroration and threat for the final blow.

I was stronger in the face of his threats than I had been in the face of his prayers.

"Who told you I was handing over that sum to her?" I resumed.

"My notary. Could any honest man have undertaken such an action without alerting me? Well, it's to prevent your ruin over a girl that I have come to Paris. Your mother left you money when she died for you to live on honorably, not for you to squander on your mistresses."

"I swear to you, Father, Marguerite did not know about this gift."

"Then why did you make it?"

"Because Marguerite, this woman you malign and whom you wish me to abandon, is sacrificing everything she possesses to live with me."

"And you accept this sacrifice? What kind of man are you, sir, to permit Mlle Marguerite to sacrifice anything to you? All right then, I've had enough. You will leave this woman. A while ago I begged you to; now I order you. I do not want such filth in my family. Pack your trunks and prepare to follow me."

"Pardon me, Father," I said, "but I will not leave."

"Because?"

"Because I have already reached the age at which one does not obey an order."

My father turned pale upon this answer.

"Very good, sir," he said. "I know what is left for me to do."

He rang.

Joseph appeared.

"Have my trunks taken to the Hôtel de Paris," he said to my servant. At the same time he entered his bedroom, and finished dressing.

When he reappeared, I went up to him.

"Do you promise, Father," I said, "to do nothing that might cause Marguerite pain?"

My father stopped, looked at me with disdain, and contented himself with the reply, "You are mad, I believe."

After which he left, slamming the door behind him.

I went down soon after, took a cabriolet, and left for Bougival.

Marguerite was waiting for me at the window.

CHAPTER XXI

"At last!" she cried, flinging her arms around my neck. "Here you are! You're so pale!"

I told her of the scene with my father.

"Ah! My God! I was afraid of that," she said. "When Joseph came to announce your father's arrival, I shuddered as if at the news of a tragedy. Poor friend! And to think that I am the one who causes you all this pain. Perhaps you would be better off to leave me than to quarrel with your father. But I haven't done anything to him. We live peacefully; we will live more peacefully still. He knows very well that you must have a mistress, and he should be happy that it is me, since I love you, and seek no more from you than your position permits. Did you tell him of our plans for the future?"

"Yes, and that is what annoyed him most of all, because he saw in that determination the proof of our mutual love."

"Then what are we to do?"

"Stay together, my good Marguerite, and let this storm pass."

"Will it pass?"

"It must."

"But your father doesn't support us?"

"What do you expect him to do?"

"What do I know? A father might do anything to make his son obey him. He will bring up my past, and will perhaps do me the honor of inventing some new story to make you leave me."

"You know very well that I love you."

"Yes, but what I also know is that, sooner or later, one must obey one's father, and you will end perhaps by letting him convince you."

"No. Marguerite, I am the one who will convince him. It's gossip from some of his friends that has made him so angry; but he's a good man, he's fair, and he will retract his first impression. Then again, after all, what does it matter to me!"

"Don't say that, Armand. I would prefer anything than to think that I have got you into trouble with your family. Let this day pass, and tomorrow return to Paris. Your father will have reflected on his end, as you will have on yours, and maybe you will get along better. Don't attack his principles; act as if you are making some concessions to his wishes. Act as if you aren't as set on me, and he will let things stay as they are. Have faith, my friend, and remain assured of one thing, which is that, come what may, your Marguerite will remain yours."

"Do you swear it to me?"

"Do I need to swear it to you?"

How sweet it is to let oneself be persuaded by a voice one loves! Marguerite and I spent the entire day talking about our plans over and over, as if we understood the need to put them into practice faster. We expected some new turn of events every moment, but luckily the day passed without bringing news.

The next day I left at ten and arrived at the hotel around noon.

My father had already gone out.

I returned to my apartment, where I hoped he might have gone. Nobody came. I went to see my notary. Nobody!

I returned to the hotel and waited until six o'clock. M. Duval did not come back.

I got on the road for Bougival.

I found Marguerite no longer waiting for me as she had the night before, but sitting in the corner by the fire, which the season already made necessary.

She was so deeply lost in her thoughts that I was able to approach her armchair without her hearing me or turning around. When I placed my lips on her forehead, she shuddered as if the kiss had woken her with a start.

"You frightened me," she said. "And your father?"

"I didn't see him. I don't know what it means. I didn't find him at his hotel, or in any of the places where there was a chance he might be."

"Well then, we'll have to try again tomorrow."

"I'd rather wait until he asks for me. I've done, I believe, everything I should do."

"No, my friend, it's hardly enough. You must return to see your father tomorrow, without fail."

"Why tomorrow as opposed to some other day?"

"Because," said Marguerite, who seemed to blush a little at the question. "Because such insistence on your part will seem lively and might help us earn our pardon more promptly."

The rest of the day Marguerite was preoccupied, distracted, sad. I was forced to repeat anything I said to her twice to get a response. She blamed her preoccupation on the fears that the events of the past two days had provoked in her.

I spent the evening reassuring her, and she made me leave the next day with an anxious insistence that I could not explain to myself.

As on the previous day, my father was not there, but as he had gone out, he had left me this letter:

"If you come back to see me today, wait for me until four o'clock; if I am not back by four o'clock, come back tomorrow to dine with me. I must speak to you."

I waited until the indicated hour. My father did not reappear. I left.

The day before, I had found Marguerite sad; today I found her feverish and agitated. Upon seeing me enter, she flung herself around my neck, but she wept for a long time in my arms. I questioned her about this sudden sorrow, whose intensity alarmed me. She gave me no definite reason, offering every excuse a woman can make when she does not want to tell the truth.

When she had calmed down a little, I told her the result of my trip; I showed her the letter from my father, observing to her that it might bode good things for us.

Upon the sight of this letter and upon my remark, her tears

increased to such a point that I called Nanine, and, fearing a nervous attack, we put the poor girl to bed. She was crying wordlessly, but held my hands and kissed them every moment.

I asked Nanine if, during my absence, her mistress had received a letter or visit that might explain the state I had found her in, but Nanine responded that nobody had come and that nothing had been brought.

However, something must have happened since the previous night, which disturbed me all the more because Marguerite was hiding it from me.

She appeared a little calmer in the evening, and, making me sit at the foot of her bed, she lengthily reassured me of her love. Then she smiled at me, but effortfully, since, despite herself, her eyes were veiled with tears. I used every means to persuade her to tell me the true cause of her sadness, but she persisted in giving me the vague reasons I already told you of.

In the end she fell asleep in my arms, but with the kind of sleep that does not refresh the body but depletes it; from time to time she would cry out, wake with a start, and after being assured I was still beside her, make me swear to love her always. I understood nothing of these intermittent outbursts of sorrow, which continued until morning. At last Marguerite fell into a fitful sleep. For two nights she had not slept.

Her repose was not of long duration.

Toward eleven o'clock Marguerite awoke and, seeing me up and about, looked around her and cried, "Aren't you gone already, then?"

"No," I said, taking her hands. "I wanted to let you sleep. It's still early."

"What time are you going to Paris?"

"At four o'clock."

"So soon? Until then, you will stay with me, won't you?"

"Without a doubt—isn't that what I always do?"

"Such happiness! Are we going to have lunch?" she asked with a distracted air.

"If you like."

"And then you will be especially sweet with me until the moment you leave?"

"Yes, and I will come back as soon as possible."

"You will come back?" she said, looking at me with haggard eyes.

"Naturally."

"That's right, you'll come back tonight, and I—I will wait for you, as I always do, and we will be happy just as we always have been ever since we've known each other."

All these words were spoken in such a halting way that they seemed to conceal thoughts so uninterruptedly painful that I trembled at every moment for fear that Marguerite would fall into delirium.

"Listen," I said, "you are sick; I cannot leave you like this. I will write to my father that he should not wait for me."

"No! No!" she cried abruptly. "Don't do that. Your father will accuse me again of keeping you from going to see him when he wants to see you. No, no, you must go—you must! Anyway, I'm not sick; I'm in excellent health. It's just that I had a bad dream, and I'm not properly awake."

From that point on Marguerite tried to seem more cheerful. She cried no more.

When the hour came for me to leave, I kissed her and asked if she would like to accompany me to the station; I hoped the walk would distract her and the air would do her good.

Above all I wanted to stay with her as long as possible.

She accepted, put on a coat, and accompanied me with Nanine, so she would not have to return home alone.

Twenty times I was on the verge of not leaving. But the hope of returning quickly and the fear of inflaming my father anew sustained me, and the train carried me off.

"Until tonight," I said to Marguerite as I left her.

She did not respond.

There was one other time that she had not responded to those very words, and the Comte de G . . . , you will recall, spent that night with her; but that time was so far off that it was if it were erased from my memory, and if I feared anything, it was certainly not that Marguerite might deceive me.

Upon arriving in Paris I hurried to see Prudence and to beg

her to go see Marguerite, hoping her vitality and gaiety might distract her.

I walked in without being announced and found Prudence at her toilette.

"Ah!" she said with an anxious air. "Is Marguerite with you?"

"No."

"How is she?"

"She is not feeling well."

"Is she not coming?"

"Was she supposed to be coming?"

Mme Duvernoy blushed and responded, with a certain embarrassment, "I meant to say, since you have come to Paris, will she not be coming here to join you?"

"No."

I looked at Prudence; she lowered her eyes, and in her countenance I thought I read the fear that my visit might be a long one.

"I have actually come to beg you, my dear Prudence, if you have nothing better to do, to go see Marguerite tonight; you can keep her company and you can sleep there. I have never seen her as she was today, and I tremble for fear that she might fall sick."

"I am dining in town," Prudence responded, "and I cannot see Marguerite tonight; but I will see her tomorrow."

I took leave of Mme Duvernoy, who seemed to me almost as preoccupied as Marguerite, and went to see my father, whose first glance attentively sized me up.

He gave me his hand.

"Your two visits pleased me, Armand," he said. "They gave me hope that you had reflected on your part, as I have reflected on mine."

"May I be permitted to ask you, Father, what has been the result of your reflections?"

"It has been, my friend, that I have exaggerated the importance of the reports that had been made to me, and that I have promised myself to be less severe with you."

"What are you saying, Father!" I cried with joy.

"I am saying, my child, that every young man must have a mistress, and, based on new information, I would rather have you be the lover of Mlle Gautier than of another."

"My excellent father! You make me so happy!"

We spoke in this way for a few moments, then sat down to dine. My father was charming throughout the dinner.

I was anxious to return to Bougival to tell Marguerite of this happy change. At every moment I looked at the clock.

"You are watching the clock," my father said. "You're impatient to leave me. Oh, young people! You would therefore sacrifice sincere affections for dubious ones?"

"Don't say that, Father! Marguerite loves me; I'm sure of it."

My father did not respond; he seemed neither to doubt me nor to believe me.

He struggled mightily to persuade me to spend the entire evening with him, and not to leave until the next day; but I had left Marguerite sick at home, I told him, and asked his permission to return to her early, promising to return the next day.

It was a fine day; he wanted to accompany me as far as the station. I had never been so happy. The future appeared to me as I had yearned to see it for a long time.

I loved my father more than I had ever loved him.

At the moment of my departure, he urged me one last time to stay; I refused.

"You really love her a lot, don't you?" he asked.

"Like a fool."

"Go, then!" And he passed his hand across his forehead as if to chase away a thought, then opened his mouth as if to tell me something, but made do with clasping my hand and left me abruptly, crying, "Till tomorrow, then!"

CHAPTER XXII

It seemed that the train was not moving.

I arrived at Bougival at eleven o'clock.

Not one window of the house was lit, and I rang, but nobody answered.

It was the first time such a thing had happened to me. At last the gardener appeared. I went in.

Nanine joined me with a light. I came to Marguerite's room.

"Where is madam?"

"Madam went to Paris," Nanine responded.

"To Paris!"

"Yes, sir."

"When?"

"An hour after you."

"Did she leave a note for you to give me?"

"Nothing."

Nanine left me.

"It is possible she was afraid," I thought, "and went to Paris to make sure the visit I'd told her I was making to see my father was not a pretext for a day of freedom."

"Maybe Prudence wrote her about some important business," I told myself when I was alone; but I had seen Prudence upon my arrival, and she had said nothing that made me suppose that she might have written to Marguerite.

All at once I remembered that question Mme Duvernoy had asked me: "Isn't she coming today, then?" when I had said Marguerite was sick. I recalled at the same moment Prudence's air of embarrassment when I had looked at her after that question, which seemed to imply a rendezvous. To this memory I added Marguerite's tears during the day, tears that my father's warm welcome had made me forget a little.

From that moment on, all the incidents of the day regrouped around my first suspicion, and fixed it so solidly in my mind that everything seemed to confirm it, right up to the paternal clemency.

Marguerite had almost insisted I go to Paris; she had affected calm when I had proposed that I stay beside her. Had I fallen into a trap? Was Marguerite deceiving me? Had she counted on being back in time for me to remain unaware of her absence, and had chance detained her? Why had she said nothing to Nanine; why had she not written me? What did those tears, that absence, this mystery, mean?

This is what I asked myself with dread, in the middle of that empty room, my eyes fixed on the clock, which, striking midnight, seemed to tell me it was too late for me to hope to see my mistress return.

All the same, after the arrangements we had just made, with the sacrifice offered and accepted, was it realistic that she would deceive me? No. I tried to reject my first suspicions.

"The poor girl must have found a buyer for her furniture, and gone to Paris to conclude the deal. She didn't want to alert me, because she knows that, though I accept it, this sale, which is necessary to our happiness together, is painful for me, and she would have been afraid of hurting my pride and my feelings by talking about it with me. She prefers to reappear only once everything is over. Prudence was obviously waiting for her for that purpose, and gave herself away in front of me. Marguerite must not have finished her business today, and she has gone to sleep at her own place, or perhaps she might even turn up here later, for she must suspect my worries, and certainly would not want to leave me to them."

But then, why those tears? Doubtless, in spite of her love for me, the poor girl must not have been able to come to terms with abandoning the luxury in the midst of which she had existed up until now, and which had made her happy and envied.

I freely pardoned Marguerite for these regrets. I waited impatiently for the chance to tell her, while covering her in kisses, that I had divined the cause of her mysterious absence.

However, the night advanced, and Marguerite did not arrive.

Anxiety tightened its grip on me little by little, oppressing my head and heart. Maybe something had happened to her! Maybe she was wounded, sick, dead! Maybe a messenger was about to arrive who would inform me of some grievous accident! Maybe the morning would find me in the same uncertainty and with the same fears!

The idea that Marguerite might have been deceiving me at the hour when I awaited her amid the terrors that her absence caused me did not return to my mind. There had to have been some cause beyond her control that had kept her away from me, and the more I thought about it, the more convinced I became that this cause could be nothing but some sort of misfortune. O, the vanity of men! You reveal yourself at every turn.

The clock struck one. I told myself I would wait one more hour, but that if at two o'clock Marguerite had not returned, I would leave for Paris.

While waiting I went to look for a book, because I didn't dare to think.

Manon Lescaut was open on the table. It seemed that here and there the pages were dampened as if by tears. After leafing through it, I closed this book, whose characters seemed void of sense to me, obscured by the veil of my doubts.

The hour passed slowly. The sky was overcast. An autumn rain lashed at the windows. The empty bed seemed at times to take on the aspect of a tomb. I was afraid.

I opened the door. I listened and heard nothing but the wind in the trees. Not one carriage passed on the road. The half hour struck sadly in the church tower.

I was beginning to hope that nobody would enter. It seemed that only a calamity could find me at this hour and in this somber weather.

The clock struck two. I waited a little longer. Only the clock disturbed the silence with its monotonous, cadenced sound.

Finally I left this room, whose smallest objects had clothed it in that mournful aspect that the lonely heart confers upon everything that surrounds it.

In the next room I found Nanine, who had fallen asleep over her needlework. At the sound of the door she woke up and asked if my mistress had returned home.

"No, but if she does, tell her I could not overcome my worry and that I have gone to Paris."

"At this hour?"

"Yes."

"But how? You will not find a carriage."

"I will go on foot."

"But it's raining."

"What do I care?"

"Madam will come home, or if she doesn't, there will be time in the day to go see what has detained her. You will get yourself killed on the road."

"There is no danger, my dear Nanine. Until tomorrow."

The good-natured girl went to get my coat, threw it over my shoulders, and offered to go wake the inn owner, Mère Arnould, and inquire if it would be possible to get a carriage, but I refused, convinced I would lose more time in this possibly fruitless attempt than it would take me to complete half the journey.

Also I needed fresh air, as well as physical exertion to exhaust the overexcitement to which I had fallen prey.

I took the key to the apartment of the rue d'Antin, and, after having said good-bye to Nanine, who had accompanied me as far as the gate, I left.

I started out running, but the earth was newly damp, which was doubly tiring. After a quarter hour of running, I was forced to stop; I was bathed in sweat. Recovering my breath, I continued on my path. The night was so dark that I trembled at every moment, thinking I might stumble into one of the trees along the roadside—looming suddenly before my eyes, they looked like giant ghosts charging at me.

I saw one or two transport wagons, which I soon left behind. A calèche approached at a full trot heading for Bougival. At the moment it passed in front of me, the hope sprang to mind that Marguerite was within.

I stopped and cried out, "Marguerite! Marguerite!"

But nobody answered, and the calèche continued on its way. I watched it recede into the distance, and continued on.

It took me two hours to reach the edge of the Place de l'Étoile.

The sight of Paris restored my strength, and at a run I descended the long avenue I had crossed so many times.

That night nobody was there.

You would have thought it was the boulevard of a dead city.

The day began to break.

When I arrived at the rue d'Antin, the great city was already stirring before completely waking.

Five o'clock struck in the Church of Saint-Roch at the moment I entered Marguerite's building.

I gave my name to the porter, who had received enough twenty-franc pieces from me to know I had the right to come visit Mlle Gautier at five o'clock in the morning.

I passed without interference.

I could have asked him if Marguerite was at home, but he might have responded no, and I preferred to remain in doubt for two minutes longer because in doubt, I still could hope.

I put my ear to the door, trying to detect a sound, a movement.

Nothing. The silence of the countryside seemed to extend all the way here.

I opened the door and entered.

All the curtains were hermetically closed.

I drew open the dining room curtains, then headed to the bedroom, and pushed open the door.

I leapt at the curtain cord and pulled it violently. The curtains flew open; a weak daylight broke through. I ran to the bed.

It was empty!

I opened the doors one after the other; I entered all the rooms.

Nobody.

It was enough to drive you mad.

I entered the dressing room, opened the window, and called out for Prudence many times.

Mme Duvernoy's window remained shut.

I then went down to see the porter and asked if Mlle Gautier had come home during the day.

"Yes," responded the man, "with Mme Duvernoy."

"She left no word for me?"

"Nothing."

"Do you know what they did next?"

"They got into a carriage."

"What sort of carriage?"

"A private carriage."

What did it all mean?

I rang at the next door.

"Where are you going, sir?" the concierge asked after having opened the door.

"To see Mme Duvernoy."

"She is not back."

"Are you sure?"

"Yes, sir, and here is even a letter that someone brought her last night and which I have not yet given to her."

And the porter showed me a letter, at which I mechanically glanced.

I recognized Marguerite's handwriting.

I took the letter.

The address bore these words:

"To Mme Duvernoy, to give to M. Duval."

"This letter is for me," I told the porter, and showed him the address.

"You are Monsieur Duval?" replied this man.

"Yes."

"Ah! I recognize you; you often come to see Mme Duvernoy."

Once in the street, I broke the seal of this letter.

A lightning bolt could have landed at my feet and I would not have been more shocked than I was by what I read there.

"By the time you read this letter, Armand, I will already be the mistress of another man. Everything, therefore, is over between us.

"Return to the side of your father, my friend, go see your sister again—that chaste young girl, unaware of all our miseries—in whose company you will quickly forget what you have suffered because of that lost girl called Marguerite Gautier, whom you once tried to love for an instant, and who owes to you the only happy moments of a life that, she hopes, will not now last long."

When I read the last word, I thought I would go mad.

At one moment I truly feared I would fall down on the street. A cloud passed before my eyes, and the blood rushed to my temples.

At last I got hold of myself. I looked around me, astonished to see the lives of others continue without being slowed by my despair.

I was not strong enough to bear alone the blow that Marguerite had brought upon me.

It was then that I remembered that my father was in the same city as I, and that in ten minutes' time I could be by his side, and that, whatever the cause of my pain, he would share it with me.

I ran like a madman, like a thief, to the Hôtel de Paris. I found the key in the door of my father's room. I entered.

He was reading.

From the slight degree of astonishment he showed in seeing me appear, you would have thought he had expected me.

I threw myself into his arms without saying a word, I gave him Marguerite's letter and, sinking to my knees beside his bed, I wept hot tears.

CHAPTER XXIII

As the ordinary routine of daily life resumed its course, I could not believe the day that broke would not resemble the ones that had preceded it. There were moments when I told myself that some circumstance I could not recall had brought me to spend the night away from Marguerite, but that if I returned to Bougival, I would find her anxious, just as I had been, and that she would ask me who it was who had kept me so far away from her.

Once existence has solidified into habit, as had happened with this love affair, it seems impossible that this habit could be broken without simultaneously shattering all the other mainsprings of life.

I was therefore forced to reread that letter from Marguerite time and again, to convince myself I had not dreamed it.

My body, succumbing to moral shock, was incapable of a single movement. My anxiety, my nighttime journey, the news of the morning, had exhausted me. My father took advantage of this total prostration of my forces to ask me to formally consent to leave with him.

I promised everything he wanted. I was incapable of enduring an argument, and I needed genuine affection to help me survive what had just happened.

I was only too happy that my father was willing to console me for such heartbreak.

All I recall is that around five o'clock that afternoon he had me step into a post chaise with him. Without telling me anything, he'd had my trunks packed, had them loaded with his own behind the carriage, and taken me off.

I had no idea of what I was doing until the city had disappeared and the solitude of the road reminded me of the emptiness of my heart.

Again I was overcome by tears.

My father understood that words, even from him, would not console me, and let me cry without saying a word, contenting himself with sometimes gripping my hand, as if to remind me that I had a friend next to me.

That night I slept a little. I dreamt of Marguerite.

I woke with a start, not understanding why I was in a carriage.

Then reality came back to me, and I let my head sink on my chest.

I did not dare talk to my father; I was too afraid he might say, "You see, I was right when I denied that woman's ability to love."

But he did not abuse his advantage, and we arrived at C . . . without his having said anything to me but words completely unrelated to the events that had caused my departure.

When I embraced my sister, I recalled the words of Marguerite's letter concerning her, but understood at once that, good as she was, my sister was incapable of making me forget my mistress.

Hunting season was open; my father thought it would provide a distraction for me. He organized shooting parties with neighbors and friends. I attended them without repugnance and without enthusiasm, with the same apathy that characterized all my actions after my departure.

We were hunting for game. I was brought to my post. I set my unloaded gun down beside me and daydreamed.

I watched the clouds pass. I let my thoughts wander across the lonely plains, and from time to time I would hear my name called by some hunter, pointing out a hare ten steps away from me.

None of these details escaped my father, and he did not let himself be deceived by my tranquil exterior. He understood very well that, defeated as it was, my heart might someday experience a terrible, perhaps dangerous reaction, and while avoiding the appearance of consoling me, he did his utmost to distract me.

My sister, naturally, had not been made aware of all that had occurred. She could not understand why I, usually so cheerful, had suddenly become so dreamy and sad.

Sometimes, surprised in the midst of my sadness by an uneasy glance from my father, I would give him my hand and clasp his as if tacitly begging his pardon for the pain that, in spite of myself, I had caused him.

A month passed this way, but it was all I could bear.

The memory of Marguerite pursued me endlessly. I had loved this woman too much, and I still did, for her to become indifferent to me at once. Whatever feelings I might have for her, I simply had to see her again, and at once.

This desire entered my mind and planted itself there with all the violence of the determination that finally reemerges in a body that has been paralyzed for a long time.

It was not in the future, in one month, in a week that I had to see Marguerite; it was the day following the very day when the idea seized me, and I went to tell my father that I was leaving him for business that called me back to Paris, but that I would return promptly.

No doubt he guessed the motive for my departure, because he urged me to stay; but, seeing that the suppression of this desire, in the excitable state I was in, might have fatal consequences for me, he hugged me and begged me, almost in tears, to return quickly to his side.

I did not sleep all the way to Paris.

Once I was there, what would I do? I did not know, but first of all I needed to find out what had become of Marguerite.

I went to my apartment to get dressed, and as the weather was good, and there was plenty of time, I went to the Champs-Élysées.

After half an hour I saw Marguerite's carriage approach from afar, from the Rond-Point at the Place de la Concorde.

She had bought back her horses, because the carriage was just as it used to be, except she was not inside it.

Hardly had I noticed this absence when, following the eyes

of others around me, I saw Marguerite, on foot, accompanied
by a woman I'd never seen before.

In passing alongside me, she turned pale, and a nervous
smile tightened her lips. As for me, the violent beating of my
heart shook my chest, but I succeeded in maintaining a chilly
expression on my face, and coldly saluted my old mistress, who
reached her carriage almost at the same time, and climbed into
it with her friend.

I knew Marguerite. Meeting me unexpectedly must have dis-
concerted her. Without doubt she had learned of my departure,
which must have calmed her in the aftermath of our rupture;
but seeing me come back, and finding herself face-to-face with
me, pale as I was, she must have understood that my return had
a purpose, and asked herself what was going to happen.

If I had come upon Marguerite unhappy—if, as a sort of
revenge, I had been able to rescue her in some way—I would
perhaps have forgiven her, and certainly would not have
thought of doing her harm. But I found her happy, at least so it
appeared; another man had returned to her the luxury I could
not provide for her. As a consequence, our rupture, initiated by
her, seemed to take on the basest character. I felt as humiliated
in my pride as in my love; she absolutely had to pay for the suffering she had caused me.

I could not be indifferent to what this woman was doing,
and surely, the thing that would hurt her the most would be my
indifference; so that was the sentiment I had to feign, not only
for her eyes, but also for the eyes of others.

Trying to put on a smiling face, I presented myself at Prudence's.

The chambermaid went to announce me and made me wait
a few moments in the living room.

At last Mme Duvernoy appeared and invited me into her
boudoir. As soon as I sat down, I heard the door of the living
room open. A light step made the parquet creak, and then the
door of the building slammed violently.

"Am I disturbing you?" I asked Prudence.

"Not at all; Marguerite was here. When she heard your
name announced, she ran away; it is she who has just left."

"She is afraid of me now?"

"No, but she believes it would be disagreeable for you to see her."

"Why then," I said, making an effort to breathe naturally, as emotion was choking me, "the poor girl has left me to get back her carriage, her furniture, and her diamonds. She has done the right thing, and I should not resent her for it. I ran into her today," I continued casually.

"Where?" said Prudence, looking at me and seeming to ask herself if this man was really the same one she had known who had been so in love.

"On the Champs-Élysées; she was with another very pretty woman. Who is that woman?"

"What does she look like?"

"A blonde, slender, with long curls, blue eyes, very elegant."

"Ah! That's Olympe, a very pretty girl, indeed."

"Who does she live with?"

"With nobody, with everybody."

"And where does she live?"

"Rue Tronchet, number . . . Ah! Wait, you would like to pursue her?"

"You never know what might happen."

"And Marguerite?"

"To tell you that I don't think of her at all anymore would be a lie, but I am one of those men for whom the manner in which an affair ends carries great weight. Marguerite sent me away me in such a light manner that I felt like a fool for having been as in love as I was, for I was truly very much in love with that girl."

You may guess in what tone I attempted to say these things; sweat poured down my forehead.

"Come now, she loved you very much, and she still loves you; the proof is that after she saw you today, she came immediately to tell me about this encounter. When she arrived, she was trembling; she was almost ill."

"Well, what did she tell you?"

"She said to me, 'No doubt he will come to see you,' and begged me to ask your forgiveness."

"I forgive her; you may tell her that. She is a good girl, but she's a girl of a certain type, and what she did to me I should have expected. I am grateful to her for her decisiveness, because today I ask myself where my idea of building a life with her would have led. It was folly."

"She will be very happy to learn that you are reconciled to the necessity in which she found herself. It was time for her to leave you, my dear. The scoundrel of a businessman she had planned to sell her furniture to had contacted her creditors to ask how much she owed them; they had taken fright, and everything was going to be sold in two days."

"And now it's all paid off?"

"Just about."

"And who provided the funds?"

"The Comte de N . . . . Ah! My dear! There are men made just for that purpose. In short, he gave her twenty thousand francs, but that was his limit. He knows Marguerite is not in love with him, but that does not keep him from being very kind to her. As you saw, he bought back her horses, he redeemed her jewels, and he gives her as much money as the duke gave her. If she would like a tranquil life, that man will stay with her for a long time."

"And what is she doing? Is she living entirely in Paris?"

"She never wanted to return to Bougival after you left. I am the one who went there and got all her things, and even yours, which I've made into a bundle that you can pick up here. Everything is there, except for a small portfolio with your monogram on it. Marguerite wanted to keep it; she has it at her place. If you are attached to it, I will ask for it back from her."

"She may keep it," I stammered, for I felt the tears rise from my heart to my eyes at the memory of the village where I had been so happy, and at the thought that Marguerite wanted to hold on to something of mine that reminded her of me.

If she had entered at that moment, my resolutions of vengeance would have disappeared, and I would have fallen at her feet.

"Besides," Prudence resumed, "I've never seen her as she is now. She hardly sleeps anymore, she goes to the balls, she has supper, she even drinks too much. Very recently, after a supper, she had to stay in bed for a week; and when the doctor permitted her to get up, she started it up again, at risk of her life. Are you going to go see her?"

"What good would that do? I came to see you—you—because you have always been kind to me, and because I knew you before I knew Marguerite. It is to you that I owe the fact that I was her lover, just as it's to you that I owe the fact that I no longer am, is that not so?"

"Ah, I should say so. I did everything I could to make her leave you, and I believe that, later, you will not hold it against me."

"In that case I owe you a double debt of gratitude," I added as I rose, because I was disgusted by this woman, seeing that she took at face value everything I said to her.

"You are going?"

"Yes."

I had learned enough.

"When will we see you again?"

"Soon. Good-bye."

"Good-bye."

Prudence led me as far as the door, and I went home with tears of rage in my eyes and a hunger for vengeance in my heart.

So Marguerite, in the end, was like all the rest, and the deep love she had for me had not been able to overcome her desire to resume her past life and her need to have a carriage and to take part in wild parties.

That is what I told myself during my sleepless nights whereas, if I had reflected as coolly as I pretended to, I might have read into Marguerite's clamorous new existence her hope of quieting a persistent thought, an unceasing memory.

Unfortunately I was overcome with fury, and sought nothing but a way to torture this poor creature.

Oh! Man can be so petty and vile when one of his small-minded passions is wounded.

This Olympe, whom I had seen her with, was, if not Marguerite's friend, at least the person she had seen most often since her return to Paris. She was going to give a ball, and since I supposed that Marguerite would be there, I sought to get an invitation, and received one.

When, seething with my painful emotions, I arrived at this ball, it was already at full tilt. People were dancing, people were even shouting, and, in one of the quadrilles, I saw Marguerite dancing with the Comte de N . . . , who seemed quite proud to show her off, and seemed to say to all the world, "This woman is mine!"

I went to lean against the mantel, just across from Marguerite, and watched her dance. Hardly had she noticed me when she became troubled. I saw her and greeted her absently with a glance and a wave.

When I reflected that, after the ball, it would not be with me that she would leave, but with this rich idiot, and when I pictured what in all likelihood would follow their return to her apartment, the blood rushed to my face, and I felt compelled to stir up trouble between them.

After the contredanse I went to greet the mistress of the house, who had put on display for the eyes of her guests her magnificent shoulders and an expanse of dazzling bosom.

The girl was beautiful—and in terms of her figure, more beautiful than Marguerite. This became even clearer to me as I saw the way the former looked at Olympe while I was talking to her. The man who would be the lover of that woman could be as proud as M. de N . . . , and she was beautiful enough to inspire a passion equal to that which Marguerite had inspired in me.

She had no lover at that time. It would not be difficult to take on that role. All that was required was to show enough gold to get oneself noticed.

My resolution was set. This woman was to be my mistress.

I commenced my role as suitor by dancing with Olympe.

Half an hour later, Marguerite, pale as a corpse, put on her pelisse and left the ball.

CHAPTER XXIV

It was already something, but it was not enough. I understood the power I had over this woman, and I cravenly abused it.

When I think that she is dead now, I ask myself if God will ever forgive the wickedness I wrought.

After the supper, which was among the most raucous ever, we began to gamble.

I sat beside Olympe and was so liberal with my money that she could not help taking notice. In an instant I won nearly two hundred louis, which I spread before me and on which she fixed ardent eyes.

I was the only one who was not completely caught up in the game, and who was focusing on her. All the rest of the night I kept winning, and it was I who gave her money to play with, because she'd lost everything she had in front of her, and probably everything she had in reserve, too.

At five o'clock in the morning we left.

I had won three hundred louis.

All the gamblers had already left; I alone had remained behind without anyone noticing, because I was not friends with any of those gentlemen.

Olympe herself lit the stairway and I was about to leave like the others when, turning to her, I said, "I must speak with you."

"Tomorrow," she said.

"No, now."

"What do you have to tell me?"

"You will see."

And I went back into her apartment.

"You lost," I said.

"Yes."

"Everything you have?"

She hesitated.

"Be frank."

"Oh well, it's true."

"I won three hundred louis. Here they are, if you will let me stay."

At that moment, I threw the gold on the table.

"And why this proposition?"

"Because I love you, by God!"

"No, but because you are in love with Marguerite, and you want to revenge yourself on her by becoming my lover. You cannot fool a woman like me, my dear friend, unfortunately. I am still too young and too beautiful to accept the role you propose."

"So you refuse?"

"Yes."

"Would you prefer to love me for nothing? It is I who would not accept in that case. Think about it, my dear Olympe—if I had sent anyone at all to you to propose that you accept those three hundred louis from me on the conditions I set, you would have accepted. I preferred to deal directly with you. Accept this without questioning my motives. Tell yourself that you are beautiful, and that there is nothing very astonishing in the idea that I might be in love with you."

Marguerite was a kept woman like Olympe, yet all the same I would never have dared say to her the first time I saw her what I had just said to this woman. It was because I loved Marguerite that I had perceived in her the instincts that this other creature lacked, and at the very moment that I proposed this arrangement, despite the extreme beauty of the woman with whom I was to conclude it, she disgusted me.

She finished by accepting, of course, and at noon I left her home as her lover; but I left her bed without carrying away the memory of the caresses and the words of love that she had believed herself obliged to render me for the six thousand francs I left her.

And yet there are men who ruined themselves over that woman.

From that day forward I subjected Marguerite to a relentless persecution. She and Olympe stopped seeing each other; you may easily understand why. I gave my new mistress a carriage, jewels. I gambled; I committed, finally, all the follies appropriate to a young man in love with a woman like Olympe. The news of my new passion spread at once.

Prudence herself was fooled, and ended by believing that I had completely forgotten Marguerite. The latter, whether because she had guessed my motives or because she was fooled like the others, responded with great dignity to the wounds I gave her on a daily basis. Only, she seemed to have fallen ill, because wherever I saw her, she appeared paler and paler, sadder and sadder. My love for her, exalted at this point until it believed itself transformed into hatred, rejoiced at the sight of this daily suffering. Many times, in circumstances in which I behaved with infamous cruelty, Marguerite cast such imploring looks at me that I blushed at the role I had assumed, and was on the brink of asking her forgiveness.

But these regrets lasted as long as a lightning flash, and Olympe, who had put all pride by the wayside, and understood that by hurting Marguerite, she could get from me everything she wanted, ceaselessly incited me against her, and insulted her every time she had occasion, with that persistent cravenness exercised by a woman whose conduct is sanctioned by a man.

Marguerite no longer went to balls or to the theater for fear of seeing Olympe and me. Direct acts of rudeness were followed by a barrage of anonymous letters, and I coaxed my mistress to tell me shameful anecdotes, which I then circulated myself, attributing them to Marguerite.

You have to be crazy to reach that point. I was like a man who, having gotten drunk on bad wine, falls into one of those nervous states in which the hand is capable of a crime that the mind has no awareness of. In the midst of all this, I played the martyr. The serenity without disdain, the dignity without contempt with which Marguerite met all my attacks, and which in my own eyes made her superior to me, enraged me further against her.

One night Olympe went I know not where, and ran into Marguerite, who this time chose not to indulge the foolish girl who insulted her, to such a point that the former was forced to leave. Olympe returned home furious, and Marguerite fainted and had to be carried off.

When she arrived home, Olympe told me what had happened, told me that Marguerite, when she saw her there alone, had wanted to get back at her for being my mistress, and that I had to write to tell her that, even in my absence, she ought to treat the woman I loved with respect.

I don't need to tell you that I consented, and that I put everything bitter, shameful, and cruel I could think of into that letter, which I sent that very day to her address.

This time the blow was too strong for the unhappy woman to bear in silence.

I was sure I would receive a reply, and resolved not to leave my apartment all day.

Around two o'clock the doorbell rang, and Prudence entered.

I tried to put on an indifferent air and asked her to what I owed her visit, but Mme Duvernoy was not in a merry mood that day, and in a tone of great emotion she told me that, since my return—which is to say, for about three weeks—I had not let one occasion pass that could cause Marguerite pain; that I had made her ill, and that the previous night's scene, and my letter of the morning, had sent her to her bed.

In brief, without reproaching me, Marguerite was asking me to spare her, and wanted me to be told that she no longer had the moral or physical force to withstand the onslaught I had let loose on her.

"If Mlle Gautier," I said to Prudence, "banishes me from her home, that is her right, but for her to insult a woman I love because that woman is my mistress is something I will never permit."

"My friend," Prudence said, "you have fallen under the influence of a girl with no heart or character. You are in love with her, it is true, but that is no reason to torture a woman who cannot defend herself."

"Have Mlle Gautier send me her Comte de N . . . and we will be even."

"You know very well she will not do that. My dear Armand, leave her alone; if you were to see her, you would be ashamed of how you have behaved. She is pale, she coughs, she does not have long now."

Prudence held out her hand, adding, "Go see her; your visit will make her very happy."

"I have no desire to see M. de N . . . ."

"M. de N . . . is never with her. She cannot stand him."

"If Marguerite is so determined to see me, she knows where I live. Let her come, but I will never again set foot on the rue d'Antin."

"And you will receive her politely?"

"Perfectly."

"Then I am sure she will come."

"Let her come."

"Will you be going out today?"

"I will be at home all night."

"I will tell her."

Prudence left.

I didn't even write to Olympe to tell her I would not be seeing her. I took no trouble with that girl. I barely spent one night with her a week. She consoled herself, I believe, with some actor from I don't know which theater from the boulevard.

I left for dinner and returned almost immediately. I had fires made everywhere, then gave Joseph the night off.

I cannot give you a full account of the diverse impressions that agitated me during an hour of waiting, but when, around nine o'clock, I heard the doorbell ring, I was filled with such emotion that, going to open the door, I was forced to lean against the wall so as not to fall over.

Luckily the foyer was in semidarkness, and the alteration of my countenance was hardly visible. Marguerite entered.

She was dressed in black, and veiled. I could hardly make out her face beneath the lace.

She passed into the living room and removed her veil.

She was as pale as marble.

"Here I am, Armand," she said. "You wanted to see me; I came."

And, letting her head fall into her hands, she dissolved in tears.

I drew near to her.

"What is wrong with you?" I said, in an altered voice.

She gripped my hand without answering me; tears muffled her voice. But a few moments later, after having regained some composure, she said to me, "You have hurt me badly, Armand, and I did nothing to you."

"Nothing?" I replied with a bitter smile.

"Nothing except what circumstances forced me to do."

I don't know if ever in your life you have felt or will ever feel what I felt at the sight of Marguerite.

The last time she had come to see me in my apartment, she had sat in the same place where she had just sat down; only, since that time, she had become the mistress of another man. Other kisses than mine had touched her lips, lips for which, in spite of myself, my own lips yearned, and yet I felt I loved this woman as much as and maybe more than I ever had.

However, it was difficult for me to continue the conversation, broaching the subject she had raised. Marguerite doubtless understood this, for she resumed, "I have come to trouble you, Armand, because I have two things to ask of you: to forgive me for what I said yesterday to Mlle Olympe, and to spare me the pain of whatever you may still have planned for me. Intentionally or not, since your return to Paris, you have hurt me so badly that I would now be incapable of bearing a quarter of the emotions that I have had to withstand up to this morning. You will have pity on me, won't you? And you will understand that for a good-hearted man, there are nobler things than to take vengeance on a woman who is as sick and sad as I am. Here, take my hand. I have a fever; I left my bed to come to ask you not for your friendship but for your indifference."

I took Marguerite's hand. It was burning hot, and still the poor woman shivered under her velvet cloak.

I rolled the armchair she sat in closer to the fire.

"Do you believe, then, that I did not suffer," I said, "the night when, after having waited for you in the country, I came to look for you in Paris, and found nothing but a letter that could only serve to drive me mad? How could you have deceived me, Marguerite, I who loved you so much!"

"Let us not speak of that, Armand; I did not come to speak of that. I wanted to see you in some other way than as an enemy, that is all, and I wanted to clasp your hand one more time. You have a young, pretty mistress whom you love, they say. Be happy with her and forget me."

"And you, you are happy, no doubt?"

"Do I have the face of a happy woman, Armand? Do not compound my sorrow, you who know better than anyone the causes and the extent of it."

"It once lay within your power to ensure that you were never unhappy, if indeed you are unhappy now, as you say."

"No, my friend; circumstances were stronger than my will. I was not obeying any girlish instincts, as you seem to suggest, but a serious necessity, for reasons you will learn one day that will make you forgive me."

"Why don't you tell me these reasons today?"

"Because they might reestablish a rapprochement that is impossible between us, and because they will estrange you from people you must not be estranged from."

"Who are these people?"

"I cannot tell you."

"In that case you are lying."

Marguerite rose and headed for the door.

I could not witness this mute and eloquent pain without being moved by it, when I compared this pale and weeping woman with the lively girl who had teased me at the Opéra-Comique.

"You must not go," I said, blocking the door.

"Why?"

"Because, in spite of what you did to me, I love you still and want to keep you here."

"In order to chase me away tomorrow, no? No, it's impossible! Our two destinies are separate. Let's not try to get back together—you will despise me, perhaps, whereas now you only hate me."

"No, Marguerite," I cried out, feeling all my love and all my desire rekindle from my contact with this woman. "No, I will forget everything, and we will be as happy as we promised each other we would be."

Marguerite shook her head in a sign of doubt and said, "Am I not your slave, your dog? Do with me as you like. Take me; I'm yours."

And taking off her coat and hat, she threw them on the sofa and began to roughly unfasten the bodice of her dress, because, as a result of one of those reactions so common with her illness, blood was rising from her heart to her head and suffocating her.

A dry and raucous cough followed.

"Tell my coachman," she said, "to drive my carriage home."

I went down myself to send the man away.

When I returned, Marguerite was lying in front of the fire, her teeth chattering with cold. I took her in my arms, undressed her without her making a movement, and carried her all frozen into my bed.

Then, sitting beside her, I tried to warm her with my caresses. She did not say a word, but she smiled at me.

Oh! It was a strange night. Marguerite's entire life seemed contained in the kisses she covered me with, and I loved her so intensely that, amid the transports of my feverish love, I asked myself if I was not trying to kill her to keep her from ever belonging to another.

A month of a love like that and the body, like the heart, would be no more than a corpse.

The morning found us both wide awake.

Marguerite was as white as a sheet. She did not say a word. Fat tears rolled from time to time from her eyes and rested on her cheek, shining like diamonds. Her exhausted arms opened occasionally to clutch me, then would fall back without strength onto the bed.

For one moment I believed I could forget what had happened

since I left Bougival, and I said to Marguerite, "Do you want us to leave, to leave Paris for good?"

"No, no," she said, almost in terror. "We would be too unhappy. I cannot bring you happiness, but as long as I have breath, I will be slave to your whims. At any hour of the day or the night that you want me, come; I will be yours. But do not join your future with mine; you will be too unhappy, and you will make me too unhappy. I am still, for the moment, a pretty girl—take advantage of that; I ask nothing more."

When she left, I was stricken by the loneliness in which she left me. Two hours after her departure, I was still sitting on the bed she had just left, looking at the pillow that retained the contours of her form, and asking myself what would become of me, between my love and my jealousy.

At five o'clock, without knowing what I was going to do, I turned up on the rue d'Antin.

It was Nanine who let me in.

"Madam cannot receive you," she told me with embarrassment.

"Why?"

"Because M. le Comte de N . . . is here, and has been told that I would not let anyone enter."

"That's right," I stammered. "I had forgotten."

I staggered home like a drunken man, and do you know what I did during the minute of jealous delirium that produced the shameful action I was going to commit—do you know what I did? I told myself that this woman was mocking me. I pictured her in her inviolable tête-à-tête with the count, repeating the same words she had told me the night before; and taking a five-hundred-franc note, I sent it to her with these words: "You left so quickly this morning that I forgot to pay you. Here is the fee for your night."

Then, when this letter was taken away, I went out as if to protect myself from instantaneous remorse for this infamous act.

I went to see Olympe, whom I found trying on dresses, and who, once we were alone, sang obscenities to me to distract me.

She was the model of the shameless hussy, without heart or

character—for me, at least; perhaps some other man might have made of her the dream I made of Marguerite.

She asked me for money; I gave it to her, and then, free to go, I went home.

Marguerite had not responded to me.

I do not need to tell you in what agitation I passed the next day.

At six thirty a commissioner brought an envelope containing my letter and the five-hundred-franc bill, not one word more.

"Who gave you that?" I said to the man.

"A woman who was leaving with her chambermaid in the mail coach to Boulogne, and who told me not to bring it until the coach had left the courtyard."

I ran to Marguerite's.

"Madam left for England today at six o'clock," the porter told me.

Nothing could keep me in Paris, neither hatred nor love. I was exhausted by all these shocks. One of my friends was about to take a trip to the Orient. I went to tell my father that I wanted to accompany him; my father gave me bank drafts and letters of introduction, and eight or ten days later I embarked at Marseille.

It was in Alexandria that I learned from an attaché at the embassy, whom I had sometimes seen at Marguerite's, of the poor girl's illness.

I then wrote her the letter whose response you know, the one I received at Toulon.

I left at once; you know the rest.

Now you have nothing left to do but to read the few pages that Julie Duprat forwarded to me, which are the indispensable complement to what I have just related to you.

CHAPTER XXV

Armand, worn out from this long narrative, which had often been interrupted by his tears, rubbed his forehead with both hands, and closed his eyes—maybe to think, maybe to try to sleep—after he had given me the pages written in Marguerite's hand.

A few moments later, quickened breathing convinced me that Armand was sleeping, but the light sleep to which the least sound puts flight.

Here is what I read, and what I describe without adding or retracting a single syllable:

"Today is the 15th of December. I have been ill for three or four days. This morning I took to my bed. The weather is gloomy; I am sad. Nobody is with me. I am thinking of you, Armand. And you, where are you as I write these lines? Far from Paris—very far, I've been told, and perhaps you have already forgotten Marguerite. Well, be happy, you to whom I owe my life's only moments of joy.

"I was not able to resist the desire to explain my conduct to you, so I wrote you a letter; but, written by a girl like me, such a letter might be regarded as a lie, unless death were to sanctify its authority and, in place of a letter, it were to become a confession.

"Today I am sick; I may die of this illness, as I have always had the presentiment that I would die young. My mother died of consumption, and the way in which I have lived until now can only have aggravated this condition, which is the only inheritance she left me. But I do not want to die without your knowing how to think of me, if upon your return you still do think of the poor girl whom you loved before you went away.

"Here is what that letter contained, which I am happy to write down again, as a new justification of my conduct:

"You will recall, Armand, how the arrival of your father surprised us at Bougival; you will remember the involuntary terror that this arrival caused me, and the scene that took place between you and him and which you described to me that night.

"The next day, while you were in Paris, and while you were waiting for your father, who did not return to the hotel, a man appeared at Bougival, and gave me a letter from M. Duval.

"That letter, which I include with this one, begged me, in the most serious terms, to get you out of the house the next day on any pretext whatsoever, and to receive your father; he wanted to speak with me, and above all asked that I tell you nothing of his plan.

"You know how adamantly I urged you to return to Paris the next day.

"You had been gone for an hour when your father arrived. I will spare you the impression that his harsh countenance made on me. Your father was steeped in the old notions that hold that every courtesan is a creature without heart and without reason, a type of gold-digging machine that is always ready, like an ironworks, to mangle the hand that reaches for it, and to tear apart without pity, without judgment, the man who brings it to life and makes it work.

"Your father had written me a letter calculated to make me agree to receive him; he did not present himself at all in person as he had in writing. There was so much haughtiness, impertinence, and even menace in his first words that I had to remind him that I was in my own home, and that I was not bound to furnish him an account of my life, except as concerned my sincere affection for his son.

"M. Duval calmed down a little, but then began to tell me that he could not bear any longer for his son to ruin himself over me; that I was beautiful, it was true, but that, beautiful as I was, I should not make use of my beauty to destroy the future of a young man by expenses like those I incurred.

"To that, there was only one way to respond, no? It was to

give him the proof that, ever since I had become your mistress, I had demanded no sacrifice of you that you could not afford to guarantee my fidelity to you. I showed him the tickets from the pawnshop, the receipts from the people to whom I'd sold the objects I could no longer keep. I told your father of my resolution to sell all my furniture to pay off my debts, and to live with you without being too heavy a burden. I told him of our happiness, of the revelation you had given me of a life that was happier and more serene, and he finished by returning my evidence to me, and giving me his hand, while begging pardon for the way he had behaved at first.

"He then said to me, 'Well, madam, it is no longer by remonstrances and threats, but by prayers that I will try to obtain from you a greater sacrifice than any of those you already have made for my son.'

"I trembled at this preamble.

"Your father came up to me, took both my hands, and continued in an affectionate tone, 'My child, don't take in the wrong way what I am going to tell you; understand only that life sometimes demands things of us that are cruel to the heart, but to which one must submit. You are a good woman, and your soul has generosities unknown to many women who may despise you, and are not worthy of you. But consider that alongside the mistress there is the family; apart from love, there is duty; and the age of passion is followed by the age in which a man, to be respected, must be solidly established in a serious position. My son has no fortune, and nonetheless he is ready to turn over to you his inheritance from his mother. If he accepted the sacrifice which you are on the point of making for his sake, he would be required by his honor and dignity to furnish you this safeguard against complete adversity. But he cannot accept this sacrifice, because society, which does not know you, would attribute to this consent an unbecoming motive that must not be attached to the name we bear. Nobody would ask if Armand loved you, or if you loved him, or if this mutual love was a joy to him and a rehabilitation for you; everyone would see only one thing, which is that Armand Duval had permitted a kept woman—pardon me, my child, for everything I am forced now to say to you—to sell everything she owned for him. Then the day of reproaches and regrets would come, you may be sure of it, for you as it does for everyone else, and you would both be bound by a chain you could not break. What would you do then? Your youth would be lost, my son's future would be destroyed, and I, his father, would gain from only one of my children the satisfaction I had hoped for from both.

"'You are young, you are beautiful, life will console you. You are noble, and the memory of a selfless action will make up the loss of many good things you have given up. In the six months that he has known you, Armand has forgotten me. Four times I have written to him and he did not once think of responding. I could have died and he would not have known it!

"'Whatever your resolve to live differently than you have in the past, Armand, who loves you, will not consent to the seclusion to which his modest means will doom you, which does not suit your beauty. Who knows what he will do next! He has gambled, I know—without your needing to tell me anything about it, I still know—but, in a moment of drunkenness, he could have lost part of what I have accumulated over many years for the dowry of my daughter, for him, and for the security of my old age. What could have happened could happen still.

"'Are you sure, besides, that the life you are leaving behind for him will not attract you again? Are you sure that you who have loved him will never love another? Will you not suffer, finally, from the fact that your connection to him will impose obstacles in the life of your lover, for which you will perhaps not be able to console him, if, with age, notions of ambition succeed his dreams of love? Reflect on all this, madam. You love Armand; prove it to him by the only means that still remain to you to prove it: in sacrificing your love to his future. No misfortune has yet come, but it will come, and perhaps it will be greater than those I foresee. Armand may become jealous of some man who loved you; he may provoke him, he may fight with him, he may be killed in the end, and think what you would suffer, facing this father who asked you to look after the life of his son.

"'Finally, my child, know everything, for I have not told you everything. Know therefore what has brought me to Paris. I have a daughter, I just told you—young, beautiful, as pure as an angel. She is in love, and she, too, has made this love the dream of her life. I wrote about all this to Armand, but, occupied with you, he did not respond. Well, my daughter is going to be married. She is marrying the man she loves; she is entering an honorable family that expects everything to be honorable in mine. The family of the man who is to become my son-in-law heard of how Armand was living in Paris, and told me he would withdraw his proposal if Armand continued to live in this manner. The future of a child who has done nothing to you, and who has the right to count on the future, is in your hands.

"'Do you have the right and do you have the strength to shatter it? In the name of your love and of your repentance, Marguerite, grant me my daughter's happiness.'

"I wept silently, my friend, before all these considerations that I had pondered so many times before, and which, in the mouth of your father, took on a more serious reality. I told myself all the things that your father did not dare say to me, and that were on his lips twenty times: that I was after all nothing but a kept woman, and that, whatever justification I gave to our liaison, it would always appear calculated; that my past life gave me no right to dream of such a future, and that I had been taking on responsibilities that my habits and my reputation could not guarantee. Finally, I loved you, Armand. The fatherly way in which M. Duval spoke to me, the chaste sentiments he evoked in me, the esteem that I might win of this loyal old man, yours that I was sure to have later—all this awoke in my heart noble thoughts that opened my eyes, and sent me into reveries of saintly vanity, unknown to me until that moment. When I thought that one day this old man, who beseeched me on behalf of his son's future, would tell his daughter to add my name to her prayers, like the name of a mysterious friend, I felt transformed, and I was proud of myself.

"The exaltation of that moment may have exaggerated the

truth of these impressions, but that is what I felt, friend, and these new sentiments quieted the advice that my memory of the happy days I spent with you had given me.

"'All right, sir,' I said to your father, drying my tears. 'Do you believe that I love your son?'

"'Yes,' said M. Duval.

"'With a love that does not come from self-interest?'

"'Yes.'

"'Do you believe that I have made this love the hope, dream, and redemption of my life?'

"'Firmly.'

"'Well, monsieur, kiss me once, as you would kiss your daughter, and I swear to you that this kiss, the only truly chaste kiss I have ever received, will give me the strength to resist my love, and that within a week your son will be returned to your side, perhaps unhappy for some time, but forever healed.'

"'You are a noble girl,' replied your father, kissing my forehead, 'and you are undertaking something for which God will reward you; but I fear that you will have no luck with my son.'

"'Oh! rest assured, sir, he will hate me.'

"I had to impose an insurmountable barrier between the two of us, for one as for the other.

"I wrote to Prudence, telling her I accepted the propositions of M. le Comte de N . . . , and that she was to tell him that I would have supper with the two of them.

"I sealed the letter and, without telling him what was in it, asked your father to have it sent to her address upon his arrival in Paris.

"He asked me nonetheless what it contained.

"'Your son's happiness,' I told him.

"Your father kissed me one last time. I felt on my forehead two tears of gratitude that were like a baptism, a remission of my former sins, and at the moment when I had consented to deliver myself to another man, I beamed with pride to think of what I would redeem with this new one.

"It was only natural, Armand; you had told me your father was the most honest man anyone could ever meet.

"M. Duval got back into his carriage and left.

"However, I was a woman, and when I saw you again, I could not keep myself from crying, but I did not weaken.

"Did I do the right thing? That is what I ask myself, as I fall sick into a bed that I will leave perhaps only when I am dead.

"You have been witness to the full measure of what I felt as the hour of our inevitable separation approached. Your father was no longer there to support me, and there was a moment when I was close to telling you everything, so horrified was I by the idea that you would hate and despise me.

"One thing you will perhaps not believe, Armand, is that I prayed to God to give me strength; the proof that he accepted my sacrifice is that he gave me the strength I begged him for.

"At this supper I still needed help, because I did not know what I was going to do; I was so afraid my courage would fail me!

"Who could have told me—me, Marguerite Gautier—that I would suffer so at the mere thought of a new lover?

"I drank to forget, and when I woke the next day I was in the bed of the count.

"That is the whole truth, friend; judge and pardon me, as I have pardoned you for all the harm you have done me since that day."

CHAPTER XXVI

"What followed that fateful night you know as well as I do, but what you do not know, what you cannot suspect, is how much I have suffered since our separation.

"I had learned your father had taken you away, but I doubted you could live apart from me for long, and the day I saw you on the Champs-Élysées, I was moved, but not stunned.

"Then began that series of days, each of which brought me a new insult from you, an insult I received almost with joy, as, besides the fact that it was proof you still loved me, it seemed to me that the more you persecuted me, the more I would be exalted in your eyes on the day when you would learn the truth.

"Don't be astonished by this joyful martyr, Armand; the love you had for me opened my heart to noble enthusiasms.

"However, at the beginning, I was not so strong.

"Between the execution of the sacrifice I had made for you and your return, a long time passed, during which I needed medicine to preserve my sanity and to blot out the life I had thrown myself back into. Prudence told you, did she not, that I went to all the fêtes, all the balls, all the wild parties?

"I had the notion that I might kill myself quickly through excess, and I believe that this hope did not delay in starting to come true. My health, of necessity, was more and more altered, and the day I sent Mme Duvernoy to ask you to spare me, I was worn ragged, body and soul.

"I will not remind you, Armand, in what way you rewarded the last proof of love I gave you, and by what outrage you chased from Paris the woman who, though she was dying, could not resist your voice when you asked her for a night of love, and who, like a madwoman, believed, for a moment, that she could knit back together the past and the present. You had the right to do what you did, Armand; my nights have not always been bought at so high a price!

"I left everything then! Olympe replaced me at M. de N . . . 's side, and took it upon herself, I am told, to tell him the reason for my departure. The Comte de G . . . was in London. He is one of those men who, believing that love affairs with girls like me are of no more consequence than any other agreeable pastime, remain friends with the women they have possessed, and have no hatred, since they have never known jealousy; he is, in short, one of those great lords who open only one corner of their hearts to us, but both sides of their wallets. I thought of him at once. I went to find him. He received me splendidly, but he was the lover of a society woman there and feared he would compromise himself if he were connected with me. He introduced me to his friends, who gave a supper for me, after which one of them took me home.

"What did you expect me to do, my friend? Kill myself? That would have been to burden your life, which I wanted to be happy, with useless remorse—and then again, why kill oneself when one is so close to death?

"I passed into the state of a body without a soul, a thing without thought. I lived for some time a sort of automatic life, then I returned to Paris and asked after you; I learned then that you had left for a long journey. There was no longer anything to sustain me. My existence became again what it had been two years before I met you. I tried to get the duke back, but I had wounded him too deeply, and old men are impatient, doubtless because they know they are not immortal. The illness took me over; day by day, I was pale, I was sad, I grew still thinner. Men who buy love like to inspect the merchandise before they take it. There were women in Paris in finer form than I was, plumper than I was; people forgot about me a little. That is the past, up until yesterday.

"Now I am quite sick. I wrote to the duke to ask him for money, as I don't have any and the creditors have come back, and bring me their notes with merciless persistence. Will the duke respond? Why are you not in Paris, Armand! You would come see me, and your visits would soothe me."

"*December 20.*

"The weather is horrible; it's snowing. I am alone at home. For three days I have had such a fever that I have been unable to write you a word. Nothing new, my friend; each day I hope vaguely for a letter from you, but it doesn't come, and no doubt it never will. Only men have the strength not to forgive. The duke has not replied to me.

"Prudence has resumed her visits to the pawnshop.

"I never stop spitting blood. Oh! I would upset you if you saw me. You are very lucky to be under a warm sky, not surrounded as I am by an icy winter that weighs down your chest. Today I got up for a little while, and through the curtains at my window I watched the life of Paris passing by, the life I thought had ended. Some faces I recognized passed by in the street, rapid, joyful, careless. Not one raised his eyes to my windows. However, some young people came by and left their names. There was a time before, when I was sick, when you—who did not know me, who had received nothing from me but an impertinence on the day I first met you—you came to get news of me every morning. Now I'm sick again. We spent six months together. I had as much love for you as the heart of a woman can hold and give, and you are far away, and you condemn me, and no word of consolation comes from you. But it is only chance that causes this abandonment, I am sure. Because if you were in Paris, you would not leave my bedside, or my room."

"*December 25.*

"My doctor forbids me to write every day. In truth my memories only heighten my fever, but yesterday I received a letter that did me some good, more for the sentiments that it expressed than for the material relief it brought me. I can therefore write to you today. This letter was from your father, and here is what it contained:

MADAM,

I have just learned that you are sick. If I were in Paris, I would go myself to learn your news; if my son were beside me, I would tell him to go find it out, but I cannot leave C . . . , and Armand is six or seven hundred leagues away. Permit me, therefore, simply to write you, Madam, and to tell you how saddened I am to hear of your illness, and to believe in my sincere wishes for your prompt recovery.

One of my good friends, M. H . . . , will present himself at your home; please receive him. He has been charged by me with a commission whose result I await impatiently.

Please accept, Madam, the assurance of my most distinguished sentiments.

"Such is the letter I received. Your father has a noble heart; love him well, my friend, for there are few men in the world as worthy of being loved. This paper signed with his name did me more good than all the prescriptions of our great doctor.

"This morning M. H . . . came. He seemed quite embarrassed by the delicate commission M. Duval had entrusted to him. He came quite simply to bring me a thousand francs from your father. At first I wanted to refuse, but M. H . . . told me that such a refusal would give offense to M. Duval, who had authorized him to give me this sum, and in future to give me anything more I might require. I accepted this service, which, on your father's part, cannot be seen as charity. If I am dead when you return, show your father what I just wrote about him, and tell him that in writing these lines, the poor girl he deigned to write that consoling letter shed tears of gratitude and prayed to God for his sake."

"*January 4.*

"I just emerged from a series of very painful days. I did not know the body could cause such suffering. Oh! The life I led! I am paying for it twice today.

"Someone was here to watch over me every night. I could no longer breathe. Delirium and cough were sharing the remnants of my poor existence.

"My dining room is filled with candy, with gifts of all kinds that my friends have brought me. No doubt there are, among those people, some who hope I will be their mistress later. If they saw what my illness has done to me, they would flee in terror.

"Prudence is giving away my New Year's presents as her own.

"A thaw is setting in, and the doctor has told me that I will be able to go out in a few days if the good weather continues."

"January 8.

"I went out yesterday in my carriage. The weather was magnificent. The Champs-Élysées was full of people. You might have said it was the first smile of the spring. Everything around me took on an air of celebration. I never suspected I could find so much joy, sweetness, and consolation in a ray of sunshine as I did yesterday.

"I saw nearly all the people I know, still cheerful, still busy with their pleasures. It is only the lucky who don't know their luck! Olympe passed by in an elegant carriage that M. de N . . . had given her. She tried to insult me with a glance. She does not know how far removed I am from such trifles. A nice boy I've known for a long time asked me if I would have supper with him, and with one of his friends who wants very much to meet me, he said.

"I smiled sadly, and gave him my hand, burning with fever.

"I've never seen a more startled expression.

"I went home at four o'clock. I ate with appetite enough.

"This outing did me good.

"If only I would get better!

"How the vision of life and happiness in others rekindles the desire to live in those who, the night before, in the solitude of their souls and the shadow of the sickroom, longed to die quickly."

"January 10.

"This hope of renewed health was nothing but a dream. Here I am again in my bed, my body covered with burning plasters. Go put this body that fetched so high a price in former times on offer, and see what you can get for it today!

"We must have done something truly wicked before we were born, or some great happiness must be in store for us after our deaths, for God to permit so many tortures of expiation, so many painful trials, in this life."

"January 12.

"I am always sick.

"The Comte de N . . . sent me money yesterday; I did not accept it. I want nothing from that man. He is the one who is responsible for the fact that you are not near me.

"Oh! Our beautiful days in Bougival! Where are you?

"If I leave this room alive, it will be to make a pilgrimage to the house where we lived together, but I will leave it only when I am dead.

"Who knows if I will be able to write to you tomorrow?"

"January 25.

"For eleven nights I have not slept. I am suffocating, and every instant I think that I will die. The doctor has ordered that nobody permit me to touch a pen. Julie Duprat, who watches over me, allows me still to write you a few lines. Will you not come back before I die, then? Is it, then, eternally over between us? It seems to me that if you were to come, I would get better. What good would getting better do?"

"January 28.

"This morning I was awoken by a loud noise. Julie, who was sleeping in my room, ran into the dining room. I heard the voices of men, against which hers fought in vain. She came back crying.

"They had come to repossess my things. I told her to let them execute what they called justice. The bailiff came in to my bedroom, his hat on his head. He opened the drawers, wrote down everything he saw, and did not seem to notice that there was a woman dying in the bed that, happily, the charity of the law allows me to keep.

"He consented to tell me as he left that I could file an appeal within nine days, but he left a guard! What is to become of me, my God! This scene made me even sicker than before. Prudence wanted to go ask for money from your father's friend; I opposed it.

"I received your letter this morning. How I needed it. Will my reply reach you in time? Will you see me again? This has been a happy day, one that has allowed me to forget all those that have passed during these last six weeks. I feel as if I were better, in spite of the mood of sadness that colored my response to you.

"After all, one must not always be unhappy.

"When I think it may happen that I will not die, that you will come back to me, that I will see spring again, that you will love me again, and that we might begin again our life of last year!

"I'm such a fool! I can hardly hold the pen with which I am writing to you this senseless dream of my heart.

"Whatever may come, I loved you well, Armand, and I would have died long ago if I did not have the memory of that love to help me, and the vague hope of seeing you again beside me."

"*February* 4.

"The Comte de G . . . came back. His mistress was unfaithful to him. He is very sad; he loved her very much. He came to tell me about it. The poor boy's business is in a bad state, which didn't prevent him from paying off my bailiff and sending away the guard.

"I spoke to him of you, and he promised to speak to you of me. How I forgot in those moments that I had been his mistress, and how he tried to make me forget it too! He has a good heart.

"The duke sent yesterday for news of me, and he came this morning. I don't know what it is that keeps the old man living. He stayed three hours at my side, and he did not say twenty words to me. Two great tears fell from his eyes when he saw me so pale. It was the memory of the death of his daughter that made him cry, no doubt.

"Now he will have seen her die twice. His back is humped, his head points to the ground, his lip is pendulous, his gaze extinguished. Age and sorrow have laid their double weight on his exhausted back. He made me no reproach. You might even have said he secretly rejoiced at the ravages the illness has worked on me. He seemed proud to be standing upright, while I, still young, was crushed by suffering.

"Bad times have returned. Nobody comes to see me. Julie watches over me, and stays beside me as much as possible. Prudence, whom I can't give as much money to as I did in the past, has started to invent pretexts to stay away.

"Now that I am near death, despite everything the doctors tell me—for I have several, which proves my illness is worsening—I almost regret having listened to your father. If I had known that I would take only one year from your future, I would not have resisted the desire to spend that year with you, and at least I would have died holding the hand of a friend. It is true that if we had lived together this year, I would not have died so soon.

"God's will be done!"

"February 5.

"Oh! Come, Armand. I suffer terribly; I am going to die, my God. I was so sad yesterday that I longed to be anywhere but at home in the evening, which promised to be as long as the night before. The duke came in the morning. The sight of this old man whom death has forgotten seems to make me die more quickly.

"Despite the burning fever that consumed me, I had myself dressed and driven to the Vaudeville. Julie put rouge on me, without it I would have looked cadaverous. I went to the box where I permitted you our first encounter. The entire time I kept my eyes fixed on the stall you had occupied that night, which yesterday was occupied by some rustic type, who laughed loudly at all the foolish things the actors said. I was taken home half-dead. I coughed and spat blood all night. Today I can no longer speak; I can hardly move my arms. My God! My God! I am going to die. I am expecting it, but I can't get used to the idea that I will suffer any more than I am already suffering, and if . . ."

After this word, the few characters Marguerite had tried to scrawl were illegible, and it was Julie Duprat who had continued.

"*February 18.*

"MONSIEUR ARMAND,

"Since the day when Marguerite wanted to go to the theater, she has grown sicker and sicker. She completely lost her voice, then the use of her limbs. What our poor friend suffers is impossible to say. I am not used to this kind of emotion, and I am continually seized by fright.

"How I wish you could be beside us! She is nearly always in delirium, but whether she is delirious or lucid, it is always your name she speaks when she is able to say a word.

"The doctor told me she doesn't have much longer. Since she has become so ill, the old duke has not returned.

"He told the doctor that the sight of her caused him too much pain.

"Mme Duvernoy is not behaving well. This woman, who thought she would be able to keep on getting money from Marguerite, at whose expense she was living almost entirely, has taken on contracts that she cannot keep, and, seeing that her neighbor is no longer useful to her, she no longer even comes to see her. Everyone is abandoning her. M. de G . . . , hounded by his debts, was forced to return to London. When he left, he sent us some money; he has done everything he could, but they came back to seize the things, and the creditors are only waiting for her death to sell it all.

"I would have liked to use my last resources to stop this, but the bailiff told me there was no point, and that there were still more seizures to come. Since she will die, it is better to abandon it all than to save it for her family, whom she did not want to see, and who never loved her. You cannot imagine the gilded misery the poor creature is dying amidst. Yesterday we had no money at all. Silver, jewels, shawls, everything has been pawned; the rest has been sold or seized. Marguerite is still conscious of what is happening around her, and she suffers body, mind, and heart. Giant tears roll down her cheeks, which are so gaunt and so pale that you would no longer recognize the face you loved so much if you could see her. She made me promise to write you when she would no longer be able, and I am writing in front of her. Her eyes are upon me, but she does not see me; her gaze is already clouded by her impending death. However, she is smiling, and all her thoughts, all her soul, are with you; I am sure of it.

"Every time anyone opens the door, her eyes light up, and she always thinks that you will walk in; then, when she sees it is not you, her face resumes its sorrowful expression, dampens with cool perspiration, and her cheeks turn purple."

"February 19, midnight.

"What a sad day today was, my poor Monsieur Armand! This morning Marguerite couldn't breathe. The doctor bled her, and her voice came back a little. The doctor advised her to see a priest. She gave her consent, and he went himself to look for an abbot at Saint-Roch.

"During this time Marguerite called me to her bedside, begged me to open her armoire, indicated a bonnet and a long chemise covered in lace, and told me in a weak voice, 'I will die after I make my confession. Afterward, dress me in those things; it's the vanity of a dying woman.'

"Then she embraced me, crying, and added, 'I can speak, but I suffocate too much when I speak. I'm suffocating! Air!'

"I dissolved in tears. I opened the window, and a few instants later the priest walked in.

"I went straight up to him.

"When he realized whom he was attending, he seemed to be afraid he would receive a poor welcome.

"'Come in bravely, Father,' I said to him.

"He stayed a short time in the room of the sick woman, and when he left he said to me, 'She lived like a sinner, but she will die like a Christian.'

"A few moments later he returned accompanied by a choir-boy who carried a crucifix, and by a sacristan who walked before them, ringing a bell to announce that God was coming to the dying woman.

"All three of them entered this bedroom that had at other times echoed with so many strange words, but that at this hour was nothing short of a holy tabernacle.

"I fell to my knees. I don't know how long the impression that this spectacle made on me lasted, but I do not think that, until that moment, any other human occurrence had impressed me so much.

"The priest anointed the feet, hands, and forehead of the dying woman with holy oils, recited a short prayer, and Marguerite was ready to depart for Heaven, where she will go without a doubt, if God has observed the trials of her life and the sanctity of her death.

"Since that moment she has not said a word and has not made a movement. Twenty times I would have thought she was dead, had I not heard her labored breathing."

"*February 20, five o'clock.*

"Everything is over.

"Marguerite entered her final agony at about two o'clock. Never has a martyr suffered such tortures, judging from her cries. Two or three times she rose up in her bed, as if she were trying to grab back the life that was climbing toward God.

"Two or three times, as well, she spoke your name, then everything went quiet; she fell back exhausted on her bed. Silent tears flowed from her eyes, and she was dead.

"I approached her then. I called out to her, and when she did not respond, I closed her eyes and kissed her forehead.

"Poor, dear Marguerite. I wished I had been a holy woman, so that kiss might have recommended you to God.

"Then I dressed her as she had asked me to do, I went to find a priest at Saint-Roch, I lit two candles for her, and I prayed for an hour in the church.

"I gave money that came from her to the poor.

"I am not well versed in religion, but I think the good Lord will recognize that my tears were genuine, my prayer fervent, my alms sincere, and he will have pity on that woman who, dying young and beautiful, only had me to close her eyes and bury her."

"*February* 22.

"Today the burial took place. Many of Marguerite's friends came to the church. Some wept sincerely. When the procession took the road to Montmartre, only two men were in it: the Comte de G . . . , who had come back for that purpose from London, and the duke, who walked with the support of two footmen.

"I write you these details from her home, in the midst of my tears and in front of the lamp that burns sadly next to a dinner I have been unable to touch, as you may well imagine, but which Nanine made for me, as I had not eaten for more than twenty-four hours.

"My memory cannot long retain these sad impressions, as my life does not belong to me any more than Marguerite's belonged to her; that is why I give you all these details in the very places where they occurred, for fear that, should a long time pass between them and your return, I would not be able to relay them to you in all their sad exactness."

CHAPTER XXVII

"Have you read it?" Armand asked when I had finished this manuscript.

"I understand what you must have suffered, my friend, if everything I've read is true!"

"My father confirmed it to me in a letter."

We spoke for some time more of the sad destiny that had just come to a close, and I went home to rest a little.

Armand, still sad, but somewhat relieved from having related this history, recovered quickly, and together we went to visit Prudence and Julie Duprat.

Prudence had just gone bankrupt. She told us that Marguerite was responsible, that she had lent her a lot of money for which she had made promissory notes she could not redeem, since Marguerite had died without returning them to her, and had not given her any receipts she could present as a creditor.

With the help of this fable that Mme Duvernoy spread everywhere as an excuse for her bad business practices, she got a thousand-franc bill out of Armand, who didn't believe her, but who acted as if he did out of respect for anything connected with his mistress.

Then we went to see Julie Duprat, who related to us the sad events she had witnessed, shedding sincere tears in memory of her friend.

Finally we went to Marguerite's tomb, on which the first rays of April sunshine were making the first leaves break their buds.

Armand had one last duty to fulfill, which was to rejoin his father. He wanted me to accompany him.

We arrived at C . . . , where I saw M. Duval just as I had

pictured him from the portrait his son had drawn of him: tall, dignified, benevolent.

He welcomed Armand with tears of happiness, and affectionately shook my hand. I soon perceived that, for this tax collector, fatherly feeling dominated all other sentiments.

His daughter, named Blanche, had that clarity of eye and gaze, that serenity of the mouth, that showed that her soul could conceive none but holy thoughts and her lips could pronounce none but pious words. She smiled at her brother's return, not knowing, this chaste young girl, that far away from her, a courtesan had sacrificed her own happiness at the mere invocation of her name.

I stayed for some time with this happy family, all of them fussing over the man who had brought his heart to them to be healed.

I returned to Paris, where I wrote this story just as it was told to me. It has only one merit, though this may yet be challenged: that it is true.

I do not draw from this narrative the conclusion that all girls like Marguerite are capable of doing what she did—far from it—but I know that one of them experienced in her life a profound love, that she suffered for it, and died of it. I have told the reader what I have learned. It was a duty.

I am no apostle of vice, but I will let the echo of noble misfortune ring out everywhere I hear it in prayer.

The story of Marguerite is an exception, I repeat; had it been a general case, it would not have been worth the trouble of writing down.

THE STORY OF PENGUIN CLASSICS

Before 1946 ... "Classics" are mainly the domain of academics and students; readable editions for everyone else are almost unheard of. This all changes when a little-known classicist, E. V. Rieu, presents Penguin founder Allen Lane with the translation of Homer's *Odyssey* that he has been working on in his spare time.

1946 Penguin Classics debuts with *The Odyssey*, which promptly sells three million copies. Suddenly, classics are no longer for the privileged few.

1950s Rieu, now series editor, turns to professional writers for the best modern, readable translations, including Dorothy L. Sayers's *Inferno* and Robert Graves's unexpurgated *Twelve Caesars*.

1960s The Classics are given the distinctive black covers that have remained a constant throughout the life of the series. Rieu retires in 1964, hailing the Penguin Classics list as "the greatest educative force of the twentieth century."

1970s A new generation of translators swells the Penguin Classics ranks, introducing readers of English to classics of world literature from more than twenty languages. The list grows to encompass more history, philosophy, science, religion, and politics.

1980s The Penguin American Library launches with titles such as *Uncle Tom's Cabin* and joins forces with Penguin Classics to provide the most comprehensive library of world literature available from any paperback publisher.

1990s The launch of Penguin Audiobooks brings the classics to a listening audience for the first time, and in 1999 the worldwide launch of the Penguin Classics Web site extends their reach to the global online community.

The 21st Century Penguin Classics are completely redesigned for the first time in nearly twenty years. This world-famous series now consists of more than 1,300 titles, making the widest range of the best books ever written available to millions—and constantly redefining what makes a "classic."

The Odyssey continues ...

The best books ever written

PENGUIN 🐧 CLASSICS

SINCE 1946

CLICK ON A CLASSIC
www.penguinclassics.com

The world's greatest literature at your fingertips

Constantly updated information on more than a thousand titles,
from Icelandic sagas to ancient Indian epics, Russian drama to
Italian romance, American greats to African masterpieces

•

The latest news on recent additions to the list, updated
editions, and specially commissioned translations

•

Original essays by leading writers

•

A wealth of background material, including biographies
of every classic author from Aristotle to Zamyatin, plot
synopses, readers' and teachers' guides, useful Web links

•

Online desk and examination copy assistance for academics

•

Trivia quizzes, competitions, giveaways, news on
forthcoming screen adaptations